Praise for Susie Orm

The Balance Project

"A fast-paced tale of a twentysomething desperately trying to balance her own life while, ironically, working for a woman known as America's Darling of Balance. If you liked *The Devil Wears Prada,* you'll enjoy this charming romp, which delivers with heart, depth, and a perfectly satisfying conclusion."

> —Kristin Harmel, bestselling author of *The Sweetness of Forgetting* and *The Life Intended*

"A smart, refreshing, fast-paced read with twists and turns that will have you turning pages well past your bedtime. Schnall nails her portrayal of two heroines, in different stages of their lives, wrestling with the oft-debated question: Can women really have it all?"

> —Emily Liebert, author of *You Knew Me When* and *Those Secrets We Keep*

"Destined to become a book club favorite, Susie Orman Schnall's *The Balance Project* is a clever, compassionate look at the modern woman's quest to juggle it all. Schnall's heartfelt—and, at times, hilarious—storytelling is just like real life, and had me rooting for Lucy from page one."

> —Kristyn Kusek Lewis, author of *How Lucky You Are* and *Save Me*

"Sharp like the clicks of a stiletto, *The Balance Project* is a piercing look at the damaging illusion that women can 'have it all.' Readers will delight in watching Katherine Whitney dangle on her rapidly thinning thread as she falls into the deep abyss of pride, work, motherhood, and friendship."

   —Colleen Oakes, author of the *Elly in Bloom* series and the *Queen of Hearts* saga

"Utterly compelling and impossible to put down, *The Balance Project* speaks volumes about how important it is for women at any stage of life to find realistic and meaningful balance."

   —Melissa Amster, Founder of Chick Lit Central

On Grace

"In Schnall's debut novel, shocking news derails a woman's plans for her fortieth birthday and prompts a journey of self-discovery. . . . A cozy, conversational read featuring a lovably neurotic heroine."

   —*Kirkus Reviews*

"A telling, touching exploration of modern marriage, fidelity, and friendship, Susie Orman Schnall's debut is riddled with the little truths that make up the texture of women's daily lives. Fans of Emily Giffin will relate to this engaging read."

   —Beatriz Williams, internationally bestselling author of *The Secret Life of Violet Grant*

"A moving and vibrant debut that packs a sweet emotional punch. You'll laugh and cry along with Grace as she treads the complicated waters of marriage, motherhood, an unexpected betrayal, and a revelation that changes everything. Susie Orman Schnall is a fresh new voice in fiction."
    —Kristin Harmel, internationally bestselling author of *The Life Intended*

"Grace is an imperfect woman with a less-than-perfect life, but readers will find themselves drawn to her authenticity and grit."
    —Colleen Oakes, bestselling author of *Elly in Bloom*

"An authentic portrayal of the intricacies inherent in modern relationships. Susie Orman Schnall's debut is relatable, honest, and insightful. I look forward to seeing what's next from her."
    —Emily Liebert, bestselling author of *When We Fall*

The Balance Project

SUSIE ORMAN SCHNALL

SparkPress, a BookSparks imprint
A division of SparkPoint Studio, LLC

Published by SparkPress, a BookSparks imprint,
A division of SparkPoint Studio, LLC
Tempe, Arizona, USA, 85281
www.gosparkpress.com

ISBN: 978-1-940716-67-1 (pbk)
ISBN: 978-1-940716-66-4 (e-bk)

Cover design © Julie Metz, Ltd./metzdesign.com
Cover photo © Getty Images
Author photo © Tiffany Oelfke
Formatting by Polgarus Studio

Also by Susie Orman Schnall

On Grace

Kirkus Best Indie Books of 2014

2014 International Book Awards,
Finalist in Fiction: Chick Lit/Women's Lit

2014 Independent Publisher Book Awards,
Bronze Winner in Popular Fiction

For all the women who work at anything.
Especially the moms. . . .

"I absolutely believe you can have it all."

—Katherine Whitney, *The Balance Project*

Chapter One

Sometimes things fall apart because life has something better to come. I read these words over and over again, trying to parse their meaning, trying to relate them to my own life as Katherine and I wait in the small and windowless dressing room, the beige walls heavy with the scent of all the ambition that has previously filled them.

I didn't make that quote up. My best friend, Ava, posted it this morning on Instagram. For someone my age, twenty-five, I have a lower-than-normal interest in following my friends on social media, or so I've been told by people my age. I am wretchedly bored by duck-faced group selfies, look-at-my-exotic-dinner shots, and destination-wedding sunsets. I am, however, a keen devotee of the quote post.

"Katherine Whitney," a goateed production assistant says, peeking his head around the open door. "You're on in five minutes. Please come with me." He looks down at his clipboard as Katherine stands, pats down her dress, and smiles at me.

"Good luck, Katherine!" I say, smiling back.

"Thanks, Luce," she says as she follows the assistant toward the *Today* show set.

I sit back on the faded and itchy couch, relaxing for what seems like the first time since I woke up two hours ago—my morning a frenetic rush because I accidentally set my alarm for 6:00 *p.m.* instead of *a.m.* Luckily I woke up on my own at six fifteen, but I barely had time to throw on one of my uninspiring work outfits, brush my teeth, and put my hair up in a ponytail before I had to race down to Rockefeller Center in time to meet Katherine at seven. I managed lip gloss on the subway.

I had just *enough* time to buy a Glow juice for Katherine and an extra-large, extra-hot, full-fat, full-sugar latte for myself before meeting her in the dressing room. While she sat for hair and makeup, I read her *theSkimm* and the briefing from Brooke, her publicist, on the details for this interview. Impressively and characteristically, Katherine wasn't nervous at all.

Now that she's on her way to the set, I pick at the overflowing catering trays of cut melon and golden pastries on the small coffee table. My mouth is filled with a flaky and gooey chocolate croissant when I hear Katherine's cell phone ring. I try to chew as quickly as possible, while I search frantically through her bag looking for the phone.

"Katherine Whitney's phone," I say, just before it goes to voice mail.

"Who's this?" an angry sounding British-accented voices barks back.

"This is her assistant, Lucy Cooper," I say.

"Lucy, it's Nigel."

"Oh, hi Nigel. Good morning, sir."

"Good afternoon. Lucy, where is Katherine?" he asks urgently. "I've sent her three e-mails this morning and she hasn't returned any of them."

"It's been a busy morning. She's about to go on the *Today* show. Her interview starts in a minute or so. Can I help you with something?"

"Bollocks!" Nigel shouts. "I need you to get Katherine. There have been last-minute changes to one of the contracts for the London restaurant. I need Katherine to read them over and approve them within the next five minutes. I've just had the lawyers e-mail her the document. She needs to print it, sign it, and then have it scanned and e-mailed back. Immediately."

"Um . . . ," I stammer.

"Is there a problem, Lucy?"

"She's actually about to do a live interview with Matt Lauer, and there's no way I can interrupt that." I look at the television monitor that's on mute in the dressing room and see that Matt is introducing Katherine. I tuck Katherine's phone between my shoulder and ear, and turn up the volume on the remote.

"Katherine Whitney is here with us today," Matt Lauer says. *"As you all know, she's the wildly successful forty-five-year-old chief operating officer of Green Goddess & Company. She's been called the woman who woke up Americans to a healthy lifestyle. She's a wife and mother of two. She's a philanthropist and a fixture on the New York City social scene. And, today we celebrate the six-month anniversary of the launch of her bestselling book,* The Balance Project. *She's America's Darling of Balance, a beacon for women everywhere trying to do it all and trying to master the elusive work-life balance. Katherine, welcome. It's good to see you again."*

"Hi Matt, it's good to see you, too. Thanks so much for having me back," Katherine says in her best confident businesswoman voice.

"Lucy! Are you there?" Nigel is shouting again.

"Yes, sorry, sir, but, uh, if you could just wait maybe ten minutes, then I can get her to sign the document when her segment is over." I feel like that emoticon with the stuck-out tongue and greater-than and less-than signs for eyes.

"Bloody hell. Hold on," Nigel says impatiently. I hear him cover the phone and start speaking to someone else, but I can't understand what they're saying because it's muffled. "Okay, ten minutes is fine,

Lucy. But this needs to happen or we may miss the deadline to register the premises and then the opening will have to be delayed. Do you understand? These bloody lawyers are up my arse, and we need Katherine's sign-off. We cannot afford a delay at this point."

"I'm on it, sir." I say, as the line goes dead.

Shit!

I look up at the television to see the time in the bottom corner of the screen: 8:21. And though I may be on the verge of a nervous breakdown, Katherine is the perfect vision of serene gorgeousness. Perfectly blown-out, shoulder-length, blonde wavy hair. Sophisticated yet flirty blush-colored Alaïa dress. Very high nude Louboutin patents. Nicely done, Katherine, nicely done.

"*So, your bestselling book,* The Balance Project, *is celebrating its six-month anniversary today,*" Matt says. "*Remind our viewers how this book came about.*"

"*Two years ago,*" Katherine says, "*I gave the commencement address at my* alma mater, *the University of Michigan. I talked about a lot of things, how Green Goddess started, my thoughts on success, and I also talked about work-life balance, as it relates to both men and women. That speech went viral—*"

"*A couple million hits on YouTube, I think,*" says Matt.

"*Yes, it was amazing. And a few weeks later, I got approached to write a book. The feedback I got from the speech was overwhelming, and I realized that not only was this a hotly debated issue, with people on every side, but also women, and men, who were struggling with balance, wanted guidance. That's what this book provides.*"

Shit!

I open the e-mails on Katherine's phone and find the one from Nigel. I stick my head out of the dressing room and see the goateed production assistant walking by.

"Hey!" I shout to get his attention. "Is there somewhere I can get a document printed?"

"Sorry, we don't do that here," he says and continues down the hall.

"Wait!" I shout. "I'm desperate. Please."

He looks at me for a moment, like he's sizing me up, trying to decide what's in this for him. I guess he found something because he says, "Um, sure. Come with me."

"Thank you so much, you're a lifesaver," I say as I follow him down the hall lined with glossy photos of all the *Today* show hosts, past and present. "I don't mean to be obnoxious, but I'm on a tight deadline here, can we step up the pace a bit?" I smile at him kindly. He gives me a look that I can't quite decipher and starts to walk a little faster. I can not mess this up. If I need to dress up like Pippa Middleton and let Goatee Boy feel my boob to get this document signed and back to London, then I will make that happen. I despise these urgent, walk-on-water types of impossible requests, but in a company like Green Goddess and with a boss like Katherine Whitney it happens a lot. And even though I'm getting better at not freaking out entirely when presented with one of these situations, I absolutely hate them.

We wind our way through the back maze of *Today* show offices and, after what seems like forever, end up in a large room filled with desks.

"You can use one of the printers here," he says.

"Um, okay," I say, looking at his name badge. "Steve, is it?"

"That's me!" he says, pointing his thumbs at his chest.

"Okay, Steve. I just need to forward this e-mail to a computer that I can print off of. Can I use one of these?"

"No, sorry. I don't have access to these computers so I can't log you in."

Deep breath, Lucy.

"So, I have an e-mail on this phone," I say, holding the phone up in the air like he's never seen one before and trying not to sound impatient, "and I need somehow to get it off of this phone before I can print it."

"I wish you would have said that at the beginning. Come with me, I'll take you to Lorraine."

I'm starting to feel exasperated as we walk for another forever. I glance at Katherine's phone: 8:24. Shit! Finally we enter another office where a woman, Lorraine presumably, is sitting behind a large wooden desk answering phones on an elaborate system. She's got wild burgundy hair, heavy eye makeup, and acrylic nails polished in a navy and purple argyle pattern. We wait until she's off.

"Hey, Lorraine," Steve says in what I take to be his flirty voice.

"Hey, Stevie," she says, smiling as she cracks her gum.

"This lady," he gestures to me, "needs something printed. Can you help her?"

"Sure, honey. Anything for you." She says to him before turning to me with a smile. "How can I help, honey? Oh, wait, hold on, I gotta answer this."

By now, my palms are sweating, perspiration stains are starting to spread underneath my arms, and I feel like the entire African elephant population has decided to stampede from my esophagus straight down to my stomach. I eye a trash can next to Lorraine's desk, which will be oh so helpful if I end up having to hurl. While I wait for her to get off the phone—8:25—I look up at the television mounted near the ceiling.

Katherine and Matt sit in white leather chairs facing each other. Matt sits back comfortably in his. Katherine is eagerly on the front edge of hers. Feet firmly on the ground. The huge electronic screen behind them rotates photos of Katherine, the dust jacket of *The Balance Project*, and the Green Goddess lemon-yellow and grass-green logo.

"Why is balance such a, as you say, hotly debated issue?" Matt asks.

"Well, women make up approximately 60 percent of the American

workforce, yet they spend twice as many hours as men on child care and housework. Add to that the fact that in this economy, women often feel they need to work harder to keep and advance in their jobs. Whether this is actually true is irrelevant. It's the perception and that becomes the reality. And that reality translates into a significant amount of pressure on women just to manage what is on their plates. So it's hard. It's a challenge. And women are talking about it a lot to vent, to get ideas on how to manage it better, and to try, in many cases, to affect policy to support working women."

"And what specifically do women seem to be citing as the toughest part of this balance?"

"Oh, Matt, just about everything," Katherine laughs. "But one of the hardest things for women is to take any time for themselves. If a woman is spending more time in the office, because of that perceived or actual pressure to keep her job, that's less time that she can spend with her family and taking care of her own needs. There's this belief out there, much to the detriment of women, that any time not spent on work or family is somehow selfish. That to exercise, take time to eat well, to have lunch with a friend, to read a book, or heaven forbid sleep, that all those things should be given a lower priority than work and family, and not necessarily, but quite possibly, in that order. Women are famous for foregoing sleep to gain the extra hours they need to get by. Coffee helps."

"And green juice!" Matt says triumphantly.

"Yes! Green juice," Katherine smiles.

"Speaking of which, you and Evan Hewitt started Green Goddess almost twenty years ago, and now it's a multibillion-dollar business. You've got a successful national chain of healthy restaurants and juice bars, an e-commerce business that does over a billion dollars in sales every year, a magazine with a circulation of more than three million, and a vibrant website with more than four million unique visitors. You're at the pinnacle of your career, plus you have a husband and two small children. Do you

think *you've found balance, and if so, with all that on your plate, how?"*

"Absolutely," Katherine says.

"Really?" Disbelieving tone. So Matt.

"Really." Convincing tone. So Katherine. "But I don't think balance is something to be found. I think balance is something to be cultivated. And I feel like I've got all my ducks in a row. Green Goddess has solidified itself as the premier wellness brand in America. Revenue and earnings are growing at an accelerated rate as more and more Americans appreciate the benefits of a healthy lifestyle. We're about to open our first restaurant in London. My family is doing great. I feel fantastic. Things can't get much better than that, Matt."

"That's a lot to manage. Do you ever feel like things are out of control?"

"Sure it's a lot to manage. But, to be fair, I'm not doing it all myself. And that's something I stress in the book. You've got to build a support system. I've got people helping me at work—"

Yay, me.

". . . And at home. But for people who are doing it all on their own, I give a lot of tips in my book."

"Honey!" I hear someone saying loudly.

"Oh, right, sorry," I say to Lorraine. "So, I'm so sorry to bother you with this, and I'm in such a ridiculous hurry, but can I forward you an e-mail from this phone and then have you print it? I would be so appreciative."

"Who are you?" Lorraine asks curiously, tilting her head to the side.

"Right, yes, I'm Lucy Cooper. I'm Katherine Whitney's assistant," I say confidently.

"Katherine who?" Lorraine asks.

"Katherine Whitney," I say, pointing to the television. "She's the author of *The Balance Project*." I usually don't have to explain who Katherine is.

"Oh, right, the balance lady."

"Yes, right, the balance lady," I say, trying so hard to be patient and kind. "I'm so sorry to rush you like this but we have a very important deal going on in London now. We're expanding our restaurant business overseas, and they need this document signed, scanned, and e-mailed back in like, five minutes, so if you don't mind giving me an e-mail address I can send this to so you can print it I would be forever grateful, and I'd be happy to give you some vouchers to use at a Green Goddess juice bar." I smile at her and shift my wait nervously from one foot to the other.

"Oh, I love those juices. Sure, honey, no problem," Lorraine says. She gives me the e-mail address, and I forward her the document. As she's working on it on her end, I look back up at the television. It's amazing that Katherine can look so calm and poised while her London deal, which she has been thoroughly engrossed in lately and which is her current pet project, is in a state of cardiac arrest. If she only knew that the whole thing might be put in jeopardy if we don't get this document signed. But she knows none of that right now. Instead, she's her usual composed self with everything under control. Another thing I hope to learn someday from Katherine.

"You've been compared to another successful businesswoman with a book. Sheryl Sandberg. She took a lot of heat for Lean In: Women, Work, and the Will to Lead. *Would you say you're different from her?"*

"I have a lot of admiration for Sheryl," Katherine says. "And I think Lean In *is well researched and powerful. I know Sheryl. We've been on a lot of panels together. At a lot of conferences. Sheryl and I have a lot of similarities in the sense that we're both COOs of large companies, we both are working moms, we both have experienced a lot of success that we're— and I've talked to Sheryl about this—incredibly grateful for. But our missions with our books are different, and our messages are different. Sheryl is focusing on getting and keeping women in the conference rooms and*

especially in the boardrooms. What I'm trying to do with The Balance Project *is help those women stay there by giving them the tools to manage their lives and remain sane."*

"Is there competition between you and Sheryl?" Matt asks.

"Of course not," Katherine says. "We're in totally different business spaces. We've been really supportive of each other. She wrote an endorsement for the back cover of my book. Sheryl and I are good."

"Here you go, honey," Lorraine says.

"Thank you so much!" I say running out of her office as I try to find my way toward the set so I can catch Katherine as soon as she walks off.

"What about those vouchers?" I hear Lorraine shout.

"I'll bring them by after the interview!" I shout back, halfway down the hall.

"You can't go in there!" I turn around and see Goatee Boy holding up his hand to stop me as I screech to a halt at the edge of the set. "That's an active set," he says curtly, clearly enjoying the power he wields over this tiny jurisdiction: the set border.

"Don't worry, I'm not going anywhere. Steve," I say. "I have to get my boss to sign something as soon as she finishes her interview." This dragging interview. There's no way I'm going to get this document to Nigel in ten minutes. We're already at nine minutes. But it looks like they might be wrapping up. Katherine's phone rings again.

"Katherine Whitney's phone. This is Lucy," I say.

"Shhhhhhhhh!" Steve hisses at me. I give him a dirty look and walk away from his empire.

"Lucy. I'm trying to be calm here, but I need that document NOW!" It's Nigel. He started off calmly but ended in a really loud and angry NOW.

"Nigel, I know. I'm doing all I can. I have the document printed, and I'm just waiting for Katherine to finish her interview," I say, quietly, trying to sound professional despite the fact that I feel like a three-year-old getting screamed at by her mommy. "I'll have it signed and e-mailed back to you in a few minutes." The phone goes dead. I thought the English were supposed to have good manners. My stomach is still being trampled by those African elephants, but I tell myself to breathe. There's nothing I can do until Katherine is done. I walk back toward the set and strain to hear. . . .

"So, remind us what exactly is in The Balance Project." *Matt says.*

Oh, good lord.

Katherine sits up taller and gestures with her hands. "The Balance Project *is made up of four main sections. The first section highlights the research and statistics that confirm that, indeed, this is an issue in America. In the second section I feature interviews with successful women talking about balance. The third section gives women strategies and tips on how to achieve balance featuring the GLOW plan, which as you may know is also the name of our bestselling green juice."*

"I have one every morning," Matt says, flashing a smile.

"Fantastic," Katherine says, flashing a smile of her own, while crossing her nude patent leathers.

"And the fourth section?" Matt asks.

"The fourth section is a workbook with a variety of elements. First, it has the exact questions that I asked of all the women who are interviewed in the book, with spaces for the reader to write down her own answers. It's an enlightening exercise for women, to say the least, to truly shine light on how they're doing with this issue. I also have a section on setting priorities and managing your time. And there's a manifesto and pledge for women to fill out and commit to."

Come on, people. Wrap it up already. I'm keeping myself calm by biting on a stress-induced canker sore inside my bottom lip. Fantastic.

"Back to those interviews," Matt says. "We're not talking minor leagues here. You interviewed, among other household names, Hillary Clinton,

Michelle Obama, Marissa Mayer of Yahoo, Angelina Jolie."

"Yes, but I also interviewed women whose names you don't know. My goal is not to alienate readers by only focusing on women with resources. I certainly wanted to include the interviews with the famous women because their stories and perspectives are important and aspirational. But it was more important to me to include interviews with teachers, nurses, retail store managers, police officers, bank tellers, real estate agents. Everyday women who aren't in corner offices, who don't have secretaries, who don't have an army of nannies at hand. These are the women who can teach us the most about balance, and they are well represented in this book."

Fuck, Matt. Wrap. It. Up.

"I, along with what seems to be the whole world, have read the book and it is incredibly comprehensive," Matt says, nodding. Impressed.

"It is. What people might not know, is that we also have a robust companion website where readers can learn more, read interviews that didn't make it into the book, and most importantly, join an active community of women like themselves to share ideas and support one another."

"What one piece of advice would you give to viewers about balancing work and life?"

"To be confident about having it all. It's definitely possible. There's a lot out there about women not being able to have it all, and I don't believe that. We're all capable of succeeding in our careers, our home lives, and as women. It's just a matter of believing in yourself and doing what it takes. Doing it all is most definitely possible. It's as simple as that," Katherine says, flashing her money smile.

"As simple as that, folks. Well, there you have it. Katherine Whitney, thank you so much for joining us. The book is called The Balance Project. *We'll be back with more on* Today *after these messages."*

Cut.

Katherine and Matt stand up and I see them hug. Two people with all the time in the world. She is way too calm for someone whose deal is disintegrating along with every ounce of confidence I have in this being resolved triumphantly. I start to head toward the set but Officer Goatee Boy stops me so I tap my foot and try to get Katherine's attention by waving my arms frantically in the air.

"What are you doing?" Goatee Boy asks sarcastically.

"My job," I say as I sneer at him and continue my frantic gesticulations. Finally Katherine heads toward me.

"Lucy! What are you doing?" Katherine asks in a confused voice.

"Katherine, thank God. Okay," I say breathlessly. "Nigel called and the London lawyers need you to review some changes to the contract and sign off on them and Nigel said he needs the signed document back in ten minutes or you might miss some registration deadline and that was like fifteen minutes ago and you need to do this right now!" I say, trying to stress the urgency of my request.

"Seriously? He's so melodramatic. His final meeting with the lawyers isn't until tomorrow. We're fine," she says, giving me a sympathetic look.

I stare at her in shock. "Are you kidding me? He's such an asshole! I've been running around for the last ten minutes like a freaking beauty pageant contestant looking for butt tape."

"Oh, Luce. I'm sorry. You know Nigel."

"Yes, I know he's an asshole, or I should say arsehole, but he sounded like this was for real."

"Well, even if it is, they can wait five more minutes. I'll call him. Sorry about that," she says kindly.

"It's okay. At least he got my adrenaline pumping this morning. Hopefully, that will count as exercise."

Katherine laughs. "Did your butt-tape pursuit give you any opportunity to watch the interview?"

"Yes, there were times during my butt-tape pursuit when I had to wait for things, so I watched part of it. You were amazing. But I'm not surprised. You always nail things like that." She does.

"Thank you, Lucy. That means so much. Okay, let me call Nigel and tell him to stop abusing you," she says as she takes her phone from me and starts dialing.

I trudge behind her as we walk back toward the dressing room to collect our stuff. It's not even 9:00 a.m. Just another typical morning in the life of Lucy Cooper, the very unbalanced and overworked assistant extraordinaire to America's Darling of Balance.

Chapter Two

Katherine and I leave the NBC building and find Pancho idling on West Fiftieth Street. Pancho is Katherine's driver. He's been driving her for as long as I've been working for her, which is almost three and a half years. Black Escalade ESV. Standard New York City mode of transport for the wealthy and wannabes. Katherine is comfortably in category one. (Don't worry, I remembered to give Lorraine her vouchers.)

We hurry into the car, as a cop yells at Pancho to stop idling, and we head uptown. We'll drop Katherine at the ABC Studios building on Sixty-Seventh and Columbus where she's taping *LIVE with Kelly and Michael,* and then Pancho will take me back to the Green Goddess offices. I was supposed to go to all of Katherine's media appearances with her today, but there's too much going on back at the office. Even though this job is demanding and not exactly what I thought I'd be doing at this stage of my career, I am so appreciative of everything Katherine's done for me. She's the grow light and I'm the germinating seed.

My senior year at Duke, when I was finalizing what to do when I grew up, I decided I wanted to work on websites. Not from a tech perspective, more from a marketing and content perspective. The most opportunities were in New York City and that, along with the fact that my boyfriend Nick was at NYU Law School, made it easy for me to decide where to move upon graduation. The job market was tight, but I managed to get three interviews at companies with reputable and active digital-media departments: Martha Stewart Living Omnimedia, *Cosmopolitan* Magazine, and Green Goddess & Company.

Green Goddess was my number-one choice. My mother was a longtime subscriber to *Green Goddess Magazine* so I had been reading the magazine forever. And though I have a weakness for sugar- and fat-laden coffees and processed food-like products made mostly of partially hydrogenated oils and ingredients I can't pronounce, in my heart of hearts I was a health nut. Or would be someday. I was a little scared of working in Martha's exacting world of pastel perfection, and I wasn't what anyone in their right mind would call a "fun, fearless female," so I was thrilled when I got a call back after my interview at Green Goddess. It went something like this:

"Hi Lucy. This is Emma from Green Goddess's human resources department. We thought your interview was strong, and we think you'd be a great asset to the company. The only teensy little problem is that we ended up hiring internally for the digital-media spot. There is, however, a fabulous and highly coveted position that just opened up as the assistant to our chief financial officer. I know it's not exactly what you were hoping for, but it's a good way to get your foot in the door here at Green Goddess. I actually started in the events department even though I wanted to be in HR, and look where I am now."

Look where you are now, Emma from HR. Sitting in your tiny beige HR cubicle with its knockoff Aeron chair, dashing my digital-media dreams, and offering me a dull secretarial position with some crusty, old, number-crunching bean counter. No, thank you.

I hope you don't think me ungrateful. I realize it was a solid job offer with a paycheck and benefits in a terrible economy, but I was young. Right out of college. I had a digital dream. You can't blame a girl with a digital dream.

"Lucy," judicious Nick said when I told him of the lovely Emma from HR's offer, "Take the job. It's a great opportunity for you to get your foot in the door. You just have to work for the guy for a year or so, and then you'll be in a perfect position to get a different job there. Definitely take it."

"Lucy, dear," my mom said. "That's fantastic. I know it's not what you want to do, but it's a job, honey. And a great way to get your foot in the door. It sounds like you should not pass that up."

"Luce," my oldest brother Matt said. "It's tough out there right now. This sounds like a great opportunity to get your foot in the door."

After realizing that getting your foot in the door seemed to be highly valued by all the people I respected most in the world, I called the lovely Emma from HR back. It went something like this: "This is Lucy Cooper. Thank you so much for the opportunity. I'll take it."

I started working for Richie Cunningham, the CFO of Green Goddess, late in the summer of 2010. He was born way before *Happy Days* first aired so his name, the same as Ron Howard's character from the legendary TV show, was a coincidence, yet still a never-ending source of humor for me. I had watched a lot of *Happy Days* reruns after school with my brothers. While I was grateful to, bear with me, get my foot in the door of what was a great company to work for—supercool offices at Columbus Circle, beautiful lemon-yellow and grass-green decor with modern white desks and reclaimed wood floors, a subsidized and healthy cafeteria, free juice bar, nice people, generous benefits, and a relaxed dress code that didn't even begin to approach what I heard was going down at Condé Nast—I did not like my job one itty-bitty bit.

I realized I had to pay my dues. I had a good attitude. I did whatever Richie Cunningham asked me to do. I answered his phones politely, I fetched his turkey sandwiches on white with extra mustard and coleslaw, and I efficiently collated his dry and lifeless little

PowerPoints. I wasn't one of those whiny entitled millennials. In fact, I worked my little entry-level tail off and kept my grumbling to myself. But the work was boring. Richie Cunningham was usually, at best, moody, and at worst, plain old mean. And on occasion, Richie Cunningham had a really, really bad temper.

Sometimes he would refuse to call me Lucy and instead would call me Goosey. (Don't ask, I had no idea why then and I still don't.) And heaven forbid I didn't turn the stapler just so to ensure the staples were at perfect forty-five-degree angles. I knew his temper had nothing to do with me. I presumed, at the time, it was related to earnings and stock prices and audits and all that other financial hocus-pocus that I found terribly dull. That explanation didn't entirely make sense to me though, because as I understood it, Green Goddess was doing well. Incredibly well. Due in part, the media would report, to its brilliant COO Katherine Whitney, whom I had started to say *hello* to in passing and was starting to admire. But back to Richie Cunningham's temper. So it turned out to be not about the numbers at all. Turns out Richie Cunningham's wife (no, her name was not Lori Beth) was cheating on him with Richie Cunningham's best friend (no, his name was not Fonzie). I'll leave it at that.

But whatever was—or was not—going on in Richie Cunningham's marital bed was making my life unbearable. Still, I wanted to give it a year. I'd heard enough career-building advice to know that having a job on your résumé that lasted less than a year would prompt fastidious future employers to ask awkward questions. It had only been four months.

One day, in the middle of a truly miserable day of reporting to Mr. Mean, I was on the verge of tears. I didn't want to burst out sobbing in full view of everyone, and I knew I wouldn't make it to the general population ladies room before the tears started raining down. That bathroom was clear across the floor from my desk, which sat squarely in the middle of the senior executive wing. So I decided to sneak into the *senior executive wing's* ladies room, which only ever saw the likes of one Katherine Whitney considering she was—and still is—the only *lady* senior executive at Green Goddess. I had heard that morning from her assistant Janie that Katherine was away on business, so I took my chances that I could sneak on in and cry my little eyes out in peace.

Janie must have been confused or Katherine must have come back from her trip early, because while I was in the throes of bawling all over the exquisite grey glass and white marble of the senior executive wing's ladies room, trying to get every last tear out so I could return to my desk and my dreadful occupational circumstances, in walked Katherine Whitney, as shocked to see me as I was to see her.

"What's wrong? Are you okay?" Katherine had asked me. Concerned. It was four words more than she had ever said to me.

"Nothing, really, I'm fine," I had said, quickly wiping away my tears with my spent tissue, striving, or rather, struggling, for composure. "I'm so sorry I'm in here," I had said, hurrying toward the door.

"Wait. It's okay. And that doesn't look like fine to me."

Would you believe I told Katherine everything? The poor woman had only bargained for your standard pee and wash, and I subjected her to an entire Barbara Walters–worthy confessional. I told her about how mean Richie Cunningham was (she knew). About how I only took the job to get my foot in the door even though I wanted to be in digital media (she thought I had made a wise decision and extolled the virtues of getting one's foot in the door). About how I wanted to quit because I couldn't take one more day of working in these conditions (she advised against it). Katherine told me Richie had a way of going through assistants quite rapidly and that she and the CEO were dealing with that. And then she handed me extra tissues from the fancy senior executive tissue box and helped me on my way.

I continued to do my time, and it was only two weeks later that Janie fortuitously tendered her resignation because she was moving to Dallas for her husband's new job. The same day said resignation was fortuitously tendered, Katherine approached me and asked if I would interview to replace Janie. She said she had heard from Richie that I was a great assistant. She told me she knew that I wanted to do digital media but working for her would be a great way to learn about everything going on in the company and that she always had special projects over which I could take ownership. (Another foot in the door.) She promised me it wouldn't be a typical assistant's position and that it would be nothing like working for Richie Cunningham. *Sayonara* Richie Cunningham.

I went through the required rounds of interviews and emerged through the gauntlet triumphant. And that is how I became Katherine Whitney's assistant.

Katherine delivered on each of her campaign promises. While working for her, I have learned so much about every aspect of Green Goddess. She lets me listen in on conference calls and sit in on meetings that no other assistants attend. There have been numerous special projects. Because she wants me to learn. Because she wants me to be a successful *lady* executive just like her one day. It has not been a typical assistant's position. It has been nothing like working for Richie Cunningham. It has been a dream.

Until lately. Lately, it's been more of a nightmare. Nothing to do with Katherine. Katherine's kind and fair, she usually gets her own lunch, and she doesn't give a shit about which direction her staples face. But I'm still not working in digital media, which has slowly started to eat me up inside, a perpetual and sour-tasting yearning for my as-yet unrealized potential, and I've been way too busy with barely any time for anything else in my life.

If today is any indication, it looks like that's not going to let up anytime soon.

"Katherine Whitney's office," I say into the receiver. There are two other lines on hold. "Sorry to keep you waiting."

"This is Nancy from Dr. Browning's office. I'm calling to confirm Katherine Whitney's appointment tomorrow at eight thirty."

"Katherine Whitney's office."

"This is Eleanor from the York Agency. I'm calling to tell Ms. Whitney that we have six very qualified nannies that we'll be interviewing today. We'll follow up with her tomorrow to let her know how the screening went, and we'll hopefully have several candidates for her to consider."

"Katherine Whitney's office."

"Hey Lucy. It's Peter. Katherine told me that she's out for most of the morning, but can you make sure she calls me the minute she walks in? I have to review the final menu for London with her. It's pretty urgent."

"Katherine Whitney's office."

"This is Alexandra Nathanson from the parents association at The Cartwright School. Can you please let Katherine know she's been nominated to chair the book fair at the school next fall. Word has gotten out that she's doing such a great job as class mom in Abby's kindergarten class, and we'd love for her to take on a bigger role next year."

"Katherine Whitney's office."

"This is Nigel. Tell Katherine I must speak with her immediately."

"Katherine Whitney's office."

"Hello there, Lucy! It's Brooke! She did so great on *Today*, didn't you think? We all thought she killed it! Anyway, tell her that, and then tell her to call me. Yay! So happy! Thanks, Lucy! See you later!"

"Katherine Whitney's office."

"Hey, gorgeous."

"Hey! Katherine's phone has been blowing up this morning. I didn't even notice it was my line ringing. What's shaking, hot stuff?"

Hot stuff is also known as Nick Heston. Cutest boyfriend in the world.

"It's done."

"No."

"Yes. Ty signed the contract this morning. I'm officially his agent. Can you believe it?"

"Oh my God. I'm so happy for you! Nick, that's amazing," I say, smiling.

"I know. I can't believe it, but I have the contract right here. Wait, I'll take a picture of it and text it to you." Pause. *Click*. "Okay, let me know when you get it."

Ping.

"Got it," I say, enlarging the photo on my phone with my fingers. There it is, in script: *Ty Collins*.

"Amazing, right?' Nick asks excitedly. And then I picture him, left hand on his hip, right hand on the phone, his ridiculously handsome smile even more ridiculous, pacing around his apartment, which is now the official headquarters of the newly minted Nick Heston Sports Management, Inc.

"This changes everything for you," I say.

"I know, babe. It's really happening."

"It's amazing. All you've been working toward for so long."

"I made a reservation at Nobu downtown at seven to celebrate. Ty is coming, and he's bringing his new girlfriend. Sound good?"

"Of course I'll be there," I say. "Wouldn't miss it for anything."

"I love you, Coop. Thanks for being so great. And so sexy. Do you want to be sexy with me tonight, by the way?"

"I love you, too, Nick," I say laughing. "And," I whisper, "I *would* like to be sexy with you tonight." I hang up, look down at the boring and entirely unsexy outfit I threw on this morning, and groan.

Nick is the kind of guy, the loveliest kind, who never finds anything unfortunate with my standard black-pants-and-a-blouse look, but always compliments me when I put a little more effort into an outfit. He also, the dear, says he prefers me without makeup, which is a good thing considering my ability to successfully wield an eyeliner is comparable to my ability to successfully prepare a home-cooked meal, file my own income taxes, and match my bra to my underwear. I can do it but the results aren't always pretty.

. "Katherine Whitney's office."

"Luciebelle," Evan says approaching my desk as I hang up that last call. He peeks around and sees that Katherine isn't at her desk. "When will she be in? I need to talk to her about London." Evan runs his fingers through his perfectly coiffed light-brown hair. As usual, he's a vision of stylish chic in a slim-fitting tweed suit, camel-color cashmere scarf, and charcoal-grey bow tie.

"Early afternoon. Right now she's taping *LIVE with Kelly and Michael*. Then she's heading to SiriusXM to do an interview with *The Moms*—"

"Okay. Got it," Evan says, shaking his hair out of his piercing green eyes. "Will you tell her I need to see her as soon as she gets in?"

"For a swell guy like yourself? Anything," I say.

"Thanks, Luce."

And, with that, Evan Hewitt, cofounder and director of business development of Green Goddess, heads back to his office that is personally designed, I must add, by his dear friend Jonathan Adler with the requisite lacquer desk, snarky needlepoint pillows, and a divine every-hue-known-to-man color scheme. It's to die for, or so Evan and Katherine tell me, since I'm not known to die for things like that.

I spend the next two hours fielding calls, dodging needy coworkers, managing Katherine's social media accounts (ironic, considering I have no interest in managing my personal social media accounts), which are going crazy as a result of her media appearances this morning, and trying to keep all the balls in the air. Balls must stay in the air.

Ever since Katherine's book came out last October, exactly six months ago today, things have been busier around here than the chardonnay line at a Michael Bolton concert. The phone calls are constant, and Katherine might as well be a world leader, or a Beverly Hills plastic surgeon, considering how overloaded her schedule is. Of course we expected *The Balance Project* to sell really well, but we didn't anticipate that it would virtually change Katherine's life. That she would go from being a hard-working, unknown COO to a sought-out, oft-photographed, highly respected household name. But that's exactly what happened.

The TED Talk she did a few months ago still gets around a thousand views a day, she's been named one of *Fortune's* Most Powerful Women in Business, she's spoken at the White House, been interviewed by Oprah, and has appeared on the cover of every major magazine. Katherine's life feels like a runaway train and I'm the one racing over the perilous tracks trying to slow it down.

"Hi, I'm back," Katherine whispers when she eventually returns to the office, tilting the phone away from her mouth while still listening to her call. She approaches my desk, an extra-large Green Goddess Glow juice in hand and a huge Chloé bag on her shoulder.

"Hey," I whisper back. "Let me help you with that," I say as I grab the Chloé, easing her short journey into her office, which is personally designed, I must add, by *her* dear friend Kelly Wearstler with the requisite bronze desk, vintage leather and wood office chair, plus sofa, plus other chairs, graphic silk rug, and a divine collection of coffee-table books and *très chic* accessories. It's to die for, or so Katherine and Evan tell me, since, well, you know. . . .

I plop down on a Kelly chair across from Katherine and wait for her to finish her call. I look at my reflection in the back of a silver frame on Katherine's desk. My hazel eyes look tired and my hair looks droopy. I pull out the hair band holding my ponytail, run my fingers through my long, brown, straight hair, pull it up to the back of my head, and rewrap the hair band around it all.

"So, how did you think everything went this morning?" I ask Katherine when she's off the phone.

"Jesus. Seventeen new e-mails since I got in the elevator!" Katherine says, looking at her computer.

"And your phone has been ringing off the hook all morning. Let me grab all the messages."

I run through the Urgents, Pretty Importants, Can Waits, and finally, the Don't Bothers, which will fall to me because Katherine believes everyone deserves a reply.

"Okay. On it. Thanks, Lucy."

"Just doing my job, boss woman."

"No, really, Luce. Things have been their own brand of crazy around here lately. And if this book keeps up at a pace anything like *Lean In*, the crazy will continue for a while. Crazy good. But still crazy. You know I couldn't do any of this without you."

"Well, I'm happy for you. You deserve all this."

"Let's just hope I can hold it all together and get through all this book stuff and the restaurant opening in London. Curious scheduling, these two, happening at the same time."

"No problem. You can handle it. And you've got me. Your loyal minion. Your trusty acolyte. Your noble steed."

"Nice," Katherine says, laughing. "Nice to know I've got you in my court. Okay, enough of this lovey-dovey bullshit. Let's get to work.

We'll head out at six thirty."

"What's at six thirty?" I ask.

"It's the book celebration dinner," Katherine says. "What do you mean, what's at six thirty?"

"I didn't know anything about a book dinner."

"It's on my calendar. Look," she says pointing to her calendar program that is open on her computer. "Wednesday, six thirty, book dinner."

"I know it's on *your* calendar. But I didn't know I was invited."

"Of course you're invited," Katherine gushes, staring at her computer and taking a long drag of her juice. "What the hell kind of nonsense are you talking? Simon & Schuster is hosting it to celebrate the first six months of record-breaking sales, Brooke and the other publicists are coming, Theo will be there. You have to help with Theo. Of course you're coming."

"I kinda have something tonight," I say slowly, realizing that this conversation might end, will most definitely end, with me agreeing to Katherine's dinner and missing Nick's. "And what I'm wearing does not earn the right to attend the book dinner of a *New York Times* best seller," I say motioning to my standard-issue black pants, boring white blouse, and black ballerina flats. I am, as I've mentioned, not gifted in the sartorial arts.

"Well, you can't miss this, Lucy, and you're dressed fine. You were instrumental in getting this book done. You are first violin in this orchestra we call my life. I wouldn't feel right if you weren't there. Six thirty."

"Six thirty," I echo, sulking to my desk.

And Nick loses again.

It's not that I can't tell Katherine that I have a previous engagement. It's not like she'll fire me or hold it against me if I tell her I can't come to her dinner. It's more that I feel insanely loyal to her and to my career. There are certain sacrifices I have to make to be professional. I feel loyal to Nick as well, but he's always much better at understanding than Katherine is. So I usually let her win. Hopefully, that strategy won't come back to haunt me, but I'm not so sure.

Chapter Three

"I'm gonna be late for your dinner and I'm so sorry and Katherine needs me to go to her book party and I just found out about it and I'm so sorry and I love you and please don't be mad," I say into the phone in one breath.

"Whoa, whoa, slow down tiger. What's going on?" Nick asks.

"Ugh, Nick. Tonight is some book dinner that Katherine's publishers are throwing for her for the six-month anniversary of *The Balance Project* launch."

"Really?"

"She thought I knew about it, but of course I didn't or I wouldn't have told you I could be at Nobu at seven. But the dinner's in Tribeca, too, so I won't be that late. Just start without me, and I'll get there as soon as I can."

"Coooooop," he says, dejected, calling me by his nickname for me. The same thing he's been calling me since we met at the beginning of my freshman, his sophomore, year at Duke.

"I know. I know. I'm a terrible girlfriend. I'm so sorry. I will be there, and then I will make it up to you after dinner. I promise," I say in my sexiest voice, at least the sexiest one I can use at the office.

"Can't you get out of it?"

"No, I can't get out of it, Nick. This is my job."

"I know. But tonight is a really big deal for me."

"Hold on," I say, putting him on hold.

"Katherine Whitney's office, can you hold please?"

"Okay, I'm back, but I gotta go. I'm really sorry. You know I am," I say.

"It just seems like you're always choosing Katherine over us lately," Nick says.

"It's not that I'm *choosing*, Nick, it's that this is my job and there are certain things I have to do outside of normal business hours. You know how Katherine's life is," I say, rushing, watching the blinking hold light on Katherine's line out of the corner of my eye.

"I do understand, Coop, you know I do. You're just always so rushed, and I think it's all too much. You've been so stressed lately. I wanted to celebrate with you tonight."

"And I want to celebrate with you, too. And we will, just a little late. I appreciate your concern, Nick, it *has* all been too much lately. But can we talk about it later? The phones are ringing like crazy over here."

"Okay, hurry through your dinner. See you later."

"Keep my seat warm and my Kirin cold, and I'll be there as fast as you can say yellowtail sashimi with jalapeños. Bye."

Deep breath.

"Katherine Whitney's office. Thank you for holding."

The rest of the day speeds by in a torrent of productivity, and at 6:35 Katherine and I race out of the building to her waiting car. The chilly April air stings my cheeks, and I wrap my black coat more tightly around myself. Katherine slinks gracefully and I slump, well, ungracefully, into the backseat. Pancho hits the gas.

Katherine adjusts her earpiece and returns to a phone call that she had put on hold while we were in the elevator.

"I realize that, Peter," Katherine says, most definitely annoyed. "And I'm not concerned. Everything is going to be fine."

Peter's turn.

"Yes, I realize London is asleep and we're wasting valuable hours, but it can wait until tomorrow. Call Nigel first thing in the morning or, if it will make you feel better, set your alarm and call him at 3:00 a.m. our time. I'm really not worried at all."

Peter's turn.

"Yes. Thank you, Peter. We'll talk about it tomorrow."

"Sorry," Katherine sighs loudly, checks her phone, reads a few e-mails, responds to one, and starts another phone call.

"Sorry, Luce. I want to call the girls before they go to sleep."

As Katherine talks to her daughters (Abby is five and Jordan just turned three), I draw a happy face with my fingers on the fogged-up window. I turn the smile upside down, erase the whole thing with a quick swipe of my palm, and stare out the window as Manhattan races by in silvers, greens, mirrors, yellow blurs, and rushing heads-down pedestrians. The Green Goddess offices are at Columbus Circle on the Upper West Side, far from dinner in Tribeca but close to Katherine's apartment way up high in a fancy doorman building on Central Park West and not too far at all from my modest walk-up on Eighty-Third between Broadway and Amsterdam.

I am happy to have a moment to breathe. Between handling the incessant calls that came in for Katherine today and managing her social media accounts (tweet, retweet, favorite, post, share, like, comment, begin again), and every other little thing that I do to keep her life—personal, professional, and otherwise—in order, I realize I'm praying at the altar of busy and lighting incense to cover the stench.

I take my phone out of my tote, scroll through my Instagram feed, and read Ava's latest post: *If you want something you've never had, then you've got to do something you've never done.* The Drina Reed quote is written in big white-block letters against a scene of a person jumping off a craggy cliff into a crisp, blue sea. I imagine what it would feel like to be that brave. To just jump.

I've been thinking about what *I* want a lot lately. Both as it relates to my future with Nick and my career. The Nick part seems simple. We're happy being *Nick and Lucy*. Sure he's frustrated that I've been so busy lately, but he's building his career, too, so he understands why I have to do what I do. Lately, though, when I think about my career, I get a nervous stomach. This running around, putting out fires, existing only so that Katherine's life runs smoothly is not what I picture when I envision a perfect day in the life of Lucy's career. But I'm paying my dues. Head down, hard work, no complaints. Isn't that what I have to do at this point in my career?

"Okay. So," Katherine says, shifting her position so she can look me in the eye. "How is everything going?"

Well, my boyfriend is upset with me because not only am I missing the dinner celebrating the biggest thing that's ever happened in his career, but I've also been terribly neglectful of our relationship. Taking proper care of your balanced life is preventing me from having any semblance of balance in my own. I haven't gone for a run in months. I have been going to bed way too late and getting up way too early to keep up with everything at work. My face is a swarming mess of angry, stress-related zits. I haven't had time to do laundry, so this is the fifth time in the last two weeks that I've worn this whitish blouse, if you haven't noticed. I've been eating spicy Cheetos for dinner. And things are so busy at work that I never feel like I'll ever catch up.

"Fine," I say cheerfully. This is my job after all and I can't afford to lose it. Rent. Cable. Spicy Cheetos.

"I'm checking in because I know things have been really busy with the book and everything else. I know today, particularly, was beyond insane, and I have a feeling things are going to remain in that galaxy for quite some time."

Ugh.

Katherine's phone pings. She looks at it. She looks at me.

"Yes, today was most definitely a 9.0 on the insane scale," I say, attempting a weak smile.

"I know I ask a lot of you, Lucy, and I hope you know that I appreciate you more than I can even say."

"I know. It's all good, Katherine. Don't worry about me."

"Okay, but if things start really getting out of hand and you need me to bring in reinforcements, I can do that. My life might be out of control, but your life doesn't have to be."

"Got it. Work-life balance and all. Thanks, I'll make sure to let you know if I start taking up the bottle due to my high stress levels and lack of time to eat." I smirk. She knows my act by now.

Katherine's phone rings. "This is Katherine," she says, putting her Bluetooth back in her ear.

Dinner drags. I watch the clock, pick at my dessert, and plan my escape.

"What's the hurry, slugger?" Theo, who's sitting to my left, asks me, sensing my plot. He calls me slugger. I have no idea why. But I like it just fine.

Theo Laurent is Katherine's husband. He's a professor of economics at Columbia and completely adored by his students. Especially the ones of the female persuasion. And, he's one of my favorite people in the world. True, true, I don't know that many people, but even if I did, I'm sure Theo would still make the cut. For one thing, he likes to drink beer and I like to drink beer, and in this city of cosmos and cabernets, any friend of the lager is a friend of mine.

When Katherine said earlier that I have to "help" with Theo, she didn't mean to imply that Theo *needed* help. She just knows that at events like this, Theo could use a pal. Theo is brilliant and kind and presidentially handsome—he's always reminded me of Olivia Pope's Fitz on *Scandal*—but he's not entirely enamored by the small talk and empty mingling that goes on, on occasion, on lots of occasions, in Katherine's world. Theo's world is academic and thorough and decisive and intellectual. Sure, Katherine's world can be, too, given the right event. But Katherine's world can also be bedazzled and one-dimensional and "you look fabulous," and that's where we are tonight. So I'll help with Theo. But, to be fair, Theo also helps with me.

"Just somewhere else I'm supposed to be." I look at my phone: 8:43.

"Nick?"

"Yep."

"All good in that department?" Theo asks, taking a sip of his beer.

"Well, if you must know," I smile, chin in palm, elbow on table, "Nick's frustrated because I've been very busy lately with the daunting task of handling your lovely wife's bustling life. Handling her phones. Handling her schedule. Handling her handlers. Handling her Twitter and Facebook. I curse that Mark Zuckerberg."

Theo laughs.

"I'm trying to keep up while maintaining a rosy complexion, a sense of sanity, and a clean wardrobe. And I'm trying to watch her to see how *she* does it. But, between you and me, Theo, it's profoundly overwhelming. I'm not so good at overwhelming. I don't know how, to coin a phrase, she does it all."

"Well, she doesn't do it all. You do some. I do some. The nanny and Pancho and all the other villagers do some. But, yes, she is pretty remarkable at, as you say, doing it all. That's understandable considering she's, how did Matt Lauer put that, America's Sweetheart of Balance?"

"Darling. Darling of Balance," I say.

We laugh. That Matt Lauer.

"Well, regardless, she makes it *look* very easy. You are one lucky guy, Theo Laurent. You seem to have scored yourself one capable, competent, and well-loved lady."

"Why don't you tell her you're drowning, Lucy? I'm sure she could hire you some help."

"An assistant for the assistant?" I ask mockingly.

"Wouldn't be the first," Theo says.

"It's just a busy spell. We'll get out of it. It's a lot but I can handle it." I start to analyze why it is that I'm trying to be a martyr. Why I won't ask for help. Delegating some of the administrative work might actually be a good idea because it would free me up to do more of the special projects that I really love. But I worry that having to oversee a new assistant will be even more time-consuming. *If you want something done right, do it yourself* and all. I make a mental note to think about that more but for now, it's getting late and I want to go.

I check my watch again.

"Go," Theo says, observing my not-so-stealthy move. "I'll cover for you. We've eaten filet. We've raised a toast. We've enjoyed laughter and gaiety. Your duties, in my opinion, have been fulfilled for the night. And if America's Darling has any issue with that, well, I'll handle it."

"Thanks, Theo," I say, standing up and kissing his cheek.

It's eight forty-five, and I only have four blocks to cover to get from where I am to where my darling boy, who is hopefully not too pissed at me, is holding court at arguably the best Japanese restaurant in Manhattan. Good thing I'm not a stiletto girl or those four blocks would be ugly.

"Sorry. So sorry I'm late!" I exhale when I finally arrive at the table at Nobu, giving Nick a big smooch. Ty stands up, swallows me in a hug, and then introduces me to his girlfriend, Lauren. Latest in a long line. She won't last. We hug.

"That's all right, Coop, no worries," Nick says almost convincingly, passing me a small bottle of Kirin and gesturing to my waiting yellowtail sashimi with jalapeños. Whataguy.

I take a bite of the glistening fish and savor the deliciousness of my favorite dish. Then I attempt a toast. "I don't know if my unexcused tardiness precludes my prerogative to give a toast, but if it does, I really don't give a shit. So a toast—"

"A toast!" Nick, Ty, and Lauren announce joyfully, their considerable delight belying the indisputable truth that they're clearly at least two, if not three, toasts ahead of me.

"A toast," I continue, "to the start, rather, a continuation of a beautiful relationship. Tonight has been a long time coming. We had to get Nick through law school and those awful ball-busting years working for Grant at Actors and Athletes International, and we had to get Ty through a couple years playing at Duke and eight years of stellar athletic achievement with the Cleveland Cavaliers, and now here we are. Nick has the client of his dreams. Ty has the agent of his dreams. And it's all just so fucking awesome. Cheers!"

"Cheers!"

I've known Ty since college, and Nick met Ty several years before that. Nick and Ty played together at AAU basketball camps all through high school. They were both recruited to play basketball at Duke, and they decided to room together when they both committed—neither decision, rooming together or committing to Duke, requiring more than a second's contemplation. Unfortunately, a shocking and devastating diagnosis of hypertrophic cardiomyopathy, a heart condition, during Nick's precollege physical destroyed his dream to play Division 1 for Duke and Coach K.

Even though Nick couldn't be on the team, his grades were good enough that he was still able to matriculate. And Coach K gave him one of the highly regarded positions of team manager, which Nick took very seriously his freshman and sophomore years. Ty, who became the star of Duke's legendary team, left after his sophomore year and was the first pick in the NBA draft that year. He has played with the Cavs ever since and is regarded as the second-best player in the league, after LeBron James. Ty and LeBron are the Sheryl Sandberg and Katherine Whitney of the NBA.

"So what happens now?" I ask.

"Well," Nick says. "The official announcement of the signing will happen tomorrow morning. I'll get a nasty call from Grant, which will be amusing and intensely satisfying. I'll spend the rest of my day dealing with Ty's lawyers as well as Nike and Gatorade and the other companies he endorses. And then we'll cap off the day watching our beloved New York Knickerbockers play our now even-more-beloved Cleveland Cavaliers."

Grant Jerome is Nick's old boss at AAI, only the most-prominent sports and talent agency in the world. Nick started at AAI right out of law school but left when he thought it was a possibility that the Ty Collins deal might come through. Grant is going to have a little-girl temper tantrum (that I wish I could observe in person) because Ty signed with Nick and his one-man band. Ty had been with an agent in Los Angeles throughout his career, but Grant's been courting him aggressively since he left Duke. Luckily, my boyfriend is a brilliant attorney so he did everything by the book to avoid any accusations of "stealing a potential client" from Grant. Still, Grant's going to have a fit.

Ty hears his name called from across the restaurant, looks up, smiles, and stands up. LeBron James, Ty's Cavaliers teammate, approaches our table and gives a fist pump to Ty and Nick. AAI, specifically Grant Jerome, is LeBron's agent so LeBron knows Nick.

After Ty introduces Lauren and me, LeBron says, "This looks like some kind of celebration."

"Sure is," Ty says. "I just signed with Nick's new company."

"Damn!" LeBron says enthusiastically, flashing his infectious smile. "I thought you were with AAI, Nick."

"Was. Was with AAI. I quit a couple months ago and went out on my own."

"That's fantastic. Well congrats, guys. Gotta head back to my table. See you tomorrow, Ty. Get some sleep. Nice meeting you, ladies."

Okay, that was pretty cool. I've been a basketball fan all my life. My brothers all played college ball. I was a Cameron Crazy at Duke all four years. My boyfriend is a sports agent. I've met a lot of athletes. But LeBron is my favorite player of all time (after Magic, of course), and that was pretty cool.

"Who was that?" Lauren asks.

Really?

Delicious sushi. Another Kirin. Memories by the dozen of good times at Duke. Laughter.

"I gotta get some sleep. Big game tomorrow night," Ty says standing up and wiping his hands on his napkin. He grabs Lauren's sweater off the back of her chair and helps her put it on. Parting gesture. She'll be on the first flight back to Cleveland tomorrow morning.

"Yes, I'll see you tomorrow night at The Garden," Nick says.

"Will you be there, Lucy?" Ty asks.

"No, sorry, Ty," I say apologetically. "My boss has a book-signing event, and I have to go and help."

"She's keeping you busy, huh?"

"Yeah, but it's all good." I sneak a peek at Nick. He's looking toward the window, away from me.

"I thought you were interviewing for another job? A computer job, wasn't it?" Ty asks.

"Yeah, good memory," I say. "That's the direction I want to be heading in. A friend had told me about an opportunity a few months back, but it never panned out. In due time, I guess."

"Yeah. But you've got to make your own dreams happen, Lucy," Ty says. "Sounds a lot like you're helping to make someone else's dreams happen."

"Wasn't that the line from your last Nike commercial?" Nick asks sarcastically.

"Yeah, maybe," Ty says, laughing. "But you know I want the best for Lucy."

"We know, and that's why we love you. Thank you for looking out for me," I say to Ty.

Kisses. Hugs. Back-slapping man hugs.

"Let's go back to my place, Coop," Nick whispers in a serious voice into my ear. "There's something I need to talk to you about."

Chapter Four

As I mentioned earlier, Nick and I met my freshman, his sophomore year at Duke. Doing the math, that brings us to almost eight years of dating. Some people, namely my mother and my best friend, Ava, have encouraged, even pressured, us to do the unmentionable number two or get off the pot. But we're doing just fine. We're young. We're enjoying our twenties. We're building our careers. And we're both good with that situation. At least I am. Nick makes side comments and little jokes all the time about getting married, but if he were serious about it, he would have proposed by now.

We have separate apartments because we're both old-fashioned when it comes to living together when you're not married. But it's pretty much a farce since we spend a lot of nights together and have all the necessaries at each other's place: toothbrush, extra clothes, iPhone charger.

After more good-byes to Ty and Lauren on the sidewalk outside of Nobu, we take an UberX to Nick's apartment near Union Square. Nick has to return a call from Ty's lawyer, so I take advantage of the short ride and close my eyes. Sleep is the only thing on my mind. There seems to be something else on Nick's.

But my mind starts racing, quashing any hopes for a quick nap, however brief and ultimately unfulfilling. I capitalize on my wakefulness and try to figure out why Nick is mad at me. There are the usual reasons: I'm too busy and I'm putting my job before our relationship. But we discussed those recurring themes today, and I thought he understood why things are a bit crazier than usual right now.

Nick and I have always had an effortless relationship. We've spent years challenging each other, loving each other, supporting each other, and, most importantly, cracking each other up. I once made him a dorky (at the time I thought of it as romantic and sentimental) collage for one of our early anniversaries. I pasted on photos and words from magazines of all the things we both like and the things we'd done together. Nick loved that gift and he still has it hanging up in the back of his closet.

Sometimes, when we're in a nostalgic mood, we push all his clothes to the side and look at it. We point out the photo of us skydiving (we did it to celebrate my graduation from college; at that time of my life I wasn't afraid of jumping), two yellow labs playing (we both grew up with labs and we've always said we'll get one together someday), Sean Connery (we're both huge James Bond fans and Sean's our favorite), and Tiger Woods (inside joke, long story). There are so many memories contained in those peeling, pasted pictures. It could probably use an updating.

Maybe Nick is thinking our relationship could use one, too.

We walk up the five flights of dingy stairs to his tiny apartment in silence. He unlocks the heavy door and holds it open for me. I flip the light switch next to the door, set down my bag, and take off my shoes, which despite being flats are, at this point, killing me.

"Want a water?" Nick asks, heading toward the fridge in his small galley kitchen.

"Yes, please," I say, sweetly. I sit down on Nick's brown futon couch—yes, so very stereotypical and trite, but I swear that's what he has—and curl my legs underneath me.

Nick sets the waters down on the simple wood coffee table, sits down next to me, and starts.

"I don't want to make a big deal about this because I know it's not a big deal, but I was really bummed that you weren't there tonight."

I stare into his eyes and let him continue.

"Signing Ty is going to change everything for me. This is huge, Coop."

"I know, Nick. And I'm so happy for you. And I was there. It's been really hard lately. Katherine—"

"I'm getting tired of Katherine this, Katherine that. Like this book signing tomorrow night. Can't she have that Brooke lady help her instead of you? Isn't that her job?" He sounds annoyed.

"Yes, but Brooke and all the publicists that usually tend to her are in LA for an event, so she needs someone around."

"To tend to her?" he asks sarcastically.

"You know what I mean. Stuff comes up. She needs extra hands. Nick, I know it doesn't make any sense because *we* take care of ourselves," I say motioning to the two of us. "But this is what happens when you get all famous and successful, you need people around to help with stuff. And trust me, there is always stuff that comes up during events like this."

"Well, what if I need tending to?" Nick asks as the right side of his mouth turns up in a boyish grin.

"Well then, I will have to rush home and tend to you," I say, smiling.

"I've been so understanding lately about your job coming first," Nick says, suddenly getting very serious, "and tonight was kinda the straw that broke the camel's back."

"What do you mean?" I ask, not sure what the camel is representing here. I can't imagine the camel is representing our relationship and my choosing Door Number One tonight instead of Door Number Two could have delivered a fatal blow to our relationship.

"I mean I've been holding a lot in for the last few months because I know you've been so busy, and I haven't wanted to add more stress to your plate. I'm starting to see that you being stressed out all the time and us having barely any time together during the week is taking a toll on our relationship."

Nick might be one of the most laid-back and even-keeled people I know. It's part of the reason we have been together for so long. There is usually no drama with Nick. So I know, by how he's acting right now, that this is serious.

"I know things aren't ideal right now, Nick. But what do you want me to do?" I ask, getting flustered. "I don't know what to do. Tell me what to do. I have this job and it's a really demanding job, and I can't just waltz in at nine every morning and leave at five every night. My job doesn't work like that. And however much it's stressful and incredibly time-consuming right now, I love that job. I know it sounds insane, but despite this not being the job I thought I would be in at this point in my life, a huge part of me wants to help Katherine be successful. I believe in what she's doing. It's important for women, and I want to be a part of it."

"How can preaching—"

"We're not *preaching*," I say. Annoyed.

"Okay, how can *encouraging*. . . . Is that better?"

"Yes, thank you," I say, not loving Nick's tone.

"How can encouraging women to try to have all this stuff going on at the same time be helping them? It sure doesn't seem like your life is all that balanced, and you're at ground zero of this balance operation."

I take a deep breath and adjust myself on the sofa. Nick takes a sip of water and sets the bottle back down on the table a little harder than necessary.

"I don't exactly know, and I'm trying to figure that out. But I don't want to fight about it, Nick."

"We're not fighting. This isn't fighting. It's discussing."

"I don't see why it's that big of a deal. We're still together a lot of nights, and we have weekends. Most weekends," I say weakly.

"Yes, but you're always distracted. Always on your phone doing Katherine stuff. Always needing to change plans at the last minute. Always tired and stressed out. I respect what you're doing, and you know I've always been so supportive of your career. But this isn't, as you just said, the job you even want, and I feel like you're killing yourself for Katherine. I'm not entirely sure why you're willing to do that."

"I told you. Because I support what she's trying to do with this book. Are you suggesting I quit so I can spend my days answering your phones and making your dinner because it's not that easy to get a job these days, if you haven't noticed. And I'm not sure that you can support us both at this point, Nick. Ty Collins notwithstanding."

Didn't mean for that to come out like that.

"Oh, Coop. I'm not suggesting that. You know I'm not suggesting that. And I'm doing just fine financially. But I can tell you, since you decided to go below the belt, that this whole full-time, no-time-for-anything-else working woman is not what I'm going for long term."

"What do you mean?" I ask. My eyes start to sting.

"I mean that I'm all for you being a career woman, but when we have kids, I want a mom for my kids. Not a twenty-four-seven career woman who's only going to swoop into our lives when her e-mails slow down."

"Oh, so you want me barefoot and pregnant and Susie Homemaker? Like your mother?" I ask petulantly.

"No. Well. Maybe. It's not that I don't want you to work when we have kids. It's just that I think I had a great childhood and part of that is because my mom was around, physically and emotionally. That's what I want for my, for our, kids. Is that such a bad thing to hope for?" Nick is standing now. Pacing.

"It's not necessarily a bad thing to hope for. But it might be a bad thing to hope for with me. No one, especially not me, could ever live up to the perfection that is your opinion of your mother."

I stand up now, too, and walk toward the window. I look down onto Fourteenth Street as an ambulance tries to go crosstown in the incessant traffic. An ant in honey. The siren's blare persists, and I feel the loud pitch resonating through my body, through my bones.

It's not that Nick and I have never had this working-mom/stay-at-home-mom conversation before. It's just never seemed so all-or-nothing with him. I know how much he loved his childhood. He still has an extraordinarily close relationship with his parents and his sister. But I guess I never let myself go so far in the whole "Nick and Lucy have a baby" scenario to picture myself as an actual mother who has to make the choice to work or not. And now that I'm trying to do that, I'm not entirely sure *what* my choice would be.

"I don't know what to do here, Nick," I say from across the room. The ambulance has made it to the next block. "The facts remain that I have *this* job, and I'm not going anywhere else careerwise at this point. And I can't promise what kind of mom, working or otherwise, I'll want to be. It's unfair of you to ask me to make that decision now."

"It might be unfair, Lucy. But it's not unrealistic. I'm twenty-seven. You're almost twenty-six. We've been together for a long time. I don't want to be just your boyfriend forever. You know I want us to get married. To have kids. But we need to make sure we both want the same kind of life. If we're gonna be together."

If? I'm stunned. A little numb. I guess having a boyfriend who is one of the most laid-back and even-keeled people you know could also mean that you think your relationship is cruising along you just have a boyfriend who's laid-back and even-keeled and just not make a big deal of things. Until they get really bad. And that's where we find our dear hero and heroine now, dear readers. In the land of really bad.

Of course, we've talked about marriage before. How can you be with someone for eight years and not talk about marriage? But Nick and I come from very different families and, because of that, we have completely different perspectives on marriage. Nick's parents have been married for twenty-nine years and live in Perfect World. My parents got divorced when I was in high school and weren't exactly great marital role models. Let me rephrase that. They sucked at marriage.

My parents' marriage spiraled out of control when I was in my junior year of high school and all my brothers were already out of the house. My dad verbally abused my mom. He would embarrass her in front of her friends, threaten to leave her, and tell her, among other gems, that she was fat, worthless, and not good enough. There was one especially nasty argument toward the end of the marriage that I overheard, and I've had a pretty negative view of marriage ever since. It's hard to have a healthy view of marriage when the only live specimen you've ever seen up close was profoundly infected. There's a huge part of me that's petrified of getting married. Of having the same thing happen to me that happened to my mom. It might be an unfounded fear, especially with a guy like Nick, but my mom didn't think my dad would become like that when she first married him.

"You *know* the marriage thing is not so easy for me," I say. I feel a pit start to grow in my stomach.

"Oh, Coop, we're not gonna be like them. I'm not anything like your dad," he says softly, walking over to where I'm standing by the window. He puts his arms around me and we stay there for a moment. Being in Nick's arms always has a way of making me feel less shitty than I was feeling before.

"You do know I really, really want to marry you, don't you," Nick says as he pulls away. He lifts my chin, and looks into my eyes, a sly grin on his face.

"So you've told me, what, maybe a trillion times," I say, laughing. "I'm not so sure you still do, though, after some of the things you just said. And I'm not so sure I'm the wife of your dreams, either."

"Sorry, I know I was a little harsh tonight. It's been an emotional day. But it's important to talk about these things. We have to talk about these things, Coop," Nick says.

He leads me back to the couch and we sit down. He takes my hands in his and looks straight into my eyes. "Lucy Cooper, even though you work too much, and even though you insist on being a loyal and productive employee when so many of our peers are total fuckups, and even though you can't predict the future and know what kind of mom you want to be, I still want to marry you. And that's because I love you. I love how you think everything through, I love how you can drink any beer-guzzling college frat boy under the table, I love that you work for a health company and still eat Cheetos for dinner, I love that you're so gorgeous even when your eyes are all red and puffy, I love that you could care less about shopping, I love that you love Sean Connery, and I love that you've never backed down from how you really feel about things. For all those reasons, yes, I want to marry you."

"Yeah, yeah," I say, leaning back into the couch. I'm suddenly exhausted, the hectic day finally catching up with me.

"I'm serious, Coop. Plus, all this stuff with Katherine has to slow down soon, and then you'll realize that all you want to do is be my wife and have our babies," he says, teasing. "I know you too well for your own good. Anyway, this Katherine gig is entirely temporary. You've got to make your own dreams happen," he says imitating Ty's voice.

"I know, I know. I've got to get out of this job. It's killing me."

"Then why aren't you being more proactive about getting a new job?"

"Oh, for like a million reasons. Everything's so busy. I couldn't leave Katherine right now, and I don't have any time to look for a job anyway.

"Well, don't keep making yourself second fiddle," Nick says.

"Second fiddle? Nice expression, dork," I say, laughing.

"Takes one to know one, dork," he says as he wraps me in his arms and starts to kiss me.

"So what have we accomplished in this little *discussion*?" I ask, as I pull away from his embrace.

"Well, I think the bottom line is that we both seem to want different things, short term and long term. Short term, you want to bust your ass working for Katherine while I want you to eliminate some of the stress in your life and go for a job you really want. Long term, I want to marry you, and share a last name with you, and make multiple babies with you, and have us be a happy family while you aren't so sure about any of those things." He attempts a smile and shrugs his shoulders.

"Well, now that you've put it like that, it's pretty clear," I say.

"Yeah?" he asks expectantly.

"Yeah. It's pretty clear that you are one thoughtful and perfect boyfriend who only wants the best for me."

"True dat, Coop. True dat. So," he says, clearing his throat, "will you marry me?"

"Ha, ha, Nick."

"Someday, Lucy Cooper. Someday, I'm going to ask you for real and you know what you'll say?"

"What will I say?"

"You'll say yes."

"Oh, yeah? And how is it that you're suddenly planning on changing my mind about marriage?"

"By making you realize that you have a man who loves you and who would never do anything to hurt you or to make you feel badly about yourself. I promise you that, Lucy Cooper. I know that you believe in marriage deep inside. I've seen you cry at those Kate Hudson movies, and don't think I don't see you all swoony and teary when you watch those wedding-dress shows," he says, smiling at me. I throw a pillow at his head. "But seriously, I know that you can't stay convinced forever that marriage isn't for you, and I have a feeling you're going to change your mind very soon."

Nick scoops me up and leads me into his bedroom. He slowly undresses me, cracking me up with his jokes, and then he becomes serious as he lays me down.

"We're going to be one of those annoyingly adorable married couples, Coop. I know we will make each other extraordinarily happy," Nick says as we get into bed. As he gently trails his finger from the fingertips of my left hand up my arm, across the strap of my tank top, over my chest and down the other arm.

"I know," I say quietly, enjoying this slow lovemaking. Because our time together has been so rushed lately, sex has been, too.

He continues his gentle and leisurely exploration of my body. His light touch lingers over my lips, my breasts, my belly. I stare into his eyes and he looks at me lovingly as he bends down to kiss me.

"I love you so much," Nick says, moving a strand of hair that had settled over my eye.

"I love you, too."

As he wraps me up in his strong arms and we lie quietly, listening to the hums and humanity of New York City outside his window, I feel happy and relaxed. And mindful of how I need to make more time for this in my life.

The next morning, Thursday, I wake up to the smell of steaming coffee. I look at the clock: 7:14. I jump up because I want to be in the office by eight to catch up on work I didn't get to yesterday. As I get out of bed and walk toward the bathroom, which is attached to Nick's bedroom, I notice a trail of white rose petals on the wood floor leading from my side of the bed into the rest of the apartment under the closed bedroom door. My heart pounds, my stomach drops, my palms start to sweat. A huge smile takes residence on my face, and just as suddenly, I feel panicked. I'm no spring chicken. I have a good idea what this means.

I quickly go into the bathroom to pee and brush my teeth. Nick, who knows I love a good quote, has taped two to the mirror: "*It's okay to be scared. Being scared means that you're about to do something really, really brave.*" And "*You cannot always wait for the perfect time. Sometimes you must dare to jump.*" I smile at the thought of this beautiful man who knows my messy brain so well and head out into my future.

I open the door that leads from Nick's bedroom to the rest of the apartment, following the rose petals as I go. I see Nick as he sees me enter the living room and he immediately drops onto his knee. A loud gasp escapes my throat. There are candles lit everywhere. Rose petals covering the wood floor. A bouquet of flowers on the coffee table next to Nick. He's kneeling there with a thousand-watt smile on his handsome face. And there's something in his hand. I approach. Slowly. Pounding heart. Dropping stomach. Sweating palms.

"C'mere," he says quietly with the most adorable smile radiating from his face. He looks so sexy in a white fitted T-shirt and flannel pajama pants.

When I am directly in front of Nick, he puts what was in his hand—which I see at this point is most definitely a small jewelry box—on the table next to him and grabs both of my hands in his. Now, mind you, though I did enjoy the quick detour to the bathroom, I'm in no condition to be proposed to. My hair is a tousled mess, and I'm wearing a ratty, old tank top that I leave at Nick's and his boxers rolled up at the waist. My nails? Take a wild guess what they look like. I guess this is what you call love.

My stomach is a cesspool of fear and confusion, but somehow I'm smiling. Tears start to fill my eyes.

"Lucy, the minute I saw you that first time in college, I knew you were the girl for me. Your gorgeous smile was the first thing that I noticed. But as I got to know you, I realized how smart, funny, kind, and amazing you were. And since then, I've fallen in love with you more every single day. Last night, I started to think that maybe there's a fundamental difference with what we both want in the future. But the more I thought about it, and I stayed up late last night really thinking about all of it, the more I realized that together we can make everything work. I don't want to change any part of you, and I can't imagine my life without you. I love you for everything you are. I want to be with you for the rest of my life, and I finally want to make that official. Lucy Olivia Cooper, will you marry me?"

He drops my hands and picks up the little box on the table next to him. My body is shaking slightly; my heart is pounding not so slightly. He opens the box, faces it toward me, and I gasp again. There is a beautiful round diamond solitaire ring set in platinum staring its gorgeous little sparkly face at me. I look at Nick. Back at the diamond. Back at Nick as he takes the ring and starts to reach for my left hand.

"But, how . . . ?" I ask, looking at the ring and motioning to all the flowers.

"I've had the ring for a while. And if it's not the style you like, we can go back and you can pick out the one you want. The flowers I got down at the bodega early this morning," he says proudly.

"Nick . . . I. . . ." *That's not what I'm supposed to say.*

Nick holds the ring airborne. Millimeters from the tip of my left ring finger. His smile is large, expectant.

"I'm . . . I'm speechless. . . ." *A little better. Come on Lucy. You can do this. Nick was right. Marriage to him would be a good thing. A beautiful thing.*

"All you have to say is 'yes,'" Nick says, staring at me with love.

But yes doesn't come. What comes is, "Nick . . . I. . . ."

Nick stands up and gives me a hug. "I know this is a surprise, Coop, but I love you so much, and I want us to be married. I'm sorry this isn't a nicer proposal, but I didn't want to wait a minute longer."

He pulls away and looks at me. The ring still hovering near my left hand. A magnetic force field between it and my finger.

Something comes over me quickly and out of nowhere. Words spill out of my mouth, and I don't feel like I have control over them.

"Nick, I don't know," I start and look at him. He looks back with a shocked expression. *I don't know* is so far from what I know he was expecting. *But you love him, Lucy. He's the perfect guy for you. Don't do this.*

"I just don't think I'm ready, Nick," I say as he pulls away. "I love you so much," I continue looking at him and hold my hands out in front of me. He is staring straight ahead, straight away from me.

He lets out a resigned laugh.

"I do love you, Nick. You know I do."

"Damn it, Coop," he says and starts blowing out all the candles. Each flame extinguished feels like a sharp knife stabbing my heart. After he blows out the last candle, he leans up against the kitchen counter and stares at me.

"How can I make you understand?" I plead and start to cry. I sit down on the couch.

"Explain it to me," he says, still staring at me. His stare, so filled with love a couple minutes ago, now completely cold.

"I don't know if I can. I don't know if I want to be married. I know I want to be with you. I just don't understand why we have to be married."

"Because I believe in marriage, Coop. It's a true commitment. It's something I really want for us."

"I'm not sure I can give you that, Nick. It's just with my parents and all—"

"We're not your parents, and I'm not your dad. We've been over this a million times. Your parents knew each other for less than a year when they got married. They were kids. We've been together for so long. We know each other. We're mature enough to do this. What we would have is the type of marriage that lasts."

"I just don't know, Nick. I'm so scared."

"Of what?" Nick says.

"Of it not working. I'm really struggling with all of this."

"Oh, babe, *this* is gonna work. There's no way you and I aren't gonna work."

I cover my eyes and start to cry more heavily.

Nick takes a breath, seems to gather his thoughts, and stands up taller. I get up from the couch and walk toward him. I lean in to hug him and he pulls away. He says, "I believe in marriage. I want to marry the woman I love and start a family. And if you're not willing to do that then I'm not sure I can do this."

"Nick, please," I plead. "Don't do this. I just need some time."

"Time, Coop? Time? We've been together for eight fucking years," he says angrily. "How much more time could you possibly need? If you aren't sure about marriage by this point, then you'll never be sure. I've done all that I can in this relationship. If it's not what you want, then maybe we should both move on."

"You don't mean that. You can't mean that." I stand there, staring at him, my arms slack at my sides, tears streaming down my face.

Could he really mean that? Could he really be willing to throw away everything we have? The look on his face is a clear answer.

"I'm going to get in the shower. I think you should be gone by the time I get out. I need to be alone." With that, he walks toward the bathroom and slams the door.

I'm completely shocked. Did he just break up with me? I stare at the bathroom door, frozen, unsure of what to do next. Should I stay there and wait for him to get out of the shower so I can try to explain myself better? So I can make him understand? I want to respect that he needs to be alone right now, but if I leave, will that be the end? Will he think I don't care? After I consider all my options for a few minutes, I decide to respect his request and leave. Before I do, I lean against the bathroom door and quietly knock a couple times.

"I'm really sorry Nick. I don't want to lose you. I don't want this to be the end of us. Please can we talk about it?" I stand there quietly for a second. Then I hear the shower turn on.

I turn to leave and as I head out of the bedroom toward Nick's front door, I glance over to where the ring sits in its box on the living room table. It catches a ray of sun shining in through the window. The brightness stings my eyes as I start to cry again and leave the apartment.

Chapter Five

Failure doesn't come from falling down. Failure comes from not getting up.
Ava's quote of the day is the first thing in my Instagram feed that I look
at on the subway ride home to my apartment. I have my book in my
tote (I'm rereading *The Secret History* by Donna Tartt), but I'm too
upset over what just happened with Nick to concentrate. My head feels
like a schizophrenic fireworks show. There are colorful and noisy
explosions coming from every direction, and I don't know what to
focus on first.

While I distractedly shower and get dressed at my apartment, the
fireworks show doesn't relent. BOOM! *I'm an idiot for turning him
down.* BANG! *But you were just being honest with yourself, Lucy.* ZING!
I feel so badly for saying no. He looked so sad. BING! *Well, I got what I
deserved. He dumped me.* BOOM! BANG! ZING! BING! *I've never felt
so atrociously awful in my life.* My typically efficient getting-ready
routine turns into a pitiful display of clumsy choreography as my
cerebral synapses continue to misfire: I cut my leg shaving, I put the
wrong buttons in the wrong holes on my blouse, and I stick myself in
the eye with the mascara wand.

I walk to work in a shocked daze, and almost get hit by a cab while
crossing Seventy-Ninth Street. I resolve to not become New York City's
statistic of the day, so I stop to buy a coffee and do my best to focus as I

navigate the remaining twenty blocks. I'm in the office by nine, much later than I had hoped for, but impressive considering the circumstances. Katherine has an eight-thirty doctor's appointment this morning (Dr. Browning from yesterday's confirmation phone call is her dermatologist), so I know I'll have time to get a lot of work done before she comes in. I take a sip of my coffee and resolve to try to put the Nick situation off to a side of my brain so I can focus on work for a while. I realize that will be virtually impossible to do, but I try anyway. My workload is too heavy right now to take time off for a broken heart.

I log into the administrative area of *The Balance Project*'s companion website. I neglected it yesterday, which was entirely out of necessity and not out of design. But websites are like gardens: they need attention, updating, and constant oversight lest pests creep in. I was very involved in building and launching the website, and it's my job to manage it. Katherine was excited to award that job to me, rather than giving it to the Green Goddess digital-media department, and I was thrilled to take it on so I could get more experience in what I hope is my ultimate field.

The morning goes by calmly and, I'm surprised, considering the state of my mangled heart, I get a lot done. I take frequent breaks to check my phone, hoping for a text from Nick, but my phone is quiet. I force myself to focus on my work because the alternative, focusing on Nick, is too painful. Katherine comes in late morning and the uncharacteristic calm in Katherine Land allows her to deal with London, do countless quick phone interviews about *The Balance Project*, catch up on her e-mails, and leave me alone.

The day flies by and just when I feel like I'm about to explode from keeping my shit together all day, it's time to go to Katherine's signing at Barnes & Noble in Union Square. These signings are always a big deal mostly because there's still so much buzz about *The Balance Project*. It's number one in Amazon's business books section in three different categories. It's been on the *New York Times* and Amazon bestsellers lists for months. The five-star reviews on Amazon keep pouring in. Katherine's publishers are ecstatic. Her agent is ecstatic. And Brooke and the other publicists are ecstatic. Tonight there will be a line of smitten women out the door and a full house seated inside Barnes & Noble. Katherine did a nationwide book tour when *The Balance Project* launched, and Brooke arranged a small encore tour for the book's six-month anniversary.

I am fully aware that working women love Katherine Whitney. They pay hundreds of dollars to hear her speak at conferences. They write letters asking for career advice, informational interviews, autographs. They tweet at her and friend her and even pin her all the livelong day. But these book signings, many of which I've attended with Katherine, are something else entirely.

Here's a sample of what I've heard from Katherine's devoted "fans" when they approach her signing table: *Katherine, you are my inspiration,* from one. *Katherine, you are my role model,* from another. And on and on: *I sent a copy of your book to each of my grown daughters. . . . I admire how you're able to do it all and make it look so easy. . . . The advice in your book is a lifesaver and I use your strategies daily. . . . You are God.* Well, no one actually said that last one, but the way those ladies swoon, I wouldn't be surprised.

Tonight as Katherine signs and smiles, shakes hands and sincerely thanks those women singing her praises, I will stand off to the side— ready to replenish her spent Sharpies—and I'll think about what that would be like. What it would be like to have someone tell me I've made a difference in her life. Over Katherine's career she must have heard similar comments from thousands of women. I wonder if the praise even affects Katherine anymore or if she's heard so much of it for so long the words have become empty. Expected. Like a pretty girl who receives so many compliments on her looks that the flattery no longer registers.

I'm so proud to work for Katherine. To be a part of what she does for so many working women. The praise bestowed upon her nourishes me by association. And, as always, I'm amazed at how she always looks so calm, so energized, with piles of work waiting in the office and a beautiful happy family waiting at home. I guess you really can do it all.

It's Friday morning and I'm thinking about how amazing last night's signing went as I sit in Katherine's office, slumped across a Kelly chair, waiting for her to get off a call with Nigel. Luckily, it was so late by the time I got home last night after the signing that I collapsed in my bed, fully dressed, and went to sleep. I didn't remember my dreams when I woke up this morning, and I took a long shower so I could sort out my plan for dealing with Nick today. Showers have a way of crystallizing my emotions and helping me formulate plans. I decided that I'll call him after lunch. I hope he takes my call. I try to push him out of my thoughts because whenever I let him enter them, I feel like I've lost everything.

Katherine and I have just started going over her schedule for next week when the phone rings. I stand up to run to my desk to answer when she picks it up herself from the extension on her desk. It's on speaker.

"Katherine Whitney," she says, smiling at me, taking a sip of her omnipresent green juice.

"Kath."

It's Theo.

"Hey, hon. What's up?"

"Am I on speaker?"

"Yeah, Lucy's here."

"Hey, slugger."

"Hey, Theo."

"So, Kath, real quick. Good news. My conference got canceled for this weekend. Something about norovirus in the hotel and they don't have enough time to move it somewhere else. Good news is we can celebrate our anniversary properly after all. I booked us the weekend at Glenmere Mansion."

"Theo, that's great!" Katherine says, smiling.

"Happy anniversary," I say.

"Thanks," Katherine and Theo say in unison.

"I think this is precisely what we need, Kath," Theo says. "Time to connect, a little spa, some good old-fashioned—cover your ears, slugger—sex."

"Theo!" Katherine says, looking embarrassed.

I laugh. Theo laughs.

"Perfect. I'm in," Katherine says.

"Great. If you can leave the office at five, you can come home to kiss the girls and pack, and we can be there in time for dinner."

Glenmere Mansion is a gorgeous inn about an hour north of Manhattan in the Hudson Valley. I've never been there, but Katherine raves about it every time she goes.

Katherine returns to her e-mails and I return to my desk. I realize Katherine will be fully occupied this weekend, wrapped in an oversized white terrycloth robe, eating truffles, getting couples massages, drinking expensive red wine out of those oversized crystal glasses, having what sounds like much-needed sex with her husband—all of the things I imagine people like Katherine and Theo do in fancy Hudson Valley inns. Which means that I will be fully available all weekend long for Nick. If he'll have me.

I call him to see if he'll have dinner with me tonight. He doesn't answer his phone—I'm not really surprised, but definitely disappointed—so I leave a voice mail. And then I send a text:

Lucy: Hey, you. I've been thinking about it all so much and I really want to talk to you in person. Can you meet me at Carlo's tonight at 7? I love you.

I wait a minute hoping for a text back. Unable to focus on work just yet, I carry the phone with me to the kitchen to refill my coffee. On the way back to my desk, steaming coffee in one hand and phone in the other, I collide with someone in the hall because I'm staring at the phone, willing it to reveal a thoughtful, loving text from Nick. Instead I get no text and hot coffee splashed on my sweater, the burning feeling through the fabric less hurtful than the cruelty of the blank screen.

Later, I finalize a status report for Katherine and coordinate the details for the new nanny who will start in two weeks. Katherine's one and only nanny needs backup. Stat. Because, as every New York City working mother worth her salt knows, two kids means two nannies. If Jordan is napping, and it's time for Abby to go to Music Tots or Swim Tots or Knitting Tots (not kidding), what's the nanny to do? Wake up Jordan? Heavens no. Make Abby miss her class? Think again. Having two nannies is not that uncommon in Katherine's habitat. Don't believe me? Go to Big City Moms and look it up.

My cell rings.

"Hey," Nick says coldly when I answer. I'm surprised, and grateful, he called me back.

"Hey, thanks so much for calling me back. I really want to talk to you."

"I'm not so sure that's a great idea, Coop." He sounds distracted, and I hear him typing on his keyboard in the background.

"Then why did you call me back?" I ask gently.

"Because part of me feels like I owe it to you to hear what you have to say." His tone is cold. Any hope I had of him breaking down and telling me he'll wait for me until I'm ready for marriage is gone, gone, gone.

"Can you meet tonight?" I ask, holding my breath, nervous he'll say no. Nervous he'll say yes.

"Are you sure Katherine won't need you tonight?" He says sarcastically, condescendingly, but I don't take the bait.

"She's actually going away this weekend with Theo for their anniversary, so I'm free all weekend."

"Oh."

"Carlo's at seven?"

"Fine. Okay, I'll see you then."

He hangs up. I hold the phone out in front of me, stare at it, and sigh. The man who wanted to marry me yesterday is now someone who has no qualms about ending a phone call without a good-bye.

At four forty-five, I start getting jumpy. I'm anxious for Katherine to leave so I can get out of here early tonight. There's no work I need to do over the weekend, and I'm looking forward to having time to catch up on personal things: errands, filling Ava in on what's going on with Nick, laundry, perhaps mending my damaged relationship. If things go well tonight, I will be able to dedicate the rest of the weekend to Nick. No Katherine distractions.

I'm still not sure what I'm going to say to him tonight. I'm certainly not ready to accept his proposal. Even though part of me finds what I did repugnant and even mean, I can't blame myself for being true to what I was feeling. The more I think about it, the more I realize I did the right thing. For me. For now. Definitely not for Nick. And quite possibly not for my future. However certain I feel though, part of me is not so sure. I'm decidedly undecided.

I'm having a difficult time accepting that by rejecting Nick's proposal, I may have ended our relationship. Part of me can't believe that could be true. Our relationship is too strong. We've overcome blips before. It's made us stronger. But if, in Nick's mind, this is less a blip and more an iceberg, our relationship might be the Titanic, and we all know how *that* turned out.

What if Nick still feels how he did Thursday morning after I didn't say yes? He might tell me tonight that we've had a good ride, it was a great starter relationship for both of us, but he's moving on so he can find a good woman with wide hips and a Pinterest page filled with color-coordinated wedding-theme ideas—a woman who isn't so committed to her career. He might tell me he wants to break up. He might suggest we consciously uncouple.

The thought of that makes me say really bad and unladylike cuss words under my breath. There are all sorts of new single people things I have no idea how to navigate: swipeable dating apps, STDs, higher expectations for lady waxing. I'm petrified of having to be in the dating world again. I'm more petrified of living my life without Nick in it.

Maybe it's okay to not be so sure about what I'll say tonight. Maybe it would be better to see what Nick has to say and take it from there. I take a few deep breaths, and start to pack up my stuff to head home. Katherine is in her office putting the finishing touches on a report she needs to send to the Green Goddess board of directors. Her line rings.

I never should have picked it up.

"Katherine Whitney's office."

"Hello there, Lucy! It's Brooke! Is she around?"

"Hi Brooke. Yes, one second please."

"Katherine, Brooke's on line one," I say through the intercom.

Three minutes later, Katherine calls me into her office.

"So, good news or bad news?" Katherine asks me flatly.

"Good news."

"I'm going to be on the cover of *People* magazine."

"That's great! Bad news."

"For reasons unknown to me, but fully comprehensible to Brooke, they need to do the interview and shoot the photos this weekend. Brooke already agreed to it on my behalf."

"What about your weekend away?" I ask, feeling badly for her that her anniversary trip will be ruined.

"I feel really badly about it, but we'll just have to reschedule. These things happen. And this article is important for the book. Theo will understand."

"Sorry to hear that, but congratulations on the cover. That's amazing, Katherine," I say as I head back to my desk.

"Oh, Lucy?"

"Yes?" I turn back to Katherine.

"I'm going to need your help this weekend. Brooke and her whole team are in LA for that awards show. The shoot and interview will be at my apartment from eight to five tomorrow, and we might have to do more on Sunday if they don't get it all during the first go-round. So, bright and early tomorrow?"

No! But I have no valid excuse, and 'tis my job. So. . . .

"Okay," I say quietly as I head back to my desk, thinking about Nick. Thinking about how I won't be available tomorrow if tonight he does decide to give me another chance.

Despite the cancellation of her weekend away, Katherine still leaves the office at five and I do the same, taking the subway to my apartment rather than walking so I'll have more time to organize my pitiful and neglected home affairs before dinner with Nick.

I crank up Sam Smith and crisscross my apartment gathering pieces of clothing that never quite made it into the laundry basket. My apartment may be tiny, but I love it. It's furnished in a simple style I call Poor Single Girl Eclectic. The centerpiece of my main room is a yellow floral love seat with a pattern so busy you'd be as likely to find it in a landfill as you would in Anthropologie's furniture collection. The love seat had been in my mom's sunroom for twenty-five years before she turned it into a playroom for her grandkids. My coffee table (grey) is an old trunk I salvaged from my mom's attic. I found my carved wood headboard (white) at the Brooklyn Flea and my '50s Formica dinette set (orange) on the curb when one of my elderly neighbors died and her grieving daughter emptied the apartment. Chez Lucy will never appear in the glossy pages of a shelter magazine, but it's home, made even more homey with lots of candles, plants (dying), and framed photos of my family, friends, and Nick.

I get to Carlo's a little early so I can be sure to get "our" booth in the back corner. Carlo's is our favorite Italian restaurant on the Upper West Side. It's an old place with wood paneling on the walls, red-and-white checked tablecloths, and those red glass votive candleholders Italian restaurants are so fond of.

I order two bottles of Peroni and nurse mine while I wait for Nick. He arrives a little after seven, wearing a pair of jeans, a black button-down, and a black leather jacket that he takes off and tosses into the booth. His hair is messy and he has a look on his face that I can't decipher. I stand up to give him a kiss, but he sits down and slides his bottle of beer toward me.

"I'm not drinking tonight. I have a lot of work to do tomorrow," he says, as he places a folded piece of paper on the table in front of him.

"What's that?"

"Before I tell you about that, I have a question," he says matter-of-factly, looking straight into my eyes and clasping his hands on the table.

"Okay."

"Do you want to be with me or do you think we should call it a day and move on?"

"Seriously?"

"Yeah, Coop, seriously."

"I want to be with you." I reach my hands across the table for Nick's. He pulls his hands away and puts them down by his sides. A busboy drops a basket of sliced bread on our table along with two small glasses of tap water. "I know you're angry Nick, and I don't blame you, but I'm not ready to throw away everything we have simply because our plans for marriage are on different timetables."

"And I'm not ready to do that either. Which is why I'm sitting here. But I'm going to need you to do some things for me if we're going to be able to move beyond this with some sort of plan. I can't keep waiting with no guarantee of any sort of resolution."

"What kind of things?" I take a big sip of my beer, willing it to numb my brain. My heart.

Nick unfolds the paper and turns it to face me. At the top of the sheet, he's written "Lucy." Under it is a list.

"I've been thinking a lot about all of this since you left my apartment yesterday. And I realized that, *logically*, it doesn't make sense for us to stay together—"

"Nick!"

"Let me finish, Coop. Please. It doesn't make sense for us to stay together because we want two very different things. I want to get married and you don't. I could compromise and be with you without getting married, but that feels wrong to me. I believe in marriage. I want to be a man who gets married and has kids in a traditional family. That's just me. So that leaves you to be the one who has to compromise. If *you* think about it logically, the only way we can stay together is if you get over your fear of marriage." As Nick presents his case, I'm reminded of the fact that he is a lawyer, after all. The waiter comes over to take our order and Nick asks him for a few minutes.

"Now, you just said you want to be with me," Nick continues. "Do you still feel the same way if it means that you have to get comfortable with marriage?"

"Yeah, I guess. I mean. I don't really know what you're saying." He's got me all confused. He really is a lawyer.

"I came up with a plan of three things for you. I thought this might help clarify it all for us and make it objective rather than being all full of emotion. I know you're thinking that I'm putting it all on you, but I am 100-percent certain that I want to be married. So if that's the case, it all does fall on you."

"So, what's in your plan?"

He turns the paper back toward himself. "Number one, I think you should have a long conversation with your mom and maybe even your dad about marriage so you can address your fears and understand what happened to them from the perspective of an adult rather than as a child. Number two, I think you should start a job search for a position in digital media. Even though that has nothing to do with us getting married, it's all part of you getting unstuck from where you are right now which is unhealthy for you. And number three is to think seriously about whether you want to have kids. I know I said I want a present mom for our kids, but I'm less concerned with whether you work or not when we have kids and more concerned with knowing if you even want kids. Does that all make sense?"

We sit there in silence for a second. I look down at the list and try to absorb what he presented. As I start to say something, Nick stands up and puts his jacket on.

"I'm gonna go, Lucy. I'm not hungry, and I think I should go home. Why don't you think about the list, decide if you think it's even fair, and then let me know what you're going to do. Text me tomorrow morning and let me know if you want to move forward or not. If not, then we'll break up. If you do want to move forward, we can meet for dinner tomorrow night and start figuring it all out."

And then he leaves. He just leaves. I'm sitting there, my mouth wide open, speechless, tears forcing themselves to the surface of my eyes. Our relationship is on life support and Nick left the plug in my hands. "Pull it or don't pull it, Lucy," he seemed to say. "The choice is completely yours."

The waiter comes by again to take our order. I apologize and tell him I won't be staying. I pay for the beers and leave the restaurant, folding up the list and stuffing it into the pocket of my coat.

I call Ava on the walk home and tell her about everything that has been going on. The proposal. What I said. Our talk tonight. The list. She listens to everything I say, inserting calming encouragements in all the empty spaces. She allows me to start processing what's happened by explaining it out loud, something she knows, after all these years, that I have to do.

"Did you read the latest quote I posted?" Ava says as we're about to hang up.

"I haven't checked Instagram since this morning," I say.

"What is it you plan to do with your one wild and precious life?" Ava asks.

"What?"

"That's the quote. It's by Mary Oliver. *'What do you plan to do with your one wild and precious life?'*"

A fitting quote, I think, as I walk home and try to decide if I'm willing to do—*able* to do—the items on Nick's list. Try to decide what exactly I *am* going to do with my one wild and precious life.

Chapter Six

Lucy: Yes, Nick. I love you. Yes, I want to move forward.

I send the text to Nick as soon as I wake up on Saturday morning. I stayed up late last night thinking through all my options, making pro and con lists in my head. I kept coming back to the same place. I'm not willing to give up on our relationship. The more I thought about everything Nick said last night, the more I realized that though his delivery was far from sweet, his message was spot on. And I don't think he's being unreasonable at all. Sure, all the work falls on me, but it's work I have to do. I don't have time for any of it and it won't be easy, but I have to put in the effort. If I don't, I'll not only lose Nick, I'll also stay stuck in this unhealthy place I'm in.

Nick: Glad to hear that. Union Square Cafe at 8?

Lucy: See you then.

I've left extra time this morning so I can walk the twenty-some blocks from my apartment to Katherine's, figuring the exercise will do me good since I haven't been exactly physically active lately. I've left even a bit of extra time on top of that so I can stop at the Green Goddess Juice Bar to pick up a juice for Katherine and smoothies for the girls and Theo (per her text this morning). I'll have to stop somewhere else and grab a reinforcement coffee for myself. Green Goddess Juice does not serve coffee.

I arrive at Katherine's building energized. The brisk walk cleared my brain and now I can focus on Katherine today. There will be plenty of time to focus on Nick later. And I'm actually feeling somewhat okay because at least we have a plan.

The cute doorman winks at me (we have a little thing) as I smile and nod and make my way through the sleek lobby of Katherine's building toward the elevator bank. I see the door to her apartment is open as I head down the hall from the elevator. There are guys with cameras and lights moving equipment in. I slide by them, smoothies in hand, and realize I should have brought more.

I find Katherine standing in the middle of the apartment, which is *not* eclectic and *has* appeared in the glossy pages of a shelter magazine or three. She's in a robe directing traffic ("If you don't mind, would you please take off your shoes?") and making suggestions on what furniture they can move ("If you turn that white love seat the other way, it opens up the whole room,") and where the best light is in the apartment ("The living room with the view of Central Park really is the optimal spot").

"Oh, Lucy, you're here," Katherine says, clapping her hands and looking up to where she must think God lives, as she spots me working my way toward the kitchen to put the drinks in the fridge.

"I'm here," I trill, and she gives me the lowdown.

"I can't believe it's only eight. I feel like we've been at this for hours."

"What's going on?" I ask, leaning against her kitchen island and taking an eye-opening swig of joe.

"Well," she begins, speaking quickly and anxiously, "Jordan didn't sleep last night for some reason, so I was up all night trying to calm her because my nanny is sick, *again*, with some nasty flu this time. Thank God we finalized things with the new nanny, but I'm not sure we'll be able to manage these next two weeks with just one the way things are going. Anyway, I finally got Jordan back to sleep at six, but these dodo heads from *People* showed up an hour early, and the call from the doorman woke everyone up at seven. Abby has decided that the photographers are here *for her* so she's been in twelve different outfits and has been in my makeup bag for the last half hour. Theo is sulking and not being helpful at all because he says this is ruining our weekend and because I forgot to wish him a happy anniversary this morning. I look like a disaster because Jacki and Nathaniel are late. And to top it all off, Brooke said *People* wanted me to wear clothes from Chloé's new summer collection but the clothes never got delivered last night, so I have no idea what I'm supposed to wear." Katherine looks panicked as she catches her breath and stares at me. Stares at me in a way that assumes that somehow I'm going to fix everything.

"Excuse me, ladies," a camera guy pushes past us into the dining room.

Katherine looks like she's on the verge of tears. I've never seen Katherine on the verge of anything.

"Okay," a voice from inside me, my sergeant voice, says. "You jump in the shower. I'll get Abby and Jordan and put them in front of *Frozen* while I make their breakfast. I'll call Jacki and Nathaniel and see how far away they are and tell them to step on it. And I'll wake up Brooke in LA and tell her that we have no clothes."

"You're a lifesaver, Lucy. Thank you."

Katherine wraps her robe more tightly around her body and rushes toward her bedroom. I call about the hair and makeup, and wardrobe. Jacki and Nathaniel will be pulling up in ten minutes; Brooke was groggy but said she's on it.

A half hour later, Katherine is calmly sitting in a white leather chair at her onyx dining room table, sipping on her Glow juice and looking at her mind-blowing and very expensive view of Central Park while Jacki curls her lashes and Nathaniel curls her hair. The three of them are picking at the fruit platter I had Green Goddess send up and gossiping about the latest vegan celebrity to get caught by the paparazzi eating a burger.

Abby and Jordan sit peacefully on beanbags in the TV room, sipping on their smoothies and spooning in their Cheerios, belting "Let It Go," in their adorable sing-songy toddler voices. I broke the no-food-anywhere-but-the-kitchen rule. What's Katherine gonna do? Fire me?

I've firmly communicated the no-shoe rule to the crew and have placated them with smoothies, coffee, muffins, and croissants. Green Goddess Glow juices were not going to cut it with this group.

Eventually, a leggy blonde who's way too dressed up for a Saturday morning marches in the front door rolling a wardrobe rack behind her.

"Is this Katherine Whitney's apartment?" she asks.

I grab the rack, hand her a smoothie, and send her on her leggy blonde way.

And then I head back toward the kitchen to take a breath. And a long sip of now-cold coffee.

"Hey, slugger," I hear Theo say behind me. He's in sweats and a Columbia University T-shirt, face unshaven, face unhappy.

"Hey, Theo. Happy anniversary."

"Thanks for remembering. Nice to know someone around here did."

"I got you a smoothie," I say as I see him locate it in the stocked fridge.

"Thanks. That was nice."

"This wasn't exactly your idea of happy anniversary, huh?"

"Nope. Not exactly. But this sort of thing comes with the territory I guess." He sounds resigned.

"Theo!"

We both turn toward the dining room where Jacki and Nathaniel are putting the finishing touches on Katherine. She looks stunning. And pissed.

"Why aren't you dressed?" Katherine asks in a frustrated voice. Enraged might be a better word.

"Me?" Theo asks.

"Yes, you. They want to start with the family shots. You need to be in a suit. They said they want you in a suit."

Theo looks deflated but has clearly made a conscious decision to go along with the plan. He picks his smoothie up off the counter and sulks back toward his bedroom.

I take that as a hint that the girls need to be dressed, too, so I head into the TV room.

"Time to get your pretty dresses on, girls," I say in my happiest, Disney-princess voice.

"No!" They shout.

"It's almost the Olaf part," Abby whines.

"Well, let's get dressed and then we can watch the Olaf part. If you get dressed really fast, I'll get you guys some ice cream later."

"Ice cream!" Again in unison, and they scramble off down the hall. Bribery can be very effective with children.

I brush their teeth (princess toothbrushes), scrub their pink cheeks (princess towels), and do their fair hair (princess brushes). Then I let them each pick out a favorite dress, white tights, and party shoes, and present them to their mother.

"No. Play clothes," Katherine snaps.

"You told Theo a suit."

"Yes, but they want the girls more natural. In play clothes."

Jordan cries. She likes the dress she's wearing. Abby helps me find their play clothes. I promise toppings on the ice cream, get them changed, and then set them back in front of *Frozen* to wait for the photographers.

You may be wondering why I'm being so polite to Katherine. Why I'm not calling her on her rude behavior. You may think I'm letting her walk all over me. I can absolutely understand why you'd feel that way. But put yourself in my position. This is my boss. I'm being respectful. She's behaving uncharacteristically so I'm trying to accept it as the aberration it is. Mostly, I'm staying quiet and busting my ass to do what she asks because I don't want to make things worse by feeding into the high level of tension that is so palpable in the apartment. But inside I'm stewing, and I'm nearing my edge.

"Lucy?" I hear Katherine call frantically.

"Yep," I say finding her in the dining room.

"Call Brooke and tell her that the clothes they sent are all too big. There's nothing I can wear here. And I don't know what to do because the photographers want to start."

The doorbell rings. Katherine stares at me (*what's up with all the staring today?*) so I answer the door.

"Hi. Is this Katherine Whitney's apartment?"

"Yes."

"I'm Logan Barnes. I'm the journalist doing the interview. And this is my assistant Daniel Mahoney."

"Oh, hi. I'm Lucy Cooper, Katherine's assistant. Come on in."

I bring Logan and Daniel over to Katherine, and they start talking.

Brooke eventually calls me back and says they've had to scrap the whole Chloé plan and that Katherine is going to have to wear her own clothes.

I sidle up to Katherine and whisper that in her ear so Logan and Daniel don't hear. She takes me aside and totally freaks out, throwing an absolute hissy fit that she has to wear her own clothes. Oh, the horror.

I stand there and stare at her. Now I'm the one staring. In shock. Logan and Daniel shift uncomfortably in their seats. Though I don't think they can hear what Katherine is saying, they can clearly sense the drama. I've never seen Katherine lose it like that. And the first time she does it's about clothes? Give me a break. Clearly there's got to be something else going on here because Katherine's wardrobe is ridiculous. A stylist from Barneys comes to the office four times a year with multiple racks filled with exquisite designer clothes. Katherine selects the pieces she wants, and they magically appear in the correct sizes in her closet. She waltzes into the office every day looking like she just stepped out of a magazine spread. And not a *Green Goddess Magazine* spread. More like a *Vogue* magazine spread. So to hear her freak out about wearing her own clothes?

Jacki hears the commotion and comes over to where we are.

"Don't worry, Katherine. We'll find you something to wear," Jacki says calmly as she holds Katherine by the elbow and whisks her toward the master suite. And that closet.

"Is she always like that?" Daniel asks me quietly, snidely, as Logan gives him a not-now look. Daniel rolls his eyes and turns back to his notebook.

The day carried on like a dysfunctional family trying to convince their party guests that everything is normal. Like something out of a Wes Anderson movie. After the Wardrobe Incident, Katherine emerged from her bedroom a different person—a calm one—and proceeded to do the photo shoot and concurrent interview in a decidedly more Katherine-esque manner.

But every now and then, she'd come over to me, stress palpable, fake smile plastered, with some sort of request. *Why isn't lunch here yet? Did you put* Frozen *on again for the girls? That guy has his shoes on. I spilled some juice on my blouse; can you find the stain remover? Call Nathaniel and have him come back ASAP because they want to do some pictures with my hair in a different style.*

And with every request, Katherine got ruder and ruder. And quieter and quieter so no one heard her but me. So she could maintain the charade of America's Darling of Balance. By the middle of the day, she practically lost it every time she came to me, and I felt like she was headed for a complete breakdown. At one point, I went into Katherine's powder room, turned the faucet on full blast, and said "motherfucker" over and over again. I may have also made obscene gestures directed at Katherine through the door.

I'm taking a breather and downing a sandwich in the kitchen when Theo walks in. He's back in his sweatpants and T-shirt.

"How you holding up, slugger?"

"Okay," I say. I try to sound like I mean it. I don't need to invite Theo into my little world of hell.

"Interview seems to be going well," he says taking a sandwich from the platter and putting mustard on the bread.

"Yeah," I say. He hasn't been privy to Katherine's side (snide) conversations with me. He only sees her sitting unruffled and beautiful, bathed in light from the floor-to-ceiling windows overlooking Central Park, with doting journalists and photographers circling her like planets around a dazzling sun.

"I'll admit, she's certainly good at pulling off this whole thing," Theo says, sitting down on a kitchen stool and taking a bite of his sandwich.

"What do you mean?" I ask him, picking chocolate chips out of the brownies on the dessert platter and popping them into my mouth.

"I mean, between you and me, I think I'm starting to see cracks in our old girl. But you'd never know it looking at her holding court out there with those *People* people."

"Cracks? Really?" I'm astonished. Katherine has always had her shit together. Well, before today at least, but I had started chalking that up to lack of sleep from staying up with Jordan all night.

As if he read my mind. "I know she's always seemed to have it all together, but that's because I think the workload was perfectly manageable and in her wheelhouse, the girls were young enough, and our help situation was great. Now, with the book and London happening at the same time, it's a little more than she bargained for. The girls seem to need her more. At least they ask for her more. And our nanny, who seems to be getting sick a lot, isn't entirely working out so well. Katherine works late so many nights that we're not seeing her as often as we'd all like. Yes, indeed, I believe there are perceptible cracks."

I take a bite of a white-chocolate macadamia-nut cookie and think about what he said.

"I don't know, Theo. I think she's gonna pull it off. Not only this interview but all of it. If there's ever been a woman in control, it's Katherine."

"Yes, she's in control all right. But this balance thing is harder than it seems. And from where I stand, she's not doing it all as effortlessly as you might think."

"But she's doing it," I say. "Isn't that all that matters."

"You could argue that," the professor says. "Anyway, enough of that. She'll be fine." He finishes his sandwich and throws the paper plate in the trash.

"Are the girls still watching *Frozen?*" he asks.

"Third time."

"I'm gonna take them into the park for a while. I have my cell if Katherine needs us back for anything."

"Got it," I say as I replenish the platters with the reserves from the refrigerator.

Later in the afternoon, as the photographers start to pack up, I realize I'll have plenty of time to walk back to my apartment, shower, and change before I have to meet Nick at eight at Union Square Cafe. I might even have time to pop into a boutique on Broadway and buy something special to wear tonight. This day has been completely draining, and I can't wait to get the hell out of Katherine's apartment.

I'm sitting in the TV room watching *Frozen* while Abby and Jordan both sleep draped across me. Anna has just frozen solid.

"Noooo. Wake them up!" Katherine says loudly, angrily, startling the girls who sit up groggily. "If they sleep now, they'll never sleep tonight."

"Sorry," I say, which is way tamer than what I almost said in response to her little freak-out. I'm practically numb at this point from all of Katherine's assaults today. But I have no energy to get into it with her right now. So not worth it. "Are they done out there?" I ask.

"Yeah, just about."

"Great, because I don't want to be late for a very important date."

"Oh, Lucy, do you mind staying a little while more? Theo wants to take me out for dinner for our anniversary and the nanny, as you know, is sick. I sent her to her sister's apartment this morning, so we don't have anyone to watch the girls."

"Sorry, Katherine, but I'm going out with Nick tonight," I say. I will not allow this to happen again. I'm going to stand my ground. Who the hell does she think she is that she can inconvenience me whenever the urge strikes? I am way too tired and way too emotional from everything that's gone on today and in the last few days to deal with this shit any longer. I need to go home, get myself together, and be completely present for Nick tonight. This might be my last chance. Sorry, lady. You're going to have to order in.

"That's fine, we'll be home early," Katherine says. We're going out now so we should be home by seven thirty at the latest."

"I really can't, Katherine. I have to go home and change. I can't go out like this," I say, gesturing to my outfit.

"You can shower here, Lucy. Really, it's no problem. And you can wear anything from my closet. Abby would love to put makeup on you!"

"Please, Lucy? It's our anniversary," Theo says sweetly. Well, if Theo's asking. I have a hard time saying no to Theo.

"Yay, Lucy is our nanny. Yay, Lucy!" Jordan says sweetly.

"Are you sure you'll be home by seven thirty? I have to be down in Union Square no later than eight."

"That won't be a problem at all. We're just going local."

"Okay, but I absolutely have to be out of here no later than seven thirty."

I realize that it's not a big deal. They'll be home in plenty of time for me to meet Nick, and I'll get a nice outfit for the night out of this deal. Plus I want to find out what happens at the end of *Frozen*.

After the girls have braided my hair and adorned it with all their hair bows, Abby asks me if I have a boyfriend. I say I do, and she asks to talk to him. I let her FaceTime Nick and the two of them carry on quite an adorable conversation. Nick saw *Frozen* with his nieces so he's well versed in the saga of Anna, Elsa, and Olaf. I bring my phone to the corner of the room to talk to Nick briefly about our plans for the night. Abby teases me that we're kissing, and after I hang up with Nick, I tickle her senseless.

I bathe and feed the girls and get them dressed for bed (princess PJs). Then it's time to gussy up.

What woman in her right mind would turn down the opportunity to get ready in Katherine Whitney's luxurious master bath, replete with ginormous shower and loads of yummy-smelling, all-natural shower gels. This is my *Pretty Woman*, Julia Roberts–in-the-hotel-suite moment. Without the bubble bath. Or the charming rendition of Prince's "Kiss." ("I just want your extra time and your *mwah, mwah, mwah, mwah, mwah* kiss.") I plop the girls, and an armload of dolls, on the bathroom floor so I can keep an eye on them while I shower.

I relax for the first time today as the hot water pounds on my shoulders. I let my mind go to Nick and what's going on. I'm nervous about our dinner tonight, but I think we're going to be able to move in the right direction. After the shower, I wrap myself in a towel and then the girls take turns holding the blow-dryer up to my hair until the very last part when I smooth it with a brush. My long, brown hair is shiny and straight, and I've given it a little curl at the ends.

The girls lead me by the hands into Katherine's closet. I've never actually seen it in person. I've only imagined what it would look like. My imagination was nothing compared to the reality. It's like Lisa Vanderpump's closet but less pink. You may think it's weird that I seem so comfortable borrowing Katherine's clothes. I do, a little bit, for sure. But Katherine is cool like that, and I know she doesn't mind. Plus, despite my previously explained lack of sartorial *savoir faire*, I still know a good wardrobe when I see it.

As the girls pull things off the hangers—"Try this one on. No, try this one on!"—and I follow them hanging everything back up, I finally settle for a simple, but very sexy, black leather Derek Lam dress. Katherine and I have the same size foot, so I scan her black-high-heel section and decide on a pair of four-inch black suede and metallic leather Jimmy Choos. I stand in front of Katherine's three-way mirror and almost can't believe my eyes. I'm hoping Nick won't believe his.

I've never really been into makeup. I usually just wear lip balm to work. Sometimes lip gloss and mascara. Abby proudly shows me where Katherine keeps her makeup, and I decide to have a little fun with it. Her drawer is neat but overflowing, mostly Bobbi Brown, but with some Chanel and Laura Mercier thrown in. I am careful to use cotton balls and Q-tips instead of Katherine's brushes, but I have no choice with the eyeliner and mascara so I leave them out to remember to clean them afterwards. Abby is quite proficient, for a five-year-old, in the art of makeup application, I learn, as I let her apply my blush and lip gloss.

It's seven o'clock by the time we're done. Bedtime for the girls.

Abby and I put Jordan in her room first. We read her *A Bad Case of Stripes*, and she goes right to sleep (princess sheets).

"What about the ice cream you promised, Lucy?" Abby asks as I sit on the edge of her bed (princess sheets) a couple minutes later.

"Oh, yeah, the ice cream! I forgot," I say, giving her a kiss on the forehead and tucking her in. "I will make it up to you. I promise. I will make a plan with your mommy very soon for me to come here and take you and Jordan out for ice cream."

I read Abby *Olivia*, and when we're done, she smiles, turns her face to the side, and happily goes to sleep.

I return to the TV room and put *Frozen* on again from the beginning. I'm starting to see what all the fuss is about.

I think you know what happens next.

Chapter Seven

Despite being utterly absorbed in *Frozen*, I am aware of the time and the time is now seven-twenty. No word from Katherine. I wait another ten minutes and then I text her.

> Lucy: Timing still good? I need to start heading downtown soon.

I watch. And I wait. No answer from Katherine. Panic starts to manifest in my body. I can not be late for this dinner. So five minutes later, I send another text.

> Lucy: Katherine, I really need to go. Are you guys on your way back home?

By nine fifteen, I have texted and called Katherine four more times. I even called Theo's cell phone but I heard it ring in the apartment, so I knew he didn't have his phone with him. Just before eight, I texted Nick to tell him I wasn't going to make it in time but that I'd be there soon. He was understanding and wrote me back that it was no problem and that he'd wait for me at the bar. I have texted him several times since with status updates, delicately explaining what was going on. His first couple texts back were none too happy. And then he stopped texting back altogether.

I have paced the apartment. I have watched *Frozen*. I have watched *NCIS*. I have taken deep breaths, which are so fucking overrated. None of those things worked at calming me down. I have also tried not to cry. And not to absolutely lose it and deface expensive artwork on Katherine's walls. I'm furious. And I'm devastated that I haven't heard from Nick. I don't think I'll be able to "Well, Katherine . . ." my way out of this one. Not this time.

At nine forty-five, Katherine and Theo stroll in the door. Theo has his arm around Katherine's shoulders and they're singing a duet of some corny old-timey love song. Katherine takes one look at me and her jaw drops.

"Wowza. You look gorgeous, Lucy!"

"Didn't you get my texts?" I ask, trying to remain calm, as I start to gather my things, trying to rush out of there.

"No," she says as she searches in her bag for her phone. "Come to think of it, I didn't hear my phone all night."

"That's 'cause I turned it off," Theo says proudly.

"Well, I'm really late so I have to go." I stare at them both and shake my head in disgust.

"Oh, right, you have a date with Nick. Sorry we're late. Dinner took longer than usual, people kept coming up to our table, and then we must have lost track of time. He'll understand, right? It's not like you have any kids who are gonna wake you up at the crack of dawn tomorrow morning," she gives Theo a knowing look. "So you two can stay out as late as you want."

I can tell Katherine's buzzed, and I don't want to get into it. She starts to hand me some cash, but I push her hand away and tell her not to worry about it.

"Okay, at least let me have Pancho give you a ride," Katherine says and asks Theo to call Pancho who was probably on his way home.

Theo heads toward the house phone. I don't object. It's the quickest and certainly the cheapest way for me to get from the Upper West Side down to Union Square. "Here, take a coat," Katherine opens her hall closet and hands me a long black wool Burberry coat. "It's really cold out."

"Thanks," I say and then I leave.

"Thanks for everything you did today," Katherine calls after me down the hall, but the elevator door is closing, and I just don't want to hear it.

Lucy: I'm so sorry, Nick. I'm on my way. In the car. Should be there in 15 minutes.

When Pancho pulls up to Union Square Cafe, I practically jump out of the car while it's still moving. When I get inside, I look around the bar, scanning the faces of all the calm and happy-looking customers. I think I see Nick sitting at the bar, but when I get closer I realize it's not him. As I'm standing there, turning my head from side to side, making sure I've looked everywhere in the bar, I hear someone call my name.

"Are you Lucy?" the bartender asks, shouting over the noise of the restaurant.

"Yes," I say.

"I have a note for you from Nick."

"Thank you so much," I say, smiling, relieved as I take the small slip of folded paper from the bartender.

I walk outside, unfolding the paper as I go. I look down and read what Nick has written in careful script. And then I reread it several times, allowing the words to sink in.

Fuck you.

Every Sunday night the entire Cooper family gathers in my mom's cozy dining room for dinner. That is, at least lately, the entire Cooper family but me. My three older brothers, their families, and my mom all live in Rye, New York, a perfect little suburb about thirty miles north of New York City in Westchester County.

I loved growing up here. When I was a kid, it seemed like everything in Rye was based around families. It almost felt like small-town America—or at least what I *thought* small-town America was from seeing it depicted on TV and in the movies. Rye has community celebrations for every holiday, town leagues for every sport, a local Y, a beach, nature preserves, historic sites, and even the famed Rye Playland amusement park that was featured in the movie *Big*. Rye also has a gentrified downtown, a stretch of Purchase Street about a mile long, where you can get anything from a box of specialty macarons to the latest best seller, from a suitcase to a luxury watch, from a new pair of jeans to a fine meal. Plus you can get your hair cut, your clothes dry-cleaned, your dog groomed, your film developed, your check cashed, and pretty much anything else American capitalism can deliver.

On the cab ride from the train station, which is on one end of downtown, to my mom's I get a thrill seeing all the old stores and restaurants I used to hang out at with my friends as well as some new places I've recently started visiting. We pass Starbucks, Longford's Ice Cream, The Smoke Shop (where we bought candy, not smokes! . . . well, maybe a few smokes), a cool new decor store called Nest Inspired Home, and as we get toward the other end of the downtown area, we pass my favorite bookstore, Arcade Books, and I crane my neck to see what they're displaying in the window.

My mom, Cindy Cooper, has lived in Rye for her entire life. The house she was raised in is only a couple blocks from the house she lives in now, the house she raised her kids, us, in. It's a tidy white colonial with navy-blue shutters and a matching navy-blue front door. There's a postage-stamp lawn out front dotted with six square pavers that lead from the cracked and uneven sidewalk, where I learned to ride a bike, to the three brick steps that approach the front door. Two small lights, that are on a timer and go on every night precisely at dusk, flank the front door, and an ancient metal mailbox, where the on-foot mailman still deposits the mail every day precisely at 3:00 p.m., hangs to the right of the door. There's a narrow driveway that leads to a one-car detached garage behind the house. And attached to that garage is a basketball hoop that has seen more games than Madison Square Garden.

"Well, look who's gracing us with her presence!" My oldest brother Matt shouts joyfully in his booming voice as I get out of the cab at the curb in front of my mom's. "I thought we might see you tonight," he says and smiles at me. There's a basketball game, to no surprise, going on in the driveway.

"Hey, guys," I say, a huge smile on my face as my middle brother Tommy launches a hard chest pass to me. I shoot and it goes in. Easy. My nephews, JJ and Parker—Matt's two boys, cheer and give their Aunt Lucy a kiss.

"These two boys playing with you can't be Henry and James, now can they?" I say in mock shock. "Henry and James are *little* boys. But these two boys in front of me are huge!" I say about Henry and James May, who live next door with their mom Grace and dad Darren. I've always really liked my mom's neighbor Grace, and whenever I'm home for an extended period of time, I like to hang with her at her house and hear her hilarious stories of all the crazy moms in her kids' school. The same elementary school I went to when I was their age. Grace writes a health column for a wellness website so we always have a lot to talk about, and she's always really interested in the work I'm doing for Green Goddess. She's also really interested in what it's like to work for

Katherine Whitney.

"Why didn't you call us?" Matt asks. "I would have picked you up at the train station."

"I wanted to surprise you," I say.

"Is that Lucy I hear?" my mom asks, coming outside, wiping her hands on a dishtowel as she approaches me and gives me one of her famous Cindy Cooper hugs. I almost start to cry, it feels so good to be home, to be with my mom, but I hold it together. And soon enough I'm involved in a characteristically competitive Cooper sibling game of two-on-two. All three of my older brothers (the youngest, Sam, had come outside when my mom did) played basketball all through high school and college. Sam and Tommy played Division II ball, but Matt, my favorite brother, played for Duke which is part of the reason I wanted to go there, even though he graduated eight years before me. Because *they* were always playing basketball, *I* was always playing basketball. They needed a fourth.

We finish the game, my brothers and I sweaty and happy, my nephews hoarse from cheering, and head inside to wash up for dinner.

There are eleven of us at the table. Sam and his wife, Allie, who is pregnant with their first baby; Tommy, his wife, Kelly, and their two-year-old daughter, Ella; Matt, his wife, Shannon, and their two boys whom you already met: JJ is five and Parker is three. And my mom and I. Eleven.

My dad, as I mentioned before, no longer lives here. He and my mom finally got divorced toward the end of my senior year in high school. She ended up calling the cops on him one night when he was really drunk, and angry, and pulled a knife out of the kitchen drawer. Rye doesn't see that much crime, so when there's a domestic violence call, all the cops come. Our street was lit up like Times Square on New Year's Eve. Neighbors spilled out of *their* tidy colonials to see what was going on at the Cooper house. My dad begged my mom not to press charges. Apparently, I would find out later, she told him that the only way she wouldn't is if he would sign divorce papers and get the hell out. The very next day, he packed his car and drove to Maine, where he grew up. I haven't seen or spoken to my dad since. He tried to contact my brothers and me at the beginning, but none of us would speak with him. Eventually he gave up.

My mom had a difficult time after my dad left. She was relieved that he wasn't there anymore to mistreat her, but she had to deal with picking up the pieces and moving on with her life. Years of therapy helped her transform from the shell of a woman she had become at the hands of my father into a strong woman who no longer felt powerless, victimized, or frightened. It was a true metamorphosis. The loving, grandmotherly Cindy Cooper of today bears no resemblance to who she was seven years ago. She doesn't like to talk about it.

"It's so great to have you here, Lucy," my mom says as we pass heaping platters and bowls filled with roasted chicken, mashed potatoes, roasted vegetables, pasta, fruit salad, green salad, and steamed spinach. Cindy Cooper loves nothing more than cooking Sunday dinner for her family.

"Yeah, sorry it's been awhile. I've really missed these dinners," I say loading up my plate. "Things have been so busy at work. By Sunday afternoons, I usually want to just crash and get to bed early."

"And look at her. She looks so, what should I call that? Pretty!" Tommy says.

"Hey!" I say.

"Of course she looks pretty. She always looks pretty!" Tommy's wife, Kelly, says, smiling at me.

"Well she's come a long way from her old tomboy days," Tommy says.

"*Old* tomboy days," I say. "I just beat you in basketball!"

"True, true. You got me there," Tommy says.

"But yeah, losing my tomboy ways was no easy feat," I say, laughing. "Especially because I grew up with three older brothers telling me that I *was* a boy," I say.

"They told you you were a boy?" Allie asks. "I've never heard that story."

"We were all so happy when our parents told us there was going to be another baby. We needed a fourth for all of our games! But when she was born and she was a girl, we all cried because we didn't know any girls in our neighborhood who liked to play sports. So we decided that if we told her she was a boy, she'd like sports," Matt says proudly.

"I think *you* decided that, Matt," Tommy says.

"Whatever. Minor detail. But as she got older some of that girl stuff just came out on its own," Matt says.

"Thank the Lord for that," my mom says, spooning more mashed potatoes onto JJ's plate.

"Yeah, I'm still not what anyone would call girly, but at least I was able to grow my hair out, finally. No thanks to you, Tommy," I say, and my brothers all start to laugh.

"I don't know if you girls ever heard that story," my mom begins, clasping her hands together, looking at my three sisters-in-law.

I see Shannon and Kelly give each other knowing looks. They've heard this story before, on more than one occasion. But it might be the first for Allie.

My mom continues, "When Lucy was five, her hair was finally long enough to put into pigtails. She looked so adorable. But one afternoon I heard her screaming upstairs. I ran up and found Tommy holding a pair of scissors in one hand and both of Lucy's pigtails were on the floor beside him.

"Yeah, yeah," Tommy says. All's well that ends well. As I said, you look pretty."

"Thank you, Tommy. I'm glad you think so," I say, taking a sip of my beer.

"Speaking of people who think you're pretty, what's Nick up to tonight?" Matt asks. They get along great. Duke basketball in common and all.

"Nice segue. Nick just felt like staying home," I say, clearing my throat. I try to be nonchalant. My brothers don't catch on and continue stuffing their faces, but my three sisters-in-law and my mother know something's wrong. And the combined female empathy and concern radiating out of their eyes thicken the air. I look from face to face and then I can't help it anymore. I start to cry.

I'm sitting next to Shannon so she puts her arm around me and they all ask in their combined female voices, "What's wrong?"

I tell the whole story. About how things have been completely overwhelming at work. About how Katherine may be able to handle this balance thing, but it's not working out so well for me. (I don't let on that it might not be working out so well for her either.) About how Nick's been fluctuating between concerned and annoyed since I've put our relationship completely on the back burner. And then, the *pièce de résistance*, the proposal: "He asked me to marry him."

The room is silent. Even Ella, who's been fussy, and the two boys, who have been kicking each other under the table, sense that they should be quiet. Matt whoops with joy and slaps his thigh with his hand. But the women know better. They all look at my finger. My sad, naked finger. And then, I explain all the reasons I said no as everyone continues to eat and I continue to cry.

"That's crap," Matt says coarsely, breaking the silence when I finish my account. Ella resumes her fussing and JJ and Parker resume their under-table horseplay.

"What's crap?" Matt's wife, Shannon, asks. She and I have always been the closest among the sisters-in-law. I've known her the longest, and she's the most good-natured of the three.

"If she loves him, she should marry him, simple as that," Matt says stuffing a chicken leg into his mouth.

"Well, she's entitled to not know if she fully believes in marriage," Shannon says, defending me.

"Of course she believes in marriage," Matt says emphatically, banging his hand on the table.

"Hello, Matt, I'm right here," I say.

"Well, I'm sorry," my mom says quietly, wringing her napkin and prematurely starting to clear the table, "that I had anything to do with your having a negative impression of marriage."

"Oh, Mom," I say. "I'm not blaming anything on you. You didn't do anything wrong."

My mom looks so sad. I see her purse her lips and shake her head back and forth. I feel badly bringing it all up. She sits up straight and sternly says, "Do not make any decisions about marrying Nick based on how your father and I ended up. You two are nothing like us. Please do not form your entire opinion on the institution of marriage based on ours. That would be an absolute shame, Lucy."

"Yeah, you can't base it on Mom and Dad," Tommy says.

"They knew each other for less than a year when they got married. They were kids. You and Nick are totally different," says Matt, taking a sip of his beer.

"I know, but what if it doesn't work out?" I ask no one in particular. My appetite is completely gone. I push my plate away.

JJ and Parker politely excuse themselves from the table. Sensing a boring adult conversation, they head toward my mom's sunroom where she has a Wii player set up for them.

"You can't live your life with what ifs, Luce," Matt says, scrunching his face and gesturing with his hands. "What if I die tomorrow? What if there's a terrorist attack? What if shit. That's a stupid way to live your life, and we raised you better than that."

"Matty," my mom and Shannon bark at the same time, suggesting he ease up on me a bit.

"It's fine. Lucy can handle it," Matt says raising his voice a little. "I just don't want my little sister to live her life controlled by fear. Fear is stupid, Lucy."

"Okay, jeez," I say to Matt. "But marriage isn't for everyone. And just because you're all happily married does not mean that I have to get married also. I am my own person."

"I think what Matt's trying to say," Shannon says gently, "is that we all want the best for you, Lucy. Life is so uncertain, and no one knows what's going to happen in the future, so when something really good comes around you should grab it with everything you've got and never let it go."

"And about that whole balance thing, Lucy," Tommy's wife, Kelly, says. "It's hard. It's really, really hard. I started reading Katherine's book that you gave me and, to be honest, she makes it sound so easy. It's not." Kelly was an assistant district attorney before she had Ella. She tried to go back to work when her maternity leave ended but she said it was too stressful because her job was unpredictable and demanding. Plus, she said, she realized that she really wanted to be a full-time mom.

"Well, I do want to work, at least I think I do," I say. "How am I supposed to know now what I'm going to want to do when we have kids? And that might be a deal breaker for Nick. He says he'd be flexible, but I know he'd prefer his wife to be a stay-at-home mom. How fair is it for me to marry him when I don't know that I could give him that?"

From across the table, I see Sam and Allie give each other a look. A sad, imploring look. They've both been quiet throughout this whole conversation. Sam catches my eye.

"Look, Luce, marriage isn't easy," Sam says.

"Sam," Allie pleads quietly.

"No, Al, it's fine. They should know."

"Know what?" my mom asks in a nervous voice.

"Allie and I have been in counseling. And it's primarily for this whole reason. I want Allie to stay home when the baby is born, and she doesn't want to give up her job," Sam says.

Allie is a physical therapist. She gets up from the table and rushes to the kitchen. Kelly follows her.

"Oh, Sammy," my mom says in a disappointed voice. Primarily, I think, because of how he upset his wife but also, I'm sure, because of her concern for his marriage.

"Look, Luce." Matt pipes up again. "No one is trying to say that marriage is easy. Or that these decisions about working or not working are easy. They're not. But if you don't give things a chance because you're afraid of what *might* happen, then you might as well crawl in a hole and shrivel up because that's not living."

"I agree with Matt," Tommy says. "It's not like you barely know Nick, Luce. I mean, it's Nick we're talking about. You guys have been dating longer than Kelly and me have been together."

"And Allie and me," Sam chimes in.

"Just give it some thought," Shannon says. "Don't be so sure you want to let Nick go because you're not sure what you want out of life. And definitely don't let Nick go because you don't believe in marriage right now. That's worth thinking over some more. When a marriage is for the right reasons, and when two people know each other so well and for so long, like you and Nick have and like Matty and I have, it can be wonderful." She turns to Matt and they smile at each other.

"How do *you* feel about being a stay-at-home mom?" I ask Shannon. She had started working for a bank in town right after she graduated from college and was the manager when she had JJ. She took maternity leave, planning to go back to work, but she never did.

"Well, I wish I were home more!" Shannon says, laughing. "I'm so involved at school in JJ's class and then I'm on the parents association at Parker's nursery school plus I'm on the board at the library, so while I don't work for money, I feel busier than I was when I worked at the bank."

Right then, JJ and Parker run back to the table asking for dessert, and Sam gets up to check on Allie in the kitchen.

Matt gets up from his chair, comes over to mine, and kneels next to it. "I want you to know something," he says, clearly not wanting anyone else to hear.

"What?" I ask.

"Nick called me a couple weeks ago to ask for your hand. He said he didn't exactly know when he was going to propose but he wanted to make sure he had the family's blessing. I want you to know that he was so sincere. The things he said about you, about how he feels about you."

"Wow," I say. "I had no idea he called you."

"We all," he says gesturing around the room at my family who are now busy clearing the table and getting ready for dessert, "love Nick. And we love you, Luce. We only want the best for you. I don't want you to hold back in your life."

"I know. I understand what you've been saying. Thank you."

He gives me a kiss on top of my head and then picks up both his boys at the same time, holds them upside down, and tickles them until they cry, "Mercy, mercy."

I didn't tell Matt, or any of them, about the list or the eloquent note Nick wrote me last night. At this point, I'm not sure marrying Nick is still even an option. Not something I will get to decide. I texted him and called him a handful of times between last night and this afternoon to apologize and explain why I was late. He never wrote or called back. Maybe I should have been really angry about the note he left me, but I knew he had been drinking and I knew he didn't mean it as maliciously as it had sounded. That being said, I knew he was really angry. And I understood why he felt so hurt. I just wish he would have let me explain.

After we eat dessert and clean up the kitchen, I go outside with a cup of coffee to watch JJ, Parker, and Ella play on the ancient little swing set out back. The same one my brothers and I played on when we were little.

"Are you sure that thing's still safe?" I ask my mom, with a laugh, as I head out the back door, the rusty screen door slamming behind me.

I walk toward the orderly arrangement of aluminum chairs my mom has near the swing set and am happy to see our neighbor Grace sitting there. Her boys Henry and James are playing in our backyard with the kids.

"Hi, Grace," I say. "I'm so happy to see you."

"Hey, Lucy!" Grace says, giving me a hug. "How's life in the big city?"

"You know. Stressful. Busy."

"How's life with Madame Balance?"

"Well, Madame Balance may be very balanced conquering the worlds of business and motherhood, but *my* life trying to coordinate hers is anything but balanced."

"Oh, Lucy. No one's life is perfectly balanced. Not even Katherine Whitney's."

"I'm starting to realize that."

"I've been at this working mom thing for a few years. And I have a lot of friends who are working moms in some way or another—either they're unpaid volunteers, or they work part time from home, or they commute into the city every day and have an army of help, or a million other ways of being a working mom—and we all talk about it all the time. *How can we do it all? Can we do it all? Is there such a* thing *as balance?"*

"And?" I ask.

"I really believe, Lucy, and this is after talking to lots of women and reading loads of articles and books, including *The Balance Project*, that you can't have the idealized version of 'it all,'" she makes quotation marks in the air, "*and* be perfectly balanced at the same time. The combination of those two conditions is virtually unsustainable."

"What do you mean?"

"Well," Grace continues, "when most people think of the term 'having it all' they think of being really successful at your job, being a great wife and a great mom, and when I say great, I mean fully attentive and involved and not distracted all the time with work stuff. And on top of those two things, it also means taking really good care of yourself. But in the real world, there aren't enough hours in the day to do all those things successfully. And unfortunately, with books like *The Balance Project* and Katherine Whitney on television glorifying this idea of balancing it all, it makes most women feel incredibly inadequate."

"But Katherine does seem to have it all."

"It may seem that way, Lucy, but I can bet you that she's making sacrifices somewhere. If she's doing so well at work, which it appears that she is, then maybe either her relationship with her husband is suffering a bit or maybe she's not around for her kids as much as she and they would like. I'm not suggesting that women have to be all things to everyone. And I'm not suggesting that kids can't or shouldn't have a nanny or go to day care. Tons of my full-time working mom friends use child care and their kids are great. I'm simply suggesting that women can have a variation of 'it all'—their own definition of it—and be really happy. But when women like Katherine Whitney say something like, 'We can all be perfect at everything and look at me and how fabulous I am,' well, I think it's a huge disservice to most women out there who struggle with this immensely. Who don't have reliable or affordable child care. Who don't have the type of job where you can talk to your boss and get time off for your daughter's dance recital. Anyway, sorry, I'm going on and on. I just get so passionate about this topic, and I don't want you to think that it's as cut and dry as Katherine Whitney makes it seem."

"JJ kicked me," James cries to Grace.

"All right, time to go in," Grace says to her boys. "It's late, and it's a school night."

Henry and James run toward their house, and Grace says her good-byes to the sundry Coopers who have gathered to watch the kids play. They all start getting up, too, ready to leave.

"It was so nice to see you, Lucy," Grace says turning to me. "I hope I didn't burst your Katherine Whitney bubble in any way."

"No, no. It's fine. I thought what you said was interesting. I don't have friends with kids, just my brothers, so I don't really know what that's like at all. It all seems so hard to navigate."

"Well, that is true. And having kids is hard and frustrating in so many ways. But I wouldn't give up those two little buggers for the world. You'll see when you become a mom. It's an amazing kind of unconditional love. There's nothing like it."

"Thanks, Grace," I say and we hug good-bye.

She turns toward her house and I go into my mom's. Matt drives me to the train station, and I have a lot of time on the eight nineteen to Grand Central to think about what everyone has said to me tonight. It's all starting to make me think differently about marriage. About motherhood. And *especially* about balance.

Chapter Eight

"Hey there, Luciebelle. Is she in yet?" Evan asks, bright and early Monday morning, leaning against my desk and looking debonair, as usual.

"Hey, Evan. Nope. Not yet," I say distractedly. I've got *The Balance Project* website open on one of my monitors and I'm trying to answer e-mails on my other monitor. E-mails from Brooke about Katherine's schedule. E-mails from Abby's school about her enrichment program application that's late. Random e-mails that come into the e-mail address associated with the book's website.

Just then, Katherine rushes toward us like a turbulent cyclone approaching an unfortunate Pacific island. It appears she's limping, and she's most definitely shouting at someone on the other end of her cell.

"As I just said, we'll have it to you in two hours, Nigel, I promise," we hear Katherine bark.

Evan and I make a face at each other. Happy that neither of us is Nigel. Or Katherine.

She rushes right past Evan and me without a word and we hear her throw her bag onto her desk and huff into her chair.

Evan and Katherine have been friends since high school. They grew up in Battle Creek, Michigan, an opposite-sides-of-the-track story. Katherine was an only child with a single mom who worked two jobs, one as a secretary at Kellogg's during the day and then, once Katherine was old enough to be home at night alone, as a waitress at the Bee Bee Diner. Evan's dad was a senior executive at Kellogg's. Head of US sales or something like that. Katherine and Evan became close friends through the honor track in high school, even going to the prom together. As friends.

They stayed in touch when Evan went off to Brown and Katherine went to the University of Michigan, which she paid for through a patchwork of scholarships, a work-study job, and a small contribution from her mother's savings. Once Evan had finished with his MBA at Wharton and Katherine had impressed a lot of CEOs with her insightful work as a management consultant at McKinsey, Evan asked Katherine if she wanted to get in on the ground floor of a company he was starting: Green Goddess & Company. That was almost twenty years ago. Together they built it into the behemoth business and brand it is today.

"What's up?" I hear Evan ask Katherine as he makes his way into her office.

I push my chair back from my desk so I am closer to Katherine's office and can hear their conversation.

"Nigel is *really* making this way more difficult than it has to be," Katherine says, sighing.

"Can you get that, Lucy?" Katherine shouts at me. I hadn't even heard the phone ring.

"Katherine Whitney's office."

"Nigel on line one," I intercom to Katherine.

"Tell him I'm no longer with the company," she yells.

"Okay," I say through the intercom. "And you have the interview call with *Working Mother* in five minutes."

I scoot my chair back again.

"I can't do all this, Evan. I just can't," Katherine says, sounding exasperated.

"What, Kath? Do all what?"

"This!" I hear her yell. "London. The book. Theo."

What's wrong with Theo?

"What's wrong with Theo?" I hear Evan ask.

"He's giving me a hard time about everything these days. He used to be so understanding when I had a lot going on at work. Now he acts resentful and pissed off all the time."

I turn around and catch sight of Evan draped over a Kelly chair, tapping his well-shod foot.

"And I'm either going to shoot Nigel or he's going to give me a heart attack," Katherine says, her voice starting to get angrier. And higher pitched. "I'm just not sure which. I think we're trying to do this London launch way too soon. We need at least another month if we're gonna pull this thing off the way it should be done."

"Katherine Whitney's office."

I tell Katherine that *Working Mother* is holding on the line for the interview. She doesn't respond. I just hear silence in her office. Eventually, Evan walks out and raises his eyebrows at me as he walks toward his office. Then. . . .

"Hello, this is Katherine Whitney."

It's incontrovertible that I have a lot more pressing things to do than listen in on one of Katherine's umpteen interviews. But I can't help myself. I'm sickly interested to hear how she's going to pull this one off in the state she's in.

"It's so nice to talk to you, too. *Working Mother* is one of my favorite publications." Katherine voice is professional, calm, and in control. That woman is good.

Working Mother's turn.

"I wrote the book because I thought it was important to share what I've learned throughout my career with other women who are struggling to find balance."

Working Mother.

"I do. I do believe you can have it all. I've experienced that in my own life," Katherine says, not smugly, but confidently, earnestly.

Working Mother.

"Yes. Absolutely. There are a lot of people who say that you can't have it all. I respect their opinions. But I think a lot of women who say that are stuck in old patterns that don't allow them to reach their full potential. *The Balance Project* gives great strategies that will allow every woman to do it all. And to do it all well.

Working Mother.

"I'm fortunate in that regard because my husband Theo is so supportive of me and the long hours I devote to my career. And my girls love having a mommy who goes to an office every day. Unfortunately, I don't get to spend that much time with them in the morning and it's close to their bedtime when I get home at night, but we spend all weekend together. It's special family time. It works. They're very happy little girls."

Working Mother.

"Thank you so much. It's been great talking to you, too."

The phone rings just as Katherine hangs up with *Working Mother.*

"Katherine Whitney's office," I say into the receiver. "Nigel on line one," I intercom to Katherine.

I hear her pick up her extension and yell, "WHAT?"

I check my phone for the first time since I arrived in the office and see there's nothing from Nick, despite my having texted him last night when I got home from dinner with my family and again when I woke up this morning.

But there is a text from Ava:

Guess what?!? There's an opening in the digital media dept

at my company. Not at cosmo but for esquire. You must
apply. Check the site. xA

Ava works at *Cosmo*—she *is* a fun, fearless female—as an associate
features editor. She loves her job, and by love I mean she would make
out with her job if she could, and is very close, she tells me, to getting a
promotion. Her dream is to be a beauty editor. Her bathroom counter
is cluttered with overflowing bins of makeup and beauty products.
She's been that way since high school and has experimented with every
beauty trend from plucked and arched brows to Brooke Shields brows,
from lined lips to red lips, from Chanel Vamp to Essie Ballet Slippers
to Deborah Lippmann Boom Boom Pow, and from blue hair to short
hair to pink hair to red hair to her current brunette ombré.

I turn around and see Katherine crouched over her keyboard,
typing frantically, so I bring up the Hearst website and click on the
Careers tab. It asks me to choose between "magazines" and "television"
so I click on "magazines." Under "category" in the first drop-down
menu, I choose "digital media." And under "location" in the second
drop-down menu, I choose "New York." *Voilà.*

I scroll through the openings. (ScrumMaster? What the hell is a
ScrumMaster?) I see the job she's talking about, along with a couple
other ones that sound interesting and decide that I'll complete the
online application later tonight in the safety of my own home.

"Lucy?" Katherine calls.

I get up, grab my pad, and walk into her office.

"Hey," Katherine says, looking at her computer monitor. "One
sec." She types a reply to an e-mail and clicks send. "Sorry," she says
looking at me, but clearly distracted. "I broke the heel on my shoe
coming in this morning." She points to a sad state of Louboutin black
ankle bootie on her desk. "Do you mind running over to my shoe
repair guy on Sixty-Seventh and Columbus and asking him if he could

fix these? If, for some reason, he can't do it right away, can you go to my apartment and grab me another pair of black ankle booties? I have that dinner tonight so I need something."

"Sure, no problem," I say as Katherine hands me her apartment keys. "I haven't had a bootie call in a while." I know she's not in the mood, but I can't resist.

"Very funny, Lucy," she says, laughing. "I'll text Pancho and have him meet you outside."

"Okay," I say, appreciating that I won't have to waste valuable time running up and down the Upper West Side.

I answer a few more e-mails, grab my coat, and head outside, the sad Louboutin safely tucked into a Green Goddess reusable tote.

The shoe repair guy apparently is unable to fix heels while you wait. "Are you freaking kidding me?" I think were his exact words. So Pancho drives me to Katherine's apartment a few blocks away.

"Do you want me to ring you up?" Cute Doorman asks as I give him a smile.

"Nope, they're not home," I say, dangling the keys in the air as I walk briskly toward the open elevator.

"Are you sure?" I hear Cute Doorman ask as the elevator doors close.

"I'm sure," I say smiling at myself and redoing my ponytail in the mirrored elevator walls.

I unlock Katherine's apartment door and laugh about the fact that she has a backup pair—possibly pairs—of black ankle booties. I've always thought of black ankle booties as something that you'd only need one of. I just have boots, for God's sake. No subcategories.

I head toward Katherine's bedroom and HOLY SHIT, THEO!

Shit! Shit! My brain explodes. I stare at Katherine's bed and the lively business going on within it, and in that split second I consider my options: I can sneak quietly into the closet to get the shoes and hope the frolickers in the bed are none the wiser of my presence. I can make a noise so they are alerted to my presence. Or I can get the hell out of there and have Pancho take me to Saks to get Katherine a new pair of black ankle booties that she may or may not realize didn't come from her closet. But my decision is made for me, because as I was standing there quietly contemplating each lousy option, Theo must have heard my brain working. All of a sudden, he turns away from his lively business and spots me.

"Lucy, shit!" Theo yells.

"Oh my God!" I yell back.

Theo's co-frolicker has what looks like auburn hair. Yep, I can see that clearly now that he's no longer on top of her. She bolts up wondering what the commotion is about and I can also see that, in addition to her auburn hair, she has very large boobs, which she just realized are exposed to the air and me, so she grabs the sheets and pulls them up. The sheets, not the boobs.

"Shit!" I hear Theo say as I stand there dumbfounded.

I'm standing there staring at them. Not moving. My brain eventually responds to all the unexpected stimuli and reminds me that now would be a good time to look away.

"Shit!" I yell as I head back out the bedroom door.

"Shit!" I yell again as I realize I have to get the black ankle booties from Katherine's closet. I cannot return to the office sans black ankle booties without a good excuse and, "Well, your husband was fucking a redhead in your bed so I thought better of scrounging around in your closet for black ankle booties and got the hell out of there," will just not do.

So, I put my hand up to the side of my left eye, creating a makeshift blinder to shield me from seeing the bed, and I hotfoot it past Theo and Red straight toward Katherine's closet. "Shit!" I say over and over as I scan her vast collection of shoes until I find the black

102

ankle booties section. Yes, section. I grab a pair without much analysis and head back through the bedroom, my hand to the side, now, of my right eye.

"Lucy, wait!" Theo says.

I see him jumping into his pants and hopping pathetically around the bed to where I'm hightailing it out of the room.

"No, Theo," I roar. I turn around, can't resist, and catch a glimpse of Red squirming in the bed looking for something. Her dignity, perhaps?

"Lucy!"

"What!?!" I yell stopping in the hallway and turning around to look at Theo. His hair's all messed up. His belt is unbuckled. His chest is bare. The perfect picture of an adulterous husband. I can barely look at him.

"What?" I repeat.

"This isn't what you think," he tries.

"Got it," I say with a disgusted laugh. "Sorry I didn't knock. I didn't think anyone would be home. Neither did Katherine," I say, and I walk out of the apartment.

"Shit!" I yell as I walk through the lobby.

"Everything okay?" Cute Doorman asks with a worried look on his face.

"Shit!" I yell as I get into the Escalade.

"You all right, Lucy?" Pancho asks.

Shit.

Two seconds later my phone rings. The display says Theo. I silence it and let it go to voice mail. Even if I did want to take the call, which I don't, I don't think picking it up and having Pancho hear our conversation would be the wisest of decisions. I'm about to delete the voice mail because I really don't want to hear Theo's pathetic excuses, but I change my mind because part of me really wants to hear Theo's pathetic excuses. I can't imagine what they would be.

Pancho drops me off in front of the Green Goddess building. I start to head inside but then I stop, lean against the side of the building, and play the voice mail on my phone.

"Lucy. It's Theo. I can't even imagine what's going through your mind right now and I'm sorry you had to see that. But please call me back so I can explain. And please don't tell Katherine until I've had a chance to talk to you. Just call me back, slugger, okay? I'll explain everything."

Curiosity takes over and I call him back.

"It's Lucy," I say when he picks up.

"Yeah, I know. Hey."

I wait.

"Listen, Lucy, I'm so sorry you had to see that," Theo says.

"Yeah, you said that." I stare straight ahead at the people, the never-ending swarms of people, walking past me on the sidewalk.

"Right. I said that, okay."

I wait.

"I really don't know what to say. That was a huge mistake. I need you to not tell Katherine. If you let me handle this with her, I will."

"Fine," I say, shifting my weight from one foot to the other.

"Really, Lucy? Thanks."

"I just think— She just doesn't need this right now, Theo. This would kill her. She's about to explode as it is."

"I know that, Lucy. Trust me, I know that. But please let me handle it with her, okay?"

"Okay. I gotta go, Theo. Your wife is waiting for me," I say and hang up.

Shit.

I try to shake off any Theo-banging-Red energy before I walk into Katherine's office, the ankle booties in one hand and a sympathy Glow juice in the other.

"Thank you so much!" she says.

"No problem," I say, trying to keep my expression even. "I have the slip for the shoe repair guy. They'll be ready on Friday. Do you want me to pick them up for you?"

"No," she says, probably trying to figure out why I'm being so nice. "Pancho can get them, but thanks."

"Okay," I say, smiling.

"Lucy, can you get Peter on the phone for me or actually, can you ask him to come to my office when he gets a chance?"

"Sure, no problem," I say as I return to my desk.

I make the call Katherine asked me to make and then I stare at my computer monitor hoping that a message will reveal itself to me telling me what to do. What do you do in these situations? Do I tell Katherine about Theo? Do I call Theo and tell him I'm going to tell Katherine so he better tell her himself? I can't believe he is cheating on her. What a douche!

I check Ava's Instagram hoping today's quote post might provide inspiration about what to do. *A flower does not think of competing with the next flower. It just blooms.* Love the Sensei Ogui quote, Ava, but not helpful. Not helpful at all.

The rest of the day proceeds like the last few. No time to pee. No time to eat. No time for anything except a quick peek now and then at my phone that confirms by its absolute heartless blankness that either Nick is as busy as I am and hasn't had a second to text me back. Or that Nick doesn't want to text me back. Most likely, most definitely, the latter.

Around seven thirty, I finally leave the office and decide to walk home. The sight of me is pathetic. Tall, brown-haired girl, walking toward her cold and lonely apartment, white plastic bag filled with Chinese takeout in one hand, quiet no-text-from-her-boyfriend phone in the other. Two weights heavy on her shoulders. First weight: does said girl tell her pushed-to-the-edge boss that her husband is cheating on her with a well-endowed redhead? Second weight: does said girl tell her boyfriend that she wants to get married so she doesn't lose him forever?

I respect the fact that Nick's incredibly angry and needs space, but I can't say that I like it that much. I hate not being in touch with him. I don't remember going this long without talking to him since we started dating.

I have been thinking a lot about his list. When he first gave it to me, it felt almost aggressive. Like, *you do these things and you get me back*. I completely understood his motivation and I know his heart was in the right place, but it seemed, initially, quite one-sided. The more I consider it, though, I realize that Nick did me a huge favor. It's not only Nick I'll get back if I'm a good girl and complete my tasks. It's *me* I'll get back. All of those demons Nick wants me to conquer are the very grains of quicksand keeping me stuck, potentially drowning me, in this rut I am in. By addressing each one, I may indeed get my man. But I'll also make big strides toward much-needed self actualization. Win-win.

But there's no time for this pitiful self-reflection. I have some job applying to do. After I've finished my lo mein and applied for three different digital-media jobs at Hearst, I realize that I can actually check off something from Nick's—from our—list. It's the only bit of happiness I've felt in days.

Chapter Nine

Katherine and Theo met right out of college. They both took consulting jobs with McKinsey, both thrilled to be based out of the New York office. They had been brought up very differently: Katherine, as you know, in Michigan, only child of a single mom who worked two jobs to keep food on the table. Theo grew up the son of a prominent and very old Charleston family. And he went to the University of Virginia as every good Laurent boy had done since Thomas Jefferson himself doled out the mashed potatoes in the dining hall.

They didn't start dating right away. They occasionally saw each other at company events, but they worked so hard and traveled so much—ah, the glorified life of a McKinsey analyst—that their interactions were sporadic. And strictly platonic. Then Katherine started Green Goddess and Theo went off to get his PhD in economics at Harvard, and they lost touch. (The University of Virginia did not offer a terminal degree in economics, but still, please don't tell all the dead Laurents.)

Katherine thrived in her career at Green Goddess and joined the junior boards of several storied Manhattan charities (museum, ballet, charter school). She found small pockets of time to date the accomplished and handsome young masters of the universe her friends and business associates fixed her up with. The young masters all looking to be the lucky suitor that the intelligent, self-made, and quite beautiful Katherine Whitney selected for her very own. It was rumored, though, that Katherine Whitney ended each affair quite quickly; she was easily bored by her suitors' self-absorption. Rumor also has it Katherine, for her part, was otherwise engaged. To her career, that is, and was disinterested in being distracted by a man who would probably want her to quit her job and breed. Meanwhile, Theo was proving himself at Columbia; being a professor suited him well.

A few years later, the timing for their impending romance was better. Katherine and Theo ran into each other at a conference on "The Economics of Entrepreneurism," which was sponsored by McKinsey and held at the Grand Hyatt right next to Grand Central. They kept each other company during all the breaks, drinking coffee (Theo) and green tea (Katherine), trading stories of what had been keeping them occupied over the last many years (work), and thoroughly enjoying each other's company. Theo, who had always been shy among the ladies, as he would tell me when I met him (long, long before Red), mustered the courage to ask Katherine to accompany him to dinner that night. She was quite impressed with the Southern gentleman's slow and proper courtship and the fact that he didn't want to move her into a center-hall colonial in Scarsdale. He respected what she did, what she and Evan had created, were still creating, and he told her that her dedication to her career was part of what he liked most about her. They fell in love, and one year later graced the Vows section of *The New York Times*. That was exactly ten years ago last weekend, exactly two days before I caught Theo banging Red.

I'm nervous as hell going into the office this morning, Tuesday, and I walk to work a little more slowly than usual to put off the inevitable. I haven't decided whether to tell Katherine about Theo or whether to let it go.

When I arrive at work, Katherine is already in her office. The door is three-quarters closed so I give a little knock and walk in. I'm shocked by what I see.

Katherine is crying. I've never seen Katherine cry. I don't think it's because she's hard-hearted or cold in any way. I just don't think she gets fazed by much. When Katherine sees me, she tries to cover it up. Does she know about Theo?

"Oh, hey, Lucy. Ugh, my allergies are so bad," she says and reaches for a tissue.

This does not look like allergies, but I let it go.

"Sorry," I say.

She shakes her head and composes herself. "I need you to confirm my lunch with Evan and then can you please call Dr. Browning's office and tell them that I can't possibly come back in till next month after London. I also need you to call Brooke, please, and tell her that I can't go on Judith Regan's radio show next week because it's at the same time as the board meeting." She sighs and looks at her monitor, which I can see and hear from where I'm standing, is rapidly filling up with new e-mails.

Katherine puts her face in her hands, and I hear her sniffle.

"Katherine," I say in a sympathetic voice.

"I'm fine, Lucy, I'm fine," she says though it's unmistakable now that those are tears, not allergies. She looks up at me, grabs a tissue, attempts a smile, and then starts to dry her eyes.

"Are you sure about that?" I ask as I sit down in the Kelly chair. I wonder if Theo told her.

And then, seemingly out of nowhere and much to my surprise, it all comes pouring out, tears and words, together in a Niagara Fall.

"Everything is so insanely out of control right now."

I don't say anything. I get up to close her door. The Green Goddess gossips do not need to get wind of this. And then I let her talk. And cry.

"I don't know why I ever wrote a book about balance. I mean, really, am I really the best person to be the authority on balance? I am the worst at balance. The worst. I just can't handle everything on my plate right now. I feel like I never see the girls and Theo. Forget about taking care of myself. I'm a mess. I don't know how I possibly thought I could manage all of this. It's too much."

She pauses and then continues.

"To make matters worse, Dr. Browning didn't like something he saw on my face at the appointment last Thursday and he wanted to biopsy it but I told him I was too busy and I just bolted out of there but I have to go back and get it looked at. I'm so scared though because the last thing he took off ended up being precancerous. He gave me a really hard time when I was there last week, because I hadn't been in to see him in years but how could I go? When did I have any time to go to the dermatologist? How can I let him biopsy it? What if it's cancer? I don't have time for cancer," she says, crying harder now. "My kids need a mother. Not like they exactly have one now," she says sarcastically and returns her face to her hands.

"You know," she lifts her face up and looks into my eyes. She's calmed down a bit. "I've always had imposter syndrome, Lucy. Do you know what that is?"

I shake my head no.

"It's when you don't really believe you are who everyone thinks you are. I get all this praise and everyone thinks I'm so accomplished, but I'm just waiting for them to find out I'm a fraud. Which is ridiculous, I realize, because I've been working my ass off since as long as I can remember. I wrote every single page of that book. Nothing in my entire life got handed to me on a silver platter. I put myself through college. I worked every second to get where I am now. But for some hideously stupid reason, I feel like I don't deserve any of the attention and accolades that I'm getting."

"Why do you feel like that," I ask.

"I have no clue. But now, I'm realizing I *should* feel like that. I wrote a fricking book, for God's sake, on how I have it all and how my life is so balanced. I went on the fricking *Today* show and told Matt Lauer and the world that I have my shit together. But you know what, Lucy? You know what? My shit is anything *but* together. It might have been. At some point. But now with this book and London coming up and my nanny sick almost every day and the new one not starting for two more weeks and my husband barely looking at me because he's so mad at me for I don't know what, it's all too much. It's all too fucking much."

I start to say something, but Katherine continues.

"The worst part of it all is what I've apparently done to all those women out there. I just read an article by Dr. Elaine Ireland and she basically ripped me apart. Apparently I've done some awful thing by allowing women to think that you can have it all. To think that you can have this perfect fucking life where everyone is happy. Where you work all day at your perfect, everything's-under-control job and then you come home and make this delicious dinner and your husband is so happy to see you and your kids are so happy to see you and you haven't missed anything and no one feels neglected. Apparently that's a load of crap, Lucy. It's a goddamn load of crap. And, the worst part, the most pathetic part, is that I'm thinking that maybe, possibly, Dr. Elaine Ireland might be right. I had always thought all those unbalanced women were lazy or stuck or just couldn't get their shit together. But no. They were just too damn busy and they had no chance in hell of balancing it all. And now because they put me on TV and on magazines, me, making it all look so easy and attainable, all these women think they should be able to do all that, too. And I guess they can't. No one can. Well, some people can but either they don't have that much to do at work. Or their husbands don't need to get laid. Or their kids are too little to notice. Or they don't care that their baby is calling their nanny "Mama."

"Katherine—" I say.

"But, here's the thing, Lucy. I would never have written all that or said all that stuff on TV if it hadn't been true. It was true. I did feel balanced. I felt amazing. And, you know what, I'm going to get back to amazing. I have to stick it out a bit, and I'll get back to balance. I absolutely believe that I will get back to balance."

Katherine lowers her head onto her desks and cries.

After a couple minutes of sitting there, letting her cry, watching the e-mails pile up in her inbox, and ignoring the phones, I work up the courage to ask Katherine what I've been wondering for a few days.

"Why don't you come clean?" I ask.

"What?" she asks muffled and sniffly.

"Why don't you go back on *Today* and tell them it was all a big mistake. That you realize now you can't really have it all?" I think about what my mom's neighbor Grace told me on Sunday night and I'm kind of surprised, though not really, that she was right.

"Seriously, Lucy? Are you serious?" Katherine asks, appalled.

"Yeah, why?" I ask.

"Because you can't do that. You can't sell hundreds of thousands of copies of a book and go on the *Today* show and then tell them it was all a mistake. There are so many people whose jobs are invested in my being this Darling of Balance, or whatever ridiculous thing Matt Lauer called me. Brooke, the publishers, even Green Goddess. They're all benefiting from this public persona of mine that I'm balanced, that I have it all, that I'm some perfect specimen of a woman." Katherine grabs a handful of tissues and holds them all up to her face at once. Her eyes are so red, and I feel so badly for her. "I'm way too far down this road to come clean, Lucy. It would be impossible at this point for me to blow the cover off myself."

I shift uncomfortably in my Kelly chair and tell Katherine that I'm so sorry for her that she feels that way. "I didn't realize it had gotten so bad," I say. "For whatever it's worth, Katherine, I am totally here for you. For whatever you need. You may not be, as you say, perfect at being balanced or whatever, but you're pretty damn good at it. And you're inspiring so many women. You heard them all at Barnes & Noble."

I'm not sure I completely believe everything I'm saying, but I feel badly for Katherine so I want to comfort her. It sounds like she has no idea about Theo. Thank God because, at this point, that would completely put her over the edge, although she might be over it already.

"Thanks, Lucy. Thanks for being supportive. You know I could never in a million years do any of this without you," she says wistfully and looks at her computer screen. "Well, that's been a nice little shit show, but I don't have time for any more histrionics. I have a book to sell, a restaurant to launch, and a million other things to deal with. Thanks for hearing me out, Lucy. Let's keep this between the two of us, okay? I trust you with this private stuff, but I don't trust anyone else with it."

"Of course," I say and get up to open the door and go to my desk. I stop and turn around, "Do you need anything right now, Katherine?" I ask.

"Nothing that you can give me," she says sadly not even looking up from her computer. I close the door softly behind me.

When I get back to my desk, there's an e-mail in my inbox from Jonathan from the HR department at Hearst asking me to come in for an interview this week. Ava must have put in a good word on my behalf to get them to respond to me so quickly. I write Jonathan back and tell him thanks but I've rethought my current job situation and I'm going to stay where I am. There's no way I could desert Katherine right now.

Just then, Maggie Stern, the Green Goddess director of restaurant operations, marches up to my desk demanding to see Katherine. Maggie is the Hillary Clinton of Green Goddess. She's smart as hell, everyone's afraid of her, she wears outdated matronly suits, and if she gets her way, she just might run the place one day.

"She's on a call right now, Maggie. Sorry. But I can have her call you when she gets off," I say politely.

Maggie looks down at my phone console. "Then why isn't one of the lines lit up?" She raises her eyebrows and nods rapidly.

"Oh," I scramble. "She must have just gotten off. Hold on a sec," I say. I get up, knock gently at Katherine's door, and open it up.

One second later I'm back at my desk staring at a very impatient Maggie.

"Sorry, Maggie. She said she's in the middle of something and she'll call you in a half hour or so."

"Seriously, Lucy? Seriously?" she asks sarcastically.

"Yeah, seriously, Maggie. Sorry, but she's been really busy."

"We've all been really busy, Lucy," Maggie says condescendingly. "But we've got a restaurant to launch. Please tell her that I need to speak with her ASAP. Nigel is up my ass and we need to figure some things out." She doesn't wait for me to say anything. She turns around on her sensible loafers and marches back toward the cave from whence she came.

I e-mail Katherine (I don't think the tinny intercom would be a welcome addition to her office ambience right now) the gist of Maggie's request and hold back from telling her that the request was actually a demand.

I'm getting coffee in the kitchen a little while later when Kyle Jackson, who works in the digital-media department, comes in.

"Now, this is someone I'm really going to miss," Kyle says, looking at me with sad eyes when I turn around. Kyle is wearing skinny black jeans, a Green Day concert T-shirt, a grey zip-up hoodie, and black Converse: the height of techie fashion.

"I'm not going anywhere," I say, smiling. "At least not that I know of. Is there something I should know about my job, Kyle?" We're friends, but he's known to be kind of a jerk.

"I'm moving on, Lucy," Kyle says looking melodramatically into the distance with a smirk on his face. "Greener pastures."

"Oh, no, say it isn't so. Where are you going?"

"I got a job at a company called Gotham Web. They're doing some really cutting-edge shit. It's a great job."

"That's amazing. Congratulations."

"Thanks," he says. "I think you should apply for my job, Lucy. I know how much you want to do digital stuff. You've been bugging me with all those questions of yours for years. I can put in a good word for you with Ash if you want."

I can't very well tell him that there's no way I could leave Katherine right now. That, in fact, she just had a complete meltdown and might still actually be crying in her office. It would be heartless for me to leave Katherine knowing how intense everything is with the book and London. And with Theo. Oh, Theo. No, there's no way I could leave Katherine. Not that I'm someone irreplaceable. That's not it at all. I know someone else could do my job. It's just the timing right now isn't good. Maybe in a few weeks. But I can't tell Kyle any of that.

"Huh. Interesting," I say to Kyle. "Yeah, please, if you don't mind. That would be great. Thanks."

Kyle grabs his coffee and heads out of the kitchen. I stir some extra sugar into mine and hurry back to my desk.

There's a text from Ava waiting for me on my phone when I get back to my desk. I respond right away.

Ava: Dinner tonight? xA

Lucy: YES!

Dinner with Ava is exactly what I need.

Chapter Ten

I meet Ava at Isabella's on Columbus and Seventy-Seventh Street at eight. Isabella's is on the expensive side, but we love it there so much that sometimes we splurge. Ava and I used to get together once a week for dinner. Lately, that hasn't entirely been the case, and it's more because of my schedule than Ava's. Ava is certainly busy at *Cosmo*, but normal New York City busy. There's usually time for dinner once a week when you're normal New York City busy.

Ava and I have been best friends since high school, and we stayed best friends throughout college. I would visit her in Boston (she went to Boston University) and she would grace me with her adorable presence in Durham. I never know what I'm gonna get when I see Ava. Tonight, she's pretty subdued with her hair in a big messy bun on the top of her head, bright-red lipstick, and a ring on every finger. Including her thumbs.

"Been too long since we did this, Luce," Ava says giving me a kiss, her armful of bracelets clinking loudly.

"I know. I'm sorry," I say as we sit at a table for two. Unfortunately, it's too cold to sit outside on the large and lively patio at Isabella's, one of its biggest draws.

"So did you hear anything back from Hearst about the job?" Ava asks once we've settled in and ordered. We're splitting the fried calamari. Then Ava's getting the kale salad (to make up for the calamari) and I'm getting the bacon cheeseburger (to make up for my job and love life).

"Jobs, actually. I applied for a few. And they asked me, well Jonathan from HR asked me, to come in for an interview."

"That's great! Toast!" Ava says, lifting her glass of pinot grigio.

"Hold up, skippy. Not so fast," I say as she looks at me with questioning eyes and sets down her glass. "I wrote him back and told him I had rethought my application and was going to actually stay in my current position."

"*Why*, Luce? Why did you do that? That job sounded perfect for you. And you've been with Katherine for so long," Ava says, looking concerned.

"I know. And that job and the other ones they're looking to fill *are* perfect for me. But things are crazy busy at work, and I feel too badly leaving Katherine right now. She's not having the easiest time with everything that's on her plate. All that balance stuff, if you know what I mean." I give a fake laugh. "But things will calm down soon, and then I can start a proper job search," I say taking a sip of my lager.

We both start talking again at the same time. It seems as if Ava is going to ask me something, but she tells me to continue. So I do.

"Well, there are two big things that I need to get your opinion on," I say to her.

The first is Nick and I fill her in on everything that happened since she and I spoke Friday night after Nick presented me with his list at Carlo's. I tell her about Nick's two-word "love" letter delivered by the bartender at Union Square Cafe, my family's not-so-subtle push toward marriage, and the constant and low-grade ache all over my body.

"What are you going to do?" Ava asks as the waiter delivers our calamari.

"I'm still having a hard time getting comfortable with this whole marriage thing. However, I haven't heard from Nick and that is pure torture. So I am also having a hard time getting comfortable with not having Nick in my life at all. That is completely out of the question," I start to get emotional. "I'm willing to do the things on the list because they're things I really need to do, but after my no-show on Saturday night, and his efficiently worded missive, I have no idea what he's even thinking."

"I think you should call him and tell him you've been an idiot, and you've reconsidered, and you would love to marry him."

"Ava!"

"What? I'm serious."

"I can't do that. I'm not sure I believe that."

"Oh, please, Lucy. Get over it. Get over your whole poorly argued, long-held, self-righteous assertion that marriage is the devil. Yes, your parents made a terrible mess of things. Yes, they're horrible examples. But there are loads of good examples. I want to get married and look what happened to *my* parents. Marriage might be the devil and it might not. But what do you have to lose? Just go for it. For all you know it could be the best decision you ever make."

As I think about what she says, she changes the subject.

"Not to gloss over your fear of white dresses," Ava says, and I give her a dirty look. "Sorry. But what's the other thing you wanted to talk to me about? You know I have no patience when it comes to big news."

"I wouldn't say this is big *news* exactly but it is a big *deal*, and I need your guidance. But first, you have to swear on your own life and the life of your parents and the lives of your future children, actually, just swear on your job, that you will not tell anyone, and I mean anyone, what I'm about to tell you," I say, getting a little intense.

"Okay, jeez. I won't tell anyone," Ava says, rolling her eyes.

"This is about someone else's private life and I probably shouldn't tell you, but it's eating me up, and I don't know what to do."

"Enough with the drama, Lucy. Spill it!"

"I walked in on Katherine's husband having an affair," I whisper.

Ava's jaw drops and she looks at me in disbelief as she moves her head closer toward mine. "Where were you?" she finally asks, also in a whisper.

"Katherine asked me to pick something up at her apartment in the middle of the day yesterday. She gave me a key so I walked right into the apartment. I went into her bedroom to get what she needed and there he was. In the bed."

"Holy shit," Ava says.

"I know. It's awful. And I don't know if I'm supposed to tell Katherine. Or tell Theo that I'm going to tell her so he can tell her first. But I really want to do the right thing here. What should I do?"

"Oh, man, Lucy. I have no idea. But I wouldn't give that bastard the luxury of a warning. No way. He does not deserve that," Ava says emphatically. Her last two boyfriends cheated on her, and her dad cheated on her mom, so Ava is not a fan of the cheater.

"So you think I should tell her?" I ask.

"Maybe. One of my mom's friends told my mom about my dad, because apparently everyone knew but my mom, and my mom was so thankful her friend told her. Don't you think Katherine deserves to know? I don't know why you're protecting Theo."

"I'm not protecting Theo. I'm protecting Katherine. She's got a lot on her plate right now, and I don't feel the need to burden her with something else. And you never know the whole story. Maybe it wasn't what it looked like."

"Were they in bed together?" Ava asks me flatly.

"Yes."

"Were their clothes on?"

"No. Not exactly."

"Then, c'mon Lucy. What else could it have been?" Ava tilts her head and looks at me expectantly.

"I don't know. It's just that Theo is so great. And I can't believe he would do this to Katherine."

"Yeah, everyone thought my dad was so great, too. But great guys do shitty things. They don't always think with the right part of their bodies. But when they do these shitty things, they should have to deal with the consequences. Could you live with yourself if you didn't tell her and she went on not knowing?

"Could I *live* with myself? Isn't that a little dramatic, Ava?" I ask.

"Well, maybe a little. Anyway, I think I would tell her."

"Really?" I let out a deep exhale. Telling Katherine about Theo is so not something I'm prepared to do. But if it's the right thing to do, then I guess I should do it.

"Sorry, babe, but it's kind of woman code, and I know you like Katherine, so you pretty much have to tell her."

The busboy clears our calamari plate and we sit staring at each other in silence for a minute. I look around at the other people in the restaurant. They look so unburdened. I envy these strangers. It looks like Ava is preparing herself to say something. She finally does.

"So, I realize from the last two topics of conversation that this might not be the *best* time for what I'm about to ask you, but I told my friend I would, so here goes."

"Your friend? What friend?" I ask and make a face at her.

"Hmmm, where do I start?" Ava asks. It doesn't seem like she's taunting me by delaying. It genuinely seems as if she doesn't know where to start.

"Just start!"

"Okay, okay. So you know how I talk a lot about my friend Daniel who used to work at *Cosmo* with me?" Ava asks.

"Yes."

"Well, apparently he met you on Saturday."

"Saturday?" I ask, trying to think of where I was on Saturday.

"At Katherine's. He was working on the interview for *People*."

"Oh, yeah. I met him."

"Well, this is a long story so bear with me. As I said, Daniel used to work at *Cosmo* but now he works at the *New York Post*. His uncle Logan works for *People*, that's who he was with that day, and sometimes Daniel helps him on the weekends with projects to get more experience."

"Okay," I say. "I'm following."

"Daniel knows that I have a best friend named Lucy but he doesn't know what you do, or at least, didn't know before today what you do. So today, I had lunch with Daniel, who's a total gossip, and he started telling me about the interview he did on Saturday with his uncle. And he said the interview was with Katherine Whitney. And then he said that he kept overhearing, sometimes innocently and sometimes shamelessly eavesdropping, Katherine being a complete asshole to her assistant. So I described what you look like and he said it was definitely you. Was it you?"

"Yes," I say hesitantly. "I was at Katherine's on Saturday helping her out."

"Anyway, Daniel was basically saying Katherine seemed like a complete bitch and he thought the whole thing was, in his words, completely fucking ironic, because they were there to interview someone who's all about preaching balance and he said her life did not seem to appear that way. Although he did say that when she was with him and his uncle, she was like a complete angel."

"Katherine's going through a lot right now, Ava. She's got a lot on her plate. She got a little frustrated with everything that was going on on Saturday and she hadn't slept a lot the night before, but it wasn't a big deal. Sounds like your friend Daniel is getting a little carried away."

"Really, Lucy?" Ava asks.

"Really, Ava," I say, a little annoyed and unsure where she's going with all this.

"Because I heard some of the things she said."

"What are you talking about?" I'm starting to feel like I'm being put on the defensive.

"Daniel recorded her."

"What?" I ask, completely shocked.

"Every time he heard Katherine start up with you, he recorded it on his phone."

"Jesus, Ava. He must have been lurking around corners. I didn't even see the guy near us."

"He's a little sneaky."

"I hope you told him to erase it. That's just lame that he goes around recording people like that. And isn't that illegal?"

"I don't know."

"So what does this all have to do with me?" I ask as our dinners arrive.

Ava pauses. She seems to be mustering courage. "Well, I told him I didn't want to ask you this, but he thinks it's a really important piece, so I told him I would."

"What? Told him you would what?" Now I'm starting to feel uncomfortable.

"Okay." She takes a deep breath. "Daniel is planning on writing an exposé for the *Post* about Katherine, about how she's out there talking all about balance and that it's not all what it seems. And he wants you to give him information as an inside source from her office."

"Are you on drugs, Ava?" I ask. "No fucking way. That's disgusting."

"You said it yourself, Lucy. You said she isn't exactly killing it in this whole balance thing."

"That's not what I said, Ava. And even if she wasn't, as you say, exactly killing it in this whole balance thing, why do you think for a second I'd betray her and go behind her back feeding information to your little friend for some salacious tell-all?" I'm pissed now.

"Sorry, Luce. I'm not trying to make you angry. This is why I didn't want to ask you at all because I knew you'd react this way. But Daniel begged me."

"Well, you can tell Daniel there's no way that I'm going to be his source. Why would he want to do such a mean piece anyway?" I ask.

"Probably because it sells newspapers. But also because he said he went out with his sister later that night, who is a working mom, and she said that she gets so annoyed when women go all public, preaching how easy it all is when it's not. She has two kids and she's always saying how hard it is to balance it all. So she got kind of worked up when Daniel was telling her all that he heard and saw, and she was like 'See, see. It's not so easy. Even Katherine Whitney loses her shit.' She made him feel like he had some sort of responsibility to American women to expose Katherine to stop her from making other women feel badly about themselves. I don't know. It sounds a little ridiculous, but I'm just telling you what he told me. He was all fired up to write this article."

This balance-is-impossible argument is becoming a regular refrain. First my sister-in-law Kelly. Then Grace. Then Katherine essentially said it herself. And now Daniel's sister.

"No way, Ava. There's absolutely no way. I would never be so unethical and disloyal. And you should tell your little friend Daniel and his sister that there are hundreds of thousands, maybe millions, of women who look up to Katherine, who write her e-mails telling her how much her book is helping them."

"Sorry, Luce. I didn't mean to make you upset. I'm sorry I asked you. Please don't shoot the messenger," she says and gives me a don't-be-mad smile. I've seen that smile before. And, as usual, I can't stay mad at Ava for that long.

"Not to give you any ideas or anything, but why does he need information from me anyway?" I ask.

"Because he wants to have a legitimate source from Green Goddess."

"Oh, shit!" I say, realizing I told Ava about Theo.

"What?" Ava asks.

"I told you about Theo. Don't you dare. I mean it, Ava. Don't you dare tell Daniel or any of the people at your magazine or at any other magazine or newspaper what I told you. I never should have told anyone about that," I say and I so regret that I ever opened my mouth about it. Ava is very trustworthy and I'm not concerned she'll tell anyone but in light of this whole *Post* thing, I'm starting to regret telling her. And I feel badly because it's none of my business what happened in the first place.

"I won't tell anyone, Lucy. I promise."

"You better not, Ava. It would be so wrong."

"Okay, I get it, Lucy. You don't have to explain that to me. I know it would be wrong. Plus, I know if I did mention it to him, he would go off and write a story about it. So you have my word."

"So what have we accomplished in this most intriguing and eventful dinner so far?" I ask sarcastically. "Hmmm, you want me to reconsider my, ahem, self-righteous thoughts on marriage and accept my boyfriend's proposal, if he'll still have me."

"Right," Ava says.

"You want me to tell my boss that her husband is moonlighting."

"Yes," Ava says.

"And you want me to pull a Benedict Arnold so your friend can sensationalize Katherine, sell lots of newspapers, and make a name for himself as the next Woodward and Bernstein."

"Well, no. Not really anymore. I see your point on that one, and

I'll tell Daniel to abort mission."

"Thank you," I say as we finish our dinner and pass on dessert.

"What did you think of my quote post today, by the way?" Ava asks, smirking at me.

"I didn't see it. What did it say?"

"*The people you fight with most are the people worth fighting for.*"

Chapter Eleven

The next morning, Wednesday, I get to my desk and am relieved to find Katherine's office still empty. When nine o'clock comes and goes, I become concerned about Katherine. She's usually in by eight, there's nothing on her calendar—no breakfast out of the office that she is supposed to be at eating egg whites and blueberries—and she's not answering my texts.

By nine thirty, I've taken sixteen phone messages, four from Nigel alone, and dodged no fewer than five coworkers looking for Katherine to approve this, sign that, do this very thing this very second to keep Green Goddess in operation. She's about to miss a very important status meeting about London. And I'm trying, once again, to keep all of Katherine's balls in the air.

A little after ten, Maggie marches to my desk demanding to know where Katherine is and why she wasn't in the meeting.

"I don't know, Maggie."

"I don't buy it, Lucy. How can you not know?"

"I don't. Really. She doesn't have anything on her calendar, besides that London meeting, which I now realize by your presence at my desk, she didn't slip into without my knowledge. And she's not answering my texts. But I'll let her know that you came by."

Maggie stands there staring at me for a second, maybe deciding which kind of witch she's choosing to be. Ah, it appears she's chosen Glinda. Lucky me. "Okay, Lucy. Please do let her know that. I really need to speak with her about London like an hour ago."

"Will do," I say and give her a smile.

Maggie and Katherine would not, shall we say, be finalists in the Green Goddess BFF category. No love lost there. Katherine doesn't have anything against Maggie, she actually thinks she's incredibly smart and great at her job, but Maggie has always been a thorn in her side. Like she's got it out for Katherine. Damn woman makes me nervous.

Around eleven, with still no word from Katherine, I'm wondering if I should be taking this more seriously. What if something happened to her? I'm about to call Theo, which I really do not want to do, when Katherine comes strolling in.

"Hey," she says nonchalantly, stopping at my desk.

"Hey," I say, stunned by the nonchalance.

"Anything I need to know?" she asks, looking at her phone.

"Tons, actually," I say.

"Okay, come on in. I just need to answer an e-mail and then you can fill me in."

I give her a minute to get settled and send that e-mail and then I sit quietly on a Kelly chair waiting for her to finish what she's doing.

When she finally looks at me, I notice a small Band-Aid on her forehead.

"I've got lots of people looking for you, Katherine," I say. "I didn't know where you were this morning."

"Sorry, Lucy. Theo was giving me a hard time last night about that biopsy, so I called Dr. Browning's office first thing and he was able to see me. Things kind of got carried away and then I had to wait forever, and it all took a lot longer than I thought it would."

"Did you see all my e-mails and texts?"

"For some reason I couldn't get any cell service in the office, and when I finally got back in the car, I saw them but I knew I'd be in shortly and I had to get on the phone with Nigel on my way here. Sorry I left you hanging all morning with these sharks circling."

I follow up with Katherine on all her messages, including the lovely visit Maggie paid, and I get back to my desk.

We each work quietly for the next couple hours. I hear Katherine typing away and making phone calls. Around one thirty, Katherine intercoms me and asks if I've had lunch. I go into her office.

"I haven't and I was actually going to go down and grab something because I'm starving. Do you want me to get you something?" I ask.

"Yes, please. Can you get me a veggie wrap and a cup of whatever the soup is today? Here's some money, use it for your lunch, too," Katherine says.

"Okay, thanks," I say and head down to the cafeteria.

"So did you apply for my job yet?" Kyle asks. He's just come up behind me in the soup line.

"Not yet."

"Why not?"

"Things are so busy with Katherine right now. It's not good timing," I say, ladling soup into a small container.

"I love the lentil, too," he says when I hand him the ladle.

"It's actually for Katherine."

"You have to get her lunch?"

"I don't *have* to. I was heading down anyway, and I asked her if she wanted anything."

"I thought you always wanted to do digital media. Getting soup for your boss is not exactly living the dream, is it?" He laughs condescendingly.

"There are different roads, Kyle. And you don't have to be such a dick about it. Right now this is my road, and I'm okay with it.

Eventually, if it's meant to be, the timing will be right and then I'll move into digital media."

"Oh, so you're one of those meant-to-be girls?" he asks, as we both move to the cashier line.

"What's that supposed to mean?"

"It means you don't take charge of your life and make things happen. You just wait for fate to take over and let things happen when they're all destined to and shit?"

"No. I don't do that," I say indignantly. "I don't like how you're making all these assumptions about me, Kyle. We're work friends and all, but you don't know anything about me."

"Oh, I know girls like you, Lucy," Kyle says arrogantly, waving his hand in the air like an idiot. "You're the type of girl who loses jobs to guys like me because you're too scared to make shit happen in your life."

"Jesus, Kyle. That's a little out of line, isn't it?" I ask completely annoyed at this point. We've both paid, and we're heading toward the elevator together.

"Is it, Lucy? Is it out of line?" Kyle asks. "Or am I dead right about you?" He winks at me.

The elevator door opens and we start to walk inside. I raise my fist to punch him in the face, but think better of it at the last second. As I'm about to say something both brilliantly articulate and sufficiently insulting to shut this whole thing down, Kyle turns around and heads back to the cafeteria.

"I forgot my crackers. Catch you later, Lucy."

The elevator doors close and I want to punch the wall. But as I stand there stewing, watching the floor numbers light up one by one as I pass them by, I realize that he's not so off target with me. I certainly don't like being characterized that way by someone who barely knows me, but isn't what he said a little bit true? I *am* too scared to make shit happen in my life. I *am* waiting for the right time, waiting for things to change in Katherine's life so I can make changes in my own. But isn't that a completely backward way to look at it? Man, Kyle Jackson, you are an asshole but you pegged me on this one. Rather than thinking only of how my applying for the digital-media job will affect Katherine, I really need to think about how *not* applying for the job will affect *me*.

Right then something comes over me and I have a moment of clarity. And courage.

"Katherine, there's actually something I want to talk to you about," I say as I hand her her lunch and the change from the twenty-dollar bill.

"What's up?" she asks, eyes back on her computer monitor.

"You know Kyle Jackson who works for Ash in digital media?"

"Yeah," she says half paying attention and half typing an e-mail.

I decide to speed things up. "Well, he's leaving and they're looking to fill his job and I know how busy things are right now and I know it's not the best timing but you know how badly I've always wanted to do digital media and I've been thinking about it a lot and I don't know when there will be another opening in that department and I don't think I can pass this opportunity up." I exhale. I have Katherine's full attention now.

"Wow. Okay. Wow," Katherine says. It appears I've rendered her speechless. The phone rings. We both ignore it and allow it to go to voice mail.

I wait for Katherine to speak. My stomach is churning. I can't actually believe I said something. *You go, Lucy!*

"I didn't know you were unhappy," she finally says.

"That's not it. It's not that I'm unhappy. But when I think of my career and what I want for myself long term, I know that I want to be doing digital media. Working for you is great. You've given me so many opportunities, but I don't want to be an assistant forever."

"I don't know what I'd do without you, Lucy," Katherine says.

This is not about our close relationship. This is about Katherine knowing that I am clearly holding it all together for her. That my all-encompassing devotion to her career allows her to maintain this illusion that she is, indeed, America's Darling of Balance. And now that I've gone all bold, I'm starting to admit to myself that even though I want to apply for Kyle's job because I want to be in the digital-media department, a big part of me also doesn't want to work for Katherine anymore. That's it, hot damn. I'm tired of this shit. I want to work hard to further my own career, not someone else's.

"Oh, you'll be fine Katherine. There are a million people who could do my job."

"I don't know about that," she says, opening the bag and starting to take out her lunch. "I am devastated to think of not having you here. But that's totally selfish, and I respect the fact that you want to go in a different direction. What do you need me to do?"

I realize I've been holding my breath, and I let out a big exhale. "Thank you so much, Katherine. I really appreciate it," I say giddily. "I'm going to submit an official application for the job through HR, but I think if you could call Joan and Ash and let them know that you've given me your blessing that would be great. And a couple words of recommendation wouldn't hurt either," I say, enjoying this rush of courage I'm feeling. Joan is the head of HR and Ash is the head of the digital-media department. Katherine is the COO of the company, but she doesn't make hiring decisions at the level I'm applying for. With a good recommendation from her, however, it should be no problem at all for me to get that job. I've read the job requirements and I'm definitely qualified, my work over the past couple years on different web projects for Katherine and my most recent work on *The Balance Project* website giving me the experience I need in all the systems Green Goddess uses.

I practically do a heel click in the air walking out of her office. *Good girl, Lucy!* I feel so proud of myself.

I go online to the Green Goddess career opportunities web page and I submit an official application and my résumé, which I had updated the other night when I applied for the Hearst jobs. Then I send Katherine a quick e-mail thanking her for giving me her blessing and reminding her to give Ash and Joan a call. When I click send, I feel a rush at the same time a pit starts to form in my stomach. I can't believe what I've done. But I'm thrilled I did.

Sometimes that happens to me. When there's something that I really want to do, even though the rational part of my brain tells me not to do it, sometimes something will come over me and I'll do it. It's like the irrational, or impulsive, part of my brain takes a stun gun to the rational part and tells it to stand down for a moment while it takes over and gets shit done. I silently thank the impulsive brain cells and carry on. And I silently thank Kyle, begrudgingly, for lighting a fire under my ass.

I text Nick, whom I still haven't heard from, and tell him the good news. Hopefully, hearing that I'm making a change might make him realize that I'm starting to take control of this overworking situation. I miss him so much. I am trying to keep busy, to distract myself with work, but every time my brain senses an opening, in comes a thought of Nick. The whole thing makes me so sad.

A little while later, and still no response from Nick, Katherine calls me into her office to go over her schedule. Before we start, she tells me she spoke to Joan and Ash, and I thank her. I realize from her perspective this all really does suck. It's another wrench thrown into her life. Things are crazy with the book and London. Her husband, for God's sake, is cheating on her, something I have not yet told her. And now I've given her the unwelcome news that I want to find a new job. It's like an awful game show where they keep loading the contestant down with more and more burdens and then wait to see how long it will take her to crack.

Katherine's phone rings and she picks it up on speaker.

"Katherine Whitney."

"Hi, Katherine! It's Brooke!"

Damn woman and her exclamatory phrases.

"Hey, Brooke. What's up? I have Lucy here," Katherine says.

"Hi, Lucy!"

"Hi, Brooke," I say.

"Listen, Katherine, great news!"

Katherine and I give each other a look.

"What?" Katherine asks.

"Oprah Winfrey has pneumonia!"

"That's not great," Katherine says, smiling at me.

"No, you're right. That's not great. But she's going to be okay. She'll be fine. She just has to rest and can't fly."

"Okay . . . ," Katherine says, clearly not understanding what this has to do with her.

"Oprah Winfrey was supposed to receive the Working Woman of the Year Award from Ellevate on Saturday night but now she can't be there to speak and they need a speaker and another recipient so they want you to come! Isn't that fabulous?!"

"Not for Oprah," Katherine says.

"I know not for Oprah, but for you! It's fabulous!"

"What's Ellevate?" I ask.

"It's the new name for 85 Broads, that organization that's all about professional women, supporting them, creating networking and educational events, you know!" says Brooke.

"I know 85 Broads," Katherine says. "It's a great organization. I'm a member. Sallie Krawcheck runs it. I love Sallie. I didn't know they had changed their name," Katherine says.

"So what do you think? Saturday night?"

"What do they need me to do?"

"They're giving you a table of ten to fill and they need you to speak about your book and how professional women can do it all, and balance it all, and all that stuff that you're so good at!"

"Wow. That's great. I'd love to. Thanks, Brooke."

"Just so you know, Katherine. They're going to give you the award but they're still also going to give Oprah an award. Gayle King is going to be there to accept on Oprah's behalf. I didn't want you to be blindsided. And also so you know, they told me that you were at the top of their list to approach for next year's dinner so while they're all terribly upset about Oprah and her pneumonia, they're thrilled that they have the opportunity to give you the award considering how timely it is with your book and all. So I can tell them yes?" Brooke asks.

"Yep. You can tell them yes. Thanks, Brooke," Katherine says turning back to her monitor.

"Yay! That's so great, Katherine! I'll send over additional information this afternoon about how long your speech should be and all that. And do let me know if you want us to help you write it."

"I should be okay. I still have my dear Lucy," Katherine says, a saccharine smile directed my way.

The "still" slipping right by Brooke, she hangs up and leaves Katherine and me.

"That's so great, Katherine," I say. "Congratulations!"

"Thanks," Katherine says, seeming distracted as we continue going over her schedule.

Katherine's phone has rung no fewer than ten times since we've been in her office, but we've let it go to voice mail. When we're done with her schedule, I go back to my desk and start listening to messages. And the part of my brain that's not in use listening to and writing down messages is very excited about the whole idea of, hopefully, not having to be someone else's assistant for too much longer. I can't wait to just have my own work to worry about.

I open the calendar on my phone and stare at an entry that mocks me every time I look at it. Last week Nick invited me to a dinner tonight at eight at Nobu with Grant, his old boss from AAI. They're supposed to discuss Ty Collins, specifically Grant's feeling that Nick acted unethically by signing Ty even though Nick knew that Grant was actively courting him. Nick had originally invited me because he had thought having me there might soften Grant up. I realize I'm clearly not invited to this anymore. But in a moment of poor decision making, I make a poor decision.

At nine thirty I stand outside of Nobu, back in the black leather dress that I haven't yet given back to Katherine. I feel sexy or at least I'm pretending I do. The more I thought about this as the day went on, the more I realized this is what must be done. Maybe Nick will be willing to talk to me if he sees me in person. I'm not letting him go without a fight. It's been enough time, in my opinion. We have to talk about what happened Saturday night and figure out how we're going to move forward.

Nick and Grant's dinner was scheduled to start at eight, so I had figured they'd be wrapping up around nine thirty. And if they weren't done yet, at least all the business stuff would be over and Grant would certainly invite me to sit down. We'd always gotten along fine.

I walk through the door, and I see Nick right away at a table in the middle of the restaurant. He's dressed in a dark-grey suit with a white shirt open at the collar. And he looks amazing. I look across the table and my heart stops. That's not Grant. Unless Grant has had a fucking sex change. Nick is sitting across from a stunning blonde also wearing a dark-grey suit (hers probably has a short skirt, but I can't tell from where I'm standing) with a white shirt *way* too far open at the collar.

She's laughing and holding a pink drink in the air. A cosmo? Give me a fucking break.

I pause and tell myself not to jump to conclusions. Maybe that's Grant's date and he's in the bathroom. But I can see that the table is set for only two: Nick and Cosmo Girl. Maybe, that's Nick's sister. I thought he said she was coming into town soon. And though my eyes aren't perfect, I squint to see her a little more clearly and that is most definitely not Nick's sister.

The fact still remains that whoever it is, it's still not Grant.

I see them laughing about something and toasting, so now, I think, is an appropriate time to jump to conclusions. I start to feel sick to my stomach and realize I need some air. I go outside and walk a few feet down the block so he doesn't turn and see me through the window, as if he'd ever turn away from gorgeous Cosmo Girl.

I can't believe how much I messed this up. I should have said yes when Nick proposed. Here I was thinking he was at home in his sweats all week, watching basketball on his futon, drinking beers, and wallowing over the idea that he may not get to marry me, while, in fact, he was dressing up in his best grey suit to take some Cosmo Girl out to dinner. That, my friend, did not look like wallowing.

Did I honestly think I could get away with saying no, that Nick would realize he loves me so much and he would be willing to stay together without getting married, and we'd go on our lovely way as life partners, or lovers, or significant others, or domestic partners, or whatever the hell people like to be called these days. But how could I have been so stupid? *You're not that great, Lucy.* Why should I think that some man, that Nick, would be willing to change his values just to spend the rest of his life not being married to me? I sulk on the subway all the way home thinking that I may have dealt a fatal blow to what used to be Nick and Lucy.

When I get home I toss my stupid, well Katherine's, stupid leather dress on the floor, kick off her heels with no care if I nick them because we all know she's got plenty more in her black-high-heel section, throw on my most comfortable PJs, and open my freezer. Yes, I know, it's a complete cliché, but I do what any jilted girl would do at this point. I make love to two other men, namely Ben and Jerry. And if you've ever tried Hazed & Confused Core you won't blame me one bit.

As I'm shoving spoonfuls into my mouth, not even mindfully as my *Green Goddess Magazine* would tell me to do if I'm going to indulge in a pint of ice cream, I check my phone. Nothing. I throw it across the room and start to lose it when I see little pieces of phone-screen glass flying through the air.

I better get this new job, I think to myself as I finally set down the spoon (only because there is no ice cream left in the carton, or in my entire freezer), because if I don't, who knows if Katherine will even want me back considering she must think I'm totally disloyal at this point. I certainly don't have a boyfriend to turn to. And now I might not even have a phone (I haven't bothered to get up and assess the damage), which is the least of my problems considering the only two people who text me on a regular basis might soon both be out of my life.

Chapter Twelve

I've only been betrayed once in my life. And it was over a boy. My senior year in high school, I finally started dating Robby Sherwood. I had fallen in love with Robby Sherwood in ninth grade when he sat in front of me in first-period English. We were a goddamn formulaic teen movie. I stared at the back of his neck and didn't pay attention to Mrs. Montgomery and her insistence that we become lovers of literature. He stared straight ahead, unaware of the pathetic girl crushing on him from behind. One day he turned around and asked to borrow a pen and we became friends. But he was never interested in me romantically until we went on a class ski trip in December of our senior year.

As luck, and teen movies, would have it, he also became interested in my so-called friend Dana Mortenson on that same ski trip. As the months went by, it was no secret that Robby and I were a thing. But it was a secret, at least to me, that Dana and Robby were also a thing. I caught them kissing behind a fake palm at prom. When I asked him to choose right there and then whom he would like to be with, Robby Sherwood did not choose me.

I had thought, until that night of course, that Dana and I were good friends. Not best friends but good-enough friends that you wouldn't think she'd be sleeping with my boyfriend. And, yes, the "sleeping with" part was confirmed when Robby chose her over me because of it. I was devastated. Later that night, after I tore off my prom dress and threw on my most comfortable PJs, I had my first experience at letting Ben and Jerry soothe a broken heart. There were no Core flavors back then, but there was Chunky Monkey.

So you see when I started work today, this fine Thursday morning, I had little experience with betrayal. Little opportunity to become resistant to it, to perfect my reaction to it. Little opportunity to see it coming.

I'm getting breakfast in the cafeteria when I run into Joan from HR.

"Hi, Joan."

"Oh, hi, Lucy."

"Oatmeal?" I say, glancing at her tray.

"Yep," she says, looking like she really wants one of those oversize everything bagels the food carts sell outside our office. "I'm trying."

"Me, too," I say, gesturing to my egg white and spinach platter.

"How's life with Katherine? Things must be so exciting with the book and all," Joan says.

"Yeah, we've been really, really busy. But, I'm definitely ready to make a change."

"Oh? Are you leaving Green Goddess?"

"No. Didn't you talk to Katherine yesterday? I'm applying for Kyle Jackson's job in digital media. I submitted an application online yesterday," I say confused.

"I was in the office all day yesterday, but I didn't get a call from Katherine about you. And I listened to all my voice mails from yesterday. But my team and I are meeting about the digital-media position this afternoon so I'm sure I'll see your application. One of the associates in my department compiles all the applications for each particular job so I don't see them until we have our position meetings," Joan says, paying for her oatmeal.

"Oh, well Katherine told me she called you. Maybe I misunderstood her. But yes, I've always wanted to work in the digital-media department. In fact, that was the first job I applied for at Green Goddess. Unfortunately, the position was filled internally and I ended up working for Richie Cunningham for a few months before I started working for Katherine, but I've always intended on making my career in digital media so I really hope to be considered for the job," I say, trying to take advantage of this impromptu interview.

"We will absolutely consider you, Lucy," Joan says, smiling before she heads out of the cafeteria with her oatmeal. "I've always heard such wonderful things about you from Katherine. We'll definitely be in touch."

"Thanks!" I say and smile at Joan. I grab a fork and some napkins and head to my office utterly confused as to why Joan hadn't heard from Katherine. I could have sworn that Katherine told me she spoke to both Joan and Ash yesterday.

I decide to make a detour to the digital-media department to check in with Ash to let him know personally that I'm interested in Kyle's position.

"Girl, what is in that bag? Whew," Ash's assistant Sera says, giving me a strange look, when I come up to her desk.

"It's just eggs, Sera. Do they smell that bad?" I ask.

"Well, I'm getting a little more used to it now, so no," she says. "But at first whiff, it really was not a good thing. I hope it tastes better than it smells."

"Thanks. Me, too," I laugh. "Is Ash in?"

"Yeah, he's in there. Go ahead in."

"Thanks," I say and head toward the open door.

"Knock, knock," I say as I tap lightly on Ash's door frame.

"Hey, Lucy," Ash says, looking up from his computer. "Always nice to see you in our happy department."

"Well, I'm hoping to make it that much happier," I say, a big smile spreading on my face.

"Yeah? How's that?" he asks.

"I'm applying for Kyle's job," I say, looking confused.

"That's fantastic, Lucy," he says.

"Yeah, I've always wanted to do digital media, and jobs don't open up in this department all that often so when I found out there was an opening, I approached Katherine about it and told her I didn't want to let the opportunity slip by. She's being completely supportive about it."

"That's great," Ash says, giving me a strange look that I can't decipher.

"But, I'm confused," I say. "Didn't you talk to Katherine yesterday? She told me she called you to put in a good word for me."

"Yeah, yeah, I spoke to her. All good. We'll be in touch about an interview," Ash says looking at his computer.

I take the hint that he's got more important things to do than talk to me, so I thank him for his time and ask him to look out for my application.

As I walk out of his office, I catch Sera trying to quickly scoot her chair back to her desk. Seems I'm not the only one who eavesdrops on her boss.

"Lucy, we've always been friends, right?" Sera asks me, her voice much quieter than it was when she was attacking my innocent breakfast.

"Yeah, of course, why?" I ask.

"Come to the kitchen with me for a second," she says.

"Okay," I say.

"Ash, I'll be right back. I'm gonna grab you a coffee," Sera calls into Ash's office.

"Thanks, Sera!" I hear him call back.

Sera takes my arm and leads me into the kitchen. There's a

coffeemaker and a fruit bowl. I grab a banana to add to my breakfast.

"What's up?" I ask her.

"I'm going to tell you something but you did not, I repeat not, hear it from me. We assistants have to watch each other's backs, no?"

"Of course," I say. I have no idea where she's going with this.

"Katherine came by to talk to Ash yesterday," she whispers.

"I know. He told me he spoke to her," I say.

"I know. I heard. But you're not going to like what she had to say, so brace yourself."

"Okay, I'm braced," I say leaning against the counter.

"Well, I moved my chair back to hear what they were saying because they were talking pretty quietly, but I know what I heard and this is what Katherine said," she says and pauses.

"What? What did Katherine say?" I ask, getting a little impatient.

"She said that you were going to apply for Kyle's position and that she wanted him, Ash, to interview you and all that and act like you were being considered but she told him that he couldn't hire you."

"What?" I'm stunned. And I can feel my face turning red.

"She said, and again, I heard her very clearly, that she is way too busy right now to lose you. That things are too crazy right now with all that's going on with her to try and train a new assistant. She did say some nice things about you, Lucy, like you were irreplaceable and all that."

"Well, that's comforting," I say sarcastically.

"Sorry I had to tell you that but I heard your conversation with Ash in there and you sounded so eager. I felt like you deserve to know the truth that Katherine is not actually supporting you with this."

I feel like I've been punched in the stomach. Like I just caught Dana and Robby kissing behind the palm.

"Thanks for telling me, Sera," I say. "That really sucks."

"I know. It totally does, honey. I'm so sorry."

"Thanks."

"I hope you're not mad that I told you."

"No. Absolutely not. I'm the complete opposite of mad. I'm not happy, but I'm so glad you told me. I feel like such an idiot," I say looking into Sera's big brown eyes.

"This shit goes down all the time in this company. People stabbing each other in the backs. Don't you hear any of the stories?"

"No. I don't. I'm too busy taking care of Katherine. Maybe I should join you and the other assistants for lunch more often."

"Yeah, Lucy. You do that. You stick with us, and we'll take care of you. None of us stab each other in the back, I can promise you that."

I slowly walk back to my desk, my poor smelly eggs getting colder by the minute. And I think about what I just found out. Not only did Katherine lie to me by telling me she spoke to Joan when she didn't, but she also blatantly forbade Ash from hiring me. She selfishly, and completely behind my back, decided to keep me for her own while having me believe she's this great boss who's supporting me. She was going to have me go through the whole interview process and think that I had a chance, when really I had no chance at all. What the hell kind of boss does that? After everything I've done for her. I'll tell you what kind of boss. A pathetic boss who realizes that her life will completely fall apart if I'm not there constantly taking care of everything.

I'm boiling when I finally arrive at my desk. Katherine's door is open and I can hear her milling around in her office, but I can't bring myself to say hello.

I wake up my computer and the first e-mail I see is from Brooke. It's to Katherine and me.

Good morning, ladies! I'm so excited to share this amazing piece from today's *Huffington Post*! It's on the front page of the Business, Books, and Women channels! All three! That's incredible exposure and so rare for *HuffPo*! Enjoy!

Oh barf, Brooke. I click on the link she so graciously included in her e-mail and read the piece.

There's a lot of talk out there about having it all. About being it all. About doing it all. For Katherine Whitney, the much-admired COO of Green Goddess, having it all, being it all, and doing it all are what she's all about.

Whitney wants to help other working women achieve her brand of success and she's using the occasion of the six-month anniversary of the launch of her bestselling book, *The Balance Project*, to do just that.

"Being balanced may seem hard, but the strategies in my book will help all women take better control of their lives. Having it all is something all women can realize. It just takes a little work."

Whitney, a mother of two and wife of a professor of economics at Columbia University in New York City, credits her drive to her mother. "My mother taught me the value of having a good work ethic. She worked two jobs when I was growing up to help pay for college. And she taught me that I could be anything I want to be."

Whitney is currently riding the express train in America's business world. With Green Goddess exceeding earnings projections and convincing more and more Americans every day to lead healthier lifestyles, Whitney is at the top of her game. And women across America consider her a role model.

"I admire Katherine Whitney so much," Melissa Donaldson, a

mother of two and advertising executive, said. "She is living proof that women these days can have it all. That we can be successful in our careers and be great moms and wives. She has given me the confidence to make the most out of my life, and my family and I are all the better for it."

Not everyone, though, is a Katherine Whitney fan. There are women who believe that her declarations set women back. They say that there aren't enough hours in the day to have a full-time traditional job (meaning one without flexible hours, work-share programs, or the opportunity to work from home), commute, provide meals for your family, be available to your children and your spouse, and also take care of yourself. Or at least not enough hours to do all those things well.

It's a popular debate around the watercooler, the playground, and even in corporate boardrooms as the situation for working mothers continues to be hotly contested.

So what does Katherine Whitney say to that backlash?

"I would say women just aren't giving it a chance. They're giving up before they do all they can to make it work. I would tell them to be more thoughtful and strategic about how they structure their days, to put time in on the weekends to prepare healthy meals for the week, to delegate at home and at work, and to ask for help when they need it. Women today are so strong and in such a good position to get what they want. They just have to make it a priority."

I finish the article and roll my eyes. Katherine sure is pulling the wool over everyone's eyes, I'm realizing more and more each day. *Oh, my life is so perfect. Oh, I've got this balance thing under control. Oh, you can do it too.* Barf. Barf. Barf. It's very clear to me that Katherine's life, as evidenced by her meltdown the other day and Theo's romp with Red, is far from perfect. And it's clear that this balance thing is far from under control. In fact, right now, the only reason it is under any control at all is because I'm making it that way. And she knows it. She most definitely knows it or she wouldn't have had that conversation with Ash.

I should quit right now. Just walk in there and confront her about what I heard. But I can't do that to Sera and there's no other explanation as to where I would have heard that information. I can't tell Katherine that Ash told me himself. I could tell her that I spoke to Joan and she said she hadn't heard from her, but Katherine could make something up about having left Joan a voice mail and she must not have gotten it yet.

I certainly couldn't challenge her on that without any sort of proof, at least proof that I could reveal, to the contrary. I guess I could say that I overheard Ash talking about it and that I can't work for anyone who would betray me like that. That I trusted her implicitly and what she did is unacceptable and I can't in good conscience continue to work for someone who has so little respect for me that she would blatantly lie to my face. That would certainly be giving her what she deserves.

I muster my courage. I stand up. Take a deep breath. Roll my shoulders back. And push my chin up. Then, I march toward Katherine's office, all two steps of it, and stand in her doorway.

Katherine looks up. "Did you need something, Lucy?" she asks.

"Um, no. I was going to get a coffee. Do you want anything?"

So I lost my nerve. Big deal. I realized in that split second that by saying my piece, I'd be out of a job. And I certainly would have a hard time getting any sort of recommendation from Katherine for any other job. Quitting now would just be screwing myself over and that would be idiotic. All I know is I'm getting angrier by the minute.

"No, thanks. Did you see the *Huffington Post* piece?" she asks, smiling widely and taking a sip of her Glow juice.

"Yeah, it was really good," I say.

"I think so. I liked how it turned out. So, Lucy, I'm going to need you to help me out on Saturday night at the Ellevate dinner. Brooke unfortunately has another event she's committed to. This did come about last minute. She offered one of the girls from her office to come, but I feel much more comfortable with you. You know this whole operation. So, black tie, Saturday night, seven o'clock at the Waldorf Astoria. We'll probably have to get there a little early. And if you want, you can come by my apartment and go with us. You can even borrow a dress if you'd like."

Spare me the best friend act, Katherine. I consider telling her that I can't come on Saturday night, that I already have plans, but as I'm opening my mouth to say that, I decide otherwise. It'll give me a chance to see Theo and Katherine together and maybe give me a chance to get Theo alone and tell him that I'm planning on telling Katherine about Red. Plus, what else do I have going on this Saturday night? Ava has a date. And my boyfriend, if I can even call him that anymore, will most likely be out with Cosmo Girl. At least if I go to Katherine's event, I'll get a good meal, a few free drinks, and a nice outfit out of it.

"Sure. No problem," I say and turn to leave.

"Lucy, one more thing. Do you mind starting a draft of my speech for Saturday night? I'm so busy with London. I don't have time to work on the speech right now, and I don't want to wait till the last minute. If you could get some thoughts down, maybe an outline, then I can fill it in if I get some free time over the next couple of days."

"On it," I say and walk back to my desk.

It's at that very minute that I make a decision that might change the course of my life and will certainly change the course of Katherine's.

Chapter Thirteen

I text Ava and ask her if she's free for dinner. She says yes and that she'll meet me outside my office building at six thirty and we'll walk somewhere for dinner near Lincoln Center. I tell her that's perfect, and then I start on Katherine's speech.

As I'm working, I try to think about whether I've ever done anything that's truly mean. I come up with pranks on my brothers, telling Ava once in high school that I thought she was acting slutty with a particular David Hingham, and being so angry at my boss at Longford's (the ice cream store in Rye that I worked at a few summers) after she wrongly accused me of stealing that I told her she was the ugliest person I had ever met and she should go bury herself in a hole to save the entire human race from ever having to look at her butt-ugly face. But I don't consider any of those as truly mean. The last one might qualify, but I was provoked.

What I'm contemplating doing, as I flip through *The Balance Project* to come up with talking points for her speech, is truly mean. Positively, downright, unequivocally, unmistakably, emphatically, decisively mean. (I just looked in the thesaurus for all those words to make sure I was making myself clear.)

"Hey, don't you look supercool!" I say to Ava when she approaches me later outside my office building.

"Why, thank you," she says tipping her fedora at me. She's got her hair in two long braids sticking out from the aforementioned fedora, heavy eye makeup, and pale-pink lipstick. Supercool.

"What do you feel like eating?" I ask as we lock arms and start walking up Broadway.

"Sushi?"

"Sushi sounds perfect. How about Haru?" Haru is a great sushi bar on Amsterdam, a couple blocks from my apartment. It's always busy and has a fun vibe that Ava and I like.

"Haru it is," Ava says.

"How was your day?" I ask Ava.

"Oh, well, the life of an associate features editor at *Cosmopolitan* magazine is so glamorous and exciting. I started my day with an editorial meeting where all of the ideas I pitched were looked upon favorably by the powers that be. I had lunch with a very famous and talented journalist who we're hoping will become a regular contributor. And then the girls in the beauty department gave me an entire tote bag filled with free, full-size makeup and skincare products," Ava says.

"Wow, Ava. That's amazing!"

"Really? Really, Lucy? Are you even paying attention?"

"Sorry, I'm a little distracted."

"Well, that is so *not* how my day went. But a girl can dream. A girl can dream!" Ava says putting her arms in the air triumphantly. "What are you so distracted about?"

"Let's start with the fact that Nick might be cheating on me," I say, looking at her with my eyebrows raised.

"What?" Ava asks, stopping in the middle of the sidewalk to stare at me.

"I said 'maybe.' I'm trying not to jump to conclusions."

"How do you know?"

"I saw them," I say.

"Okay, enough of this cryptic bullshit. What the hell are you talking about?" Ava asks, so I tell her the whole story.

"Wow. Do you think he was actually on a date?" Ava asks.

"It sure looked like it," I say.

"Are you guys technically broken up?"

"Broken up?" I ask annoyed. "I have no idea. I haven't heard from him in—what is it now?—six days! But even if he thinks we're broken up, I still don't think it's appropriate that he should already be dating girls with long blonde hair who drink cosmos."

"She was drinking a cosmo?" Ava asks.

"I know. Can you believe it?"

"So what are you going to do?"

"Well, there's not much I can do. I'm not sure if you're hearing what I'm saying. He. Won't. Call. Me. Back. I can't very well accuse him of cheating on me if he won't even talk to me."

"Yeah, I see your point there. Man, this sucks. I'm sorry you had to see that."

"It's better that I saw it and know what's going on than to not know at all."

"I guess so. Speaking of not knowing at all, did you ever say anything to Katherine about Theo?" She whispers when she says "Theo."

"No," I laugh at her whisper. "And thank you for not saying it loudly. Did *you* say anything to anyone about Theo?" I ask, also whispering "Theo."

"No. C'mon Lucy. You know I wouldn't do that."

"I know."

Eventually we get to Haru and settle into a table. We order sushi and drinks, and talk about the guy she just started dating. After the waiter sets down our drinks, I look Ava squarely in the eyes with a serious expression. "So."

"So, what?" she asks, looking at me curiously.

"So, you can tell your little friend Daniel yes." I say, taking a sip of my Kirin.

"Yes, what?" Ava asks, taking a sip of her sake.

"Yes, I'll give him information on Katherine."

"What?" Ava says, choking on her sake and spitting it out all over the table.

"Ava!"

"Sorry! But it's your fault," she says as we use our napkins to mop up the sake.

"You sound surprised," I say.

"Of course, I'm surprised. Why the change of heart?"

"I found out today that Katherine did something to me that I find inexcusable and reprehensible." I tell her about Kyle's job, Joan and Ash, and what Sera told me.

"Maybe this Sera is making it up," Ava says.

"No. No way. I've known her for a long time. She wouldn't do that."

"But you've known Katherine for a long time, and I can't imagine you'd think she'd do what Sera says she did."

"Actually, I can imagine it. I mean I'm completely surprised, but when I think about it, that's how Katherine operates. She does what she needs to do to keep her life moving along."

"Do you think you should approach her to confirm it was her?" Ava asks.

"No. There are so many lies being told. Joan told me she never heard from her and Katherine told me she spoke to her. And when I think about the conversation with Ash, he did seem a little sketchy, like there was something else going on. Katherine flat out said she'd support me. She looked me straight in the eye and told me she spoke with them. Sera has zero motivation to lie to me and every motivation to tell me the truth. I believe her story."

"So you're pissed."

"Damn straight, I'm pissed!" I say. "I have done so much for that woman. Yes, it's my job and you could say I was just doing my job, but I have gone above and beyond what I should do in that job, and Katherine has told me that time and time again. So for her to sabotage my career, to betray me the way she did, hell, yeah, I'm pissed. Never been more pissed if you want to know the truth."

"Not even about Nick and that girl with the cosmo?" Ava asks warily.

"Did you have to go there, Ava?" I ask. "Sure I'm pissed about Nick, but for some reason I feel, despite what I saw going on at Nobu, that there's some reasonable explanation. Although I'm not even sure I'm entitled to one. And the main difference between the two is that I implicitly trust Nick. Well, I did. No, I still do. But I don't trust Katherine. I might have thought I did, but when I think about what she did, I can't say I'm all that surprised."

"Huh. Got it," Ava says as the waiter sets down our edamame. "So, what do you want to do?"

"I want to screw her over the way she's screwing me over," I say.

"Are you sure, Lucy? I mean, don't you think that's a little harsh?"

"No, Ava. I do not. Well I do think it's harsh and if you try to talk me out of it, I might crumble, but don't talk me out of it because I'm angry as hell and I want to knock her down a rung and pay her back for what she's doing to me. Plus, I have a few other reasons why I'm willing to do this," I say.

"And they are . . . ?" Ava asks, waving an edamame shell.

"Well, for one thing, she's a complete fraud and she knows it. She even admitted that to me. And I think she's doing a disservice to all those women out there who hang on her every word. These women are busting their asses trying to do it all, trying to be great at everything. They think it's possible because Katherine Whitney goes on television and writes a book saying it is, and they believe her. These women want to believe they can do it all and do it all well. But, you know what I've learned over the past weeks?" I ask, getting more and more agitated.

"What?"

"I've learned that it's impossible. That what Katherine is preaching is impossible and you want to know how I know that?" I ask, expectantly. Maybe a little crazily.

"How?" Ava is starting to look worried that I might lose it.

"Because for one thing there are not enough hours in the day to do your job really well, to bring up your kids really well, to handle your relationship really well, to take care of yourself really well, and then have time to actually sleep. And, also, and this will really get your goat," I say speaking more rapidly, getting more excited. "Katherine herself, America's fucking Darling of Balance, isn't even doing it. She's completely overwhelmed and miserable at work. She told me herself that her workload is insane. She has a nanny, soon-to-be two nannies, taking care of her children most of their waking hours, and her husband is fucking a redhead. She is, in her own words, a mess. So I feel it is my duty to save all the other women out there from killing themselves trying to do something that's impossible. Because all they're ultimately doing is making themselves feel terrible when they fail."

"Okay," Ava says, slowly.

"The other reason I want to do this is I feel like I would be doing Katherine a favor."

"How so?" Ava asks skeptically.

"She told me the other day that she wishes someone would blow her cover," I say, popping an edamame in my mouth.

"Really?"

"Well, no, not entirely. But she implied it. She said it wouldn't be possible for her to blow the cover off herself. I think she secretly hopes someone else will."

"C'mon, Lucy. That's ridiculous and you know it," Ava says.

"She said there are too many people invested in this whole facade of hers. That she's too far down the road. Sounded to me like she wished someone would pull the plug on the operation and save her from herself," I say.

"Put her out of her misery, so to speak?" Ava asks, grinning at me.

"Exactly," I say. I sit back in my chair, breathe deeply, and take a long slow sip of my beer.

"Well, it sounds like you've made up your mind."

"I have. And please don't try to discourage me."

"Me? Never. I'll support you in anything you do, Luce. Well, almost anything."

"So what do we do from here?" I ask.

Ava pulls out her phone and starts texting. I peer over the table.

"What are you doing?" I ask.

"Texting Daniel."

I drink my beer and sit quietly as Ava types and waits. Reads, types back, and waits. Reads, types back, and waits.

"Okay, here's the deal," Ava says. "Daniel has already started writing the piece and he's really excited that you're going to give him the office perspective. He says you can be anonymous, and he wants to know if he can call you tonight."

"Yes," I say.

"What time can he call you?"

"Jeez, Ava. I don't know. But I'm so fired up about this that I just want to down this sushi, finish this beer, and go home to talk to him. How does that sound?" I ask.

"Check!"

Twenty minutes later I'm sitting on my bed, drinking a cup of terrible instant coffee, and staring at the phone in my hand. I'm waiting for Daniel to call.

When the phone rings, I startle and spill a couple drops of coffee on my comforter.

"This is Lucy," I say.

"Hi, Lucy. It's Daniel," he says.

"Hi."

"Thanks so much for doing this."

"Yeah, and I'm starting to have second thoughts, so let's do this before my conscience catches up with me. While I'm still feeling like this is the right thing to do."

"I completely understand. You can totally trust me, Lucy."

"So what do you want to know?" I ask.

Ten minutes later, I hang up with Daniel and stand up to shake out my legs. I realize I'm shaking a little, and I'm not sure if it's caffeine or vitriol I feel coursing through my veins. After I wash up and brush my teeth, I get into bed and lie there, looking up through the dark at the ceiling. I hear the traffic outside my window. Suddenly, what usually seems like background noise sounds very loud. I start to sweat and then bolt out of bed and make it to the toilet just as I start to vomit. When I'm done, I sit on the bathroom floor and lean against the wall. I look up at the bathroom mirror and read the quote (by one of my favorite authors, Elizabeth Gilbert) that I had taped onto it last week: *Embrace the glorious mess that you are.* Glorious mess, indeed. And about to get a whole lot messier.

Chapter Fourteen

Lucy: STOP. Do NOT run the piece. Second thoughts. Call me!!

I text the number Daniel called me from last night. I wait a couple minutes. No response. I call him. No answer. I text Ava something similar. When I don't immediately hear back, I call her. No answer. I leave a voice mail and frantically continue to call her every four minutes as I get ready for work.

When I woke up this morning, after a restless night's sleep, it took me a while to realize why I felt so awful. Then I remembered my conversation with Daniel, and I instantly regretted what I had done. So I scrambled, actually fell (it wasn't pretty), out of my bed and ran the two steps into my bathroom where my phone was charging to text Daniel. Sure, I'm furious with Katherine for what she did to me. But feeding that information to Daniel and allowing him to use me as a source to write an article about her?

What I will find out later is that while I've been texting Ava in a state of frenzy, she's been ohming and downward dogging her way to tranquility. While I realize, truly realize, the extent of the damage I could cause to Katherine by being the source for that article, Ava is blissfully unaware that her phone is vibrating like crazy on the other side of the yoga studio wall.

When she finally does get back to me, as I'm walking, trudging, to work, she decides that the nature of the correspondence requires a phone call instead of a text.

"Luce?"

"Ava, finally! Where were you? Did you get my messages?"

"I was in yoga. Sorry. Yes, I got them."

"So, did you call Daniel? I really, really don't want that to run, Ava. Please say you spoke to Daniel and he's erasing all evidence of what I talked to him about."

Crickets.

"Ava?" I ask, urgently, desperately.

"Oh my God, Lucy. Please sit down. Please find somewhere safe to go so I can tell you what I'm about to tell you. Please step away from any and all curbs and bus stops."

"What?" I ask hysterically.

"It's already done," Ava says quietly.

"What's that? I don't think I heard what you said," I say furiously.

"Oh my God, Lucy. It's on the front page of today's *Post* and it's on the home page of the newspaper's website. Daniel texted me the link this morning. I'm so sorry. But it's going to be okay. I promise. Katherine will never know it was you. Daniel understands that this is 100-percent confidential. He is so trustworthy. He'll never tell. And I'll never tell. And you're going to be fine. Please don't worry," Ava says, speaking so quickly. Sounding so worried.

"Fuck! Ava, what am I going to do? I can't believe I could do something so awful." I'm walking around in tiny circles now, near the plate-glass window of a bank on Broadway. "Yes, Katherine did something awful to me, but this is so much more awful, Ava. How could I be so stupid?" I start to bang my forehead lightly against the glass until I see the look of complete fear on the face of the bank manager whose office is on the other side.

"Really, Lucy. It's going to be okay. Here's what you have to do. Go get a coffee and one of those big street-vendor bagels that you like. Then take a deep breath and walk into your office like everything is absolutely normal. Sit down, wait for Katherine to come in, and go through your day. Like nothing ever happened. Because, remember, *you*, Lucy Cooper, were not the source for that article. Some anonymous person was the source for that article. No one would ever think it was you. And when you, quote unquote, find out about the article, because inevitably someone will come up to you and tell you that an article about Katherine is in the *Post*, act surprised and then appalled, and then help Katherine deal with it like you would if you honestly did not know anything about it."

"Jesus, Ava. This is awful."

"I know, Lucy. It's awful, but do what I said and everything will be okay. I promise. Do you want me to come meet you somewhere?"

"No," I say, calming down a little. "I'll be okay."

So I did what she said.

"Good morning!" The guy in the bagel cart outside my office says to me, in his chipper bagel-guy voice as I order a cinnamon raisin with cream cheese and a large coffee all done up. I want to shoot him and his good morning.

I walk into the office, and I'm shocked to see Brooke sitting in my chair, cell phone to her ear, yapping away, high-heeled boots on my desk. When she sees me she gets off her phone, stands up, smooths her leather skirt, and says, "Thank God you're here!"

Act surprised to see her, Lucy.

"Um, hi, Brooke. What's going on?"

"Did you not see it?" She asks with shock, her mouth wide open, her palm splayed dramatically, but not ironically, on her chest.

"See what?" I ask.

159

She's holding a newspaper that she proceeds to shove in my face. I unfold it and my eyes go wide at the headline on the front page that reads "America's Darling of Balance Is a Fraud" under which is an exceptionally unflattering photo of Katherine.

"Oh my God," I say, truly shocked. I start to read.

Women everywhere have hopped onto the Katherine Whitney bandwagon ever since her bestselling book *The Balance Project* came out six months ago. These women are impressed with Whitney's confidence, her success as the COO of Green Goddess & Company, her movie-star looks and designer clothes, her Upper West Side apartment with enviable views of Central Park, even her courtside Knicks seats. Most of all, they're impressed with her ability to have it all and make it look so effortless.

But sources are blowing Katherine Whitney's cover and revealing that she doesn't balance her life as effortlessly as she purports in her book and in her interviews. They confirm that Whitney doesn't have it all, at all.

An anonymous source, who works with Whitney at Green Goddess & Co., calls her an outright fraud. "Katherine's life is a complete mess. It's everything *but* balanced. It's a well-known fact in the office that she's an absolute nightmare to work with. Everyone does their best to keep their distance from Katherine."

The source also revealed that Simon & Schuster recently pulled the plug on a proposed follow-up book to *The Balance Project* when they got word that much of Whitney's life is a pretense.

Turns out "doing it all" is not so easy after all. Especially for working moms. According to a former nanny, "Katherine's daughters are nightmares. They constantly whine and cry, and they act like complete spoiled brats. They rarely see their mother and the family has a hard time holding on to nannies because Katherine is so demanding."

A mother at the prestigious Cartwright School, where Whitney's older daughter is in kindergarten, acknowledged that Whitney signs up for committees so she can be perceived as an involved parent. "She doesn't come to any of the meetings and doesn't do any of the work required of her. It's a joke when you see Katherine Whitney's name on a committee list. Everyone knows she doesn't ever lift a finger. She is so high on herself that, to be honest, no one cares that she doesn't show up. It's almost easier if she doesn't."

The mother also admitted that she heard from numerous people that Whitney has recently undergone some type of plastic surgery.

The Green Goddess & Co. employee added, "Katherine makes a lot of effort to cover up all her shortcomings. Her livelihood is entirely tied into convincing American working women that she should be their role model. Her carefully constructed facade would completely fall apart if people found out the truth."

Women's advocates are calling for Whitney to admit her charade to the world. They say it's no longer acceptable for her to be the face of balance for American women when everything she says is a lie. Katherine Whitney, the jig is up.

I know I'm the Green Goddess source but those are not my quotes. And the quotes from the nanny and Cartwright School mother? I have no idea if those are true.

"Oh my God, Brooke. This is awful!" I say, meaning it.

"I know! Isn't it? Such hate!"

"Does Katherine know?" I ask, slowly making my way over to my side of the desk, switching places with Brooke. I set my coffee and bagel bag on my desk and wake up my computer. The e-mails start downloading like a downpour on a stifling-hot summer night.

"I don't think so. I haven't heard from her. I didn't want to call her and have this conversation over the phone, so as soon as I found out about it this morning, I came right over to see her in person. But this article has gone viral. It's everywhere."

"What are you going to do?" I ask.

"I'm going to use every tool in my damage control toolbox to fix this. And we *will* fix this. Don't you worry," Brooke says.

We both turn at the same time to see Katherine walking down the hall toward my desk. She's on her cell. She nears my desk, and we see her surprise at seeing Brooke register on her face. She hangs up her cell but not before I hear her say, in an impatient voice, "I said, we'll talk about it later, Theo."

"Brooke, what a surprise. I didn't know we had a meeting," Katherine says, smiling at Brooke. "Was it left off my calendar by mistake, Lucy?" she asks, looking at me.

I start to talk, but Brooke, thankfully, interrupts.

"No, Katherine. Something unexpected came up. Let's go into your office, sit down, and talk about it."

The two of them walk in, Katherine in the lead, and Brooke shuts the door behind them.

I open my browser and call up the *New York Post* website. I read the article again, and it seems even worse on a big screen. Plus, there are terrible and awkward photos of Katherine throughout. The *Post* is known to be sensational, but still.

"WHAT????" I hear Katherine yell through her office walls.

My stomach feels as if it's on that *Perfect Storm* boat with Mark Wahlberg, and I actually grab my garbage can because I think I might vomit. I put my head down and stare at a snag in the carpet. Within a few minutes, I feel like I can sit up again.

I look back at my screen and see the comments, which are in the hundreds already. For every one comment supporting Katherine, there are at least ten, if not more, saying awful things. Truly awful things. About someone they don't even know. And every time I refresh the page, the numbers on those little social media share buttons increase exponentially.

"Hi, Lucy."

I look up, startled to be taken out of my reverie. "Hi, Maggie."

"Is Katherine in there?"

"Yes, but she's in a meeting."

"In a meeting, meeting? Or in a—" and she makes little air quotes with her fingers, "meeting?"

"No, Maggie. She's actually in a meeting, with a person, but I'll let her know you stopped by."

Maggie walks away. What a bitch.

I'm about to reimmerse myself in the hell that is the *New York Post* when I see Evan marching down the hall toward me. He darts right by my desk and straight into Katherine's office. He slams the door.

I start panicking and imagine that the reason he didn't look at me was because they suspect it was me. But I can't imagine that they would suspect it was me. Who in their right mind would even *begin* to suspect it was me? I'm so loyal to Katherine. I'm like the most loyal assistant ever. Or so they think. Plus, Katherine would never suspect me because she doesn't know that I know what she said to Ash. So I'm okay. I take a deep breath. I'm okay.

"Lucy, can you come in here?" Katherine asks sternly through the intercom.

I jump up and am through the door in an instant. Brooke and Evan are in the Kelly chairs. I stand behind them. Katherine is in tears.

"Do you have any idea who the anonymous source is?" she asks. Brooke and Evan turn around to stare at me.

"No, Katherine. I'm so sorry. I have no idea. It's awful. Is there anything I can do?"

Katherine continues crying and Brooke gives me a look like I can go back to my desk. That's all they wanted to ask. I honestly didn't get the sense they were suspicious.

The three of them stay locked in the war room for another hour. On occasion I hear raised voices. And once in a while, Katherine's phone line lights up but I don't know who she's calling. In the meantime, I'm fielding calls and taking messages. I can tell almost immediately whether the caller is aware of the article. It's an audible version of the head tilt you do when you walk up to someone whose loved one has recently died.

Eventually Brooke comes out of Katherine's office and closes the door behind her. She leans next to my chair and says in a hushed tone, "So we've got a plan, and I want to fill you in."

"Okay," I say, grabbing my pad and a pen.

"Katherine is booked on the *Today* show tomorrow morning so we can get out in front of this and address it head-on. It's the weekend version so that's not ideal, but it's the best we can do since today is Friday. The plan is to make it seem like there's someone in the office who has it out for Katherine, that things with Katherine are just fine and dandy, and this is just another case of the *Post* printing untruths. We'll spin it that way. She mentioned she suspects someone named Maggie but she's not going to name names in the press. And she can easily dismiss the other two sources by calling them a disgruntled former household employee and a jealous and competitive private-school mother with too much time on her French-manicured hands. She might even suggest that the *Post* made the sources up as they've been known to do. I've canceled my trip this weekend so I'll be around, but Katherine says she'd like you to be with her at *Today* tomorrow morning as well. She trusts you and she wants reinforcements at her side. I'll e-mail you where you have to be and when. I spoke to Ellevate and got them comfortable with keeping Katherine for tomorrow night's award dinner, but we're going to have to make that speech shine like the diamonds they only show the VIP customers in the Tiffany concierge rooms. Can you help with that?"

"Of course," I say softly. I've never seen this side of Brooke. She's dropped her excessive enthusiasm and is acting completely professional and in command. Someone you'd want on your side if your trustworthy assistant ever decides to ruin your life.

"Now, there will be a lot of people calling today. I need you to be command central. If the caller acts like they don't know anything about the article, then carry on with business as usual. Take messages. Say that Katherine is busy and that she'll call them back. She'll let you know when or if she's ready to start taking calls today. If anyone calls about the article and wants a comment, tell them that Katherine's public relations firm is handling those calls and then give them my direct number. And whatever you do, make absolutely no comments to anyone. Certainly not to the press but not even to your boyfriend, best friend, manicurist, pizza guy, mother, or anyone else for that matter. Got it?"

"Got it, Brooke. Thanks. Katherine's really lucky to have you."

"Well, that's nice of you to say, Lucy, but this is what I do," she says and stands up ready to leave.

"Brooke?" I ask.

"Yes?"

"Are you going to be able to find out who the source is?"

"You bet your oversized bagel I will. That's the easy part. A couple phone calls and a little Brooke intimidation, and I'll find out for sure. Plus, we've been on the phone with the lawyers to see if we've got a libel case. This clearly seems to fit the bill. The big problem is that even though *we* know most of the article is untrue, the public will want to believe what's in print. Katherine's reputation is damaged no matter what the truth is. And every tweet, like, share, and comment makes it exponentially worse. But no time for that right now. Right now it's about protecting Katherine and making this whole thing old news."

I force a smile and she walks away.

Shit.

The news about the article travels around the Green Goddess office like a Bugatti Veyron Super Sport on the autobahn. Katherine keeps her door closed most of the day so whenever someone walks by my desk and sees the closed door, he or she (it's mostly shes) stops at my desk and asks, in her best library voice, one of three things: (1) How is she doing? (2) Was the article true? (3) Do you know who the office source is? Some of the inquiring minds stick around hoping I'll go all Perez Hilton and spill sordid details, but inevitably the conversation is cut short when the phone rings. I give a little smile and wave, and the inquiring mind is off on her nosy way.

And oh how the phone does ring. I direct calls to Brooke and take loads of messages. And despite my raging guilt and justifiable fear that Brooke will channel her inner Nancy Drew and find out I'm the source, outwardly I act pretty calmly.

That Daniel better keep his mouth shut. I'm almost tempted to send him a fake bloody finger in a box or whatever mob bosses do to keep people quiet. Maybe it's supposed to be a bloody tongue. Anyway, I'm not sending any bloody body parts. Mostly because I don't want any proof of my connection to him. I just can't believe he butchered my comments so egregiously. I'm praying to God, the universe, to anyone who will listen that Katherine does not find out.

Pretty late in the afternoon, Katherine calls me into her office.

"Hey," she says, as I plop down in a Kelly chair.

"Hey," I say. "How are you doing?" And though it was me who helped put her into this situation, I'm genuinely concerned.

"Been better," she says, stifling a sad laugh.

"Do you want me to go over the messages?" I ask.

"Yes, but first I want you to help me think of who could have been the source."

"Katherine, I have no idea who would have done this."

"I have an idea," Katherine says.

"Oh? Who?" I ask.

"Well, first I thought of the people who are closest to me at work. Those people are you and Evan. Evan has a financial interest in keeping my stock high. And you would never do such a thing, so that canceled the two of you out right away."

I nod and hope that my eyes don't reveal my burning shame and intense guilt.

"Then I tried to come up with a list of people who may think I have wronged them in some way and people who may have it out for me. And to be honest, I can only think of one person?"

"Who?" I ask.

"Maggie Stern. She hates me. She's made that abundantly clear for years. She makes our working relationship incredibly difficult and despite my efforts over the years to try and unruffle her feathers, it's never gotten easier with her. I know, from reliable sources, that she'd like my job someday. So why couldn't it be her? She has the motivation. She's got the personality. And she's got the venom. The only thing she doesn't have right now is time because she's so busy with London." Another stifled laugh.

"Do you think Maggie would do that?" I ask.

"I guess it's possible. Hell, anything's possible. I wouldn't have thought it was possible that the *Post* would misrepresent me so severely. That whole school committee thing is patently untrue. I don't know if they found some bitchy woman to make it up or if they faked a source. I've only had two nannies before my current one, and I honestly don't think either would have said such things. Plus, I think they both moved back to their home countries, which makes the veracity of those statements even more questionable. The Simon & Schuster thing. Lie. And the plastic surgery. Hilarious! Also a lie. So I guess it's possible that they made up the Green Goddess source as well. That just feels so personal for some reason because, as you and I both know, my life has been a little trickier than usual lately. So that part of the article is partially true. I don't know why they had to be so vicious. It really does not make any sense to me. Anyway," she says with a little shake of her hair, trying, maybe, to get that bad energy off of her, "I've got a job to do and a speech to make so I have no time to dwell on this now. There's plenty of time for that later. Were you able to make any progress on the speech in between answering all those phone calls?"

I could not feel any worse.

"Yeah, a little. I had to scrap the outline I wrote yesterday because I figured you'd have to address the article."

"Yes. The elephant in the ballroom."

"So I wrote some things out. Do you want me to go get the outline?"

"Yes, please. That would be great, Lucy."

I start to get up and walk out her door but Katherine says, "Lucy?"

"Yeah?" I ask, stopping in the doorway.

"Can you do me a favor and keep your ears to the ground and see what you can find out though the Green Goddess grapevine? If there's anything you think I should know, I would appreciate it if you could tell me as soon as possible."

"Of course, Katherine." I say as I pause and look straight at the horrible mess I've created.

Chapter Fifteen

I feel awful when I wake up Saturday morning to get ready to meet Katherine and Brooke at *Today*. It's as if someone took my entire sense of morality and right versus wrong and pulverized it in one of those expensive Vitamix blenders with lots of spoiled kale and chia seeds. And then made me drink it. And when I look in the mirror, I notice a just plain awesome stress zit in full bloom on the tip of my nose. Good morning, Lucy, here's a gift for you. But I have no right to complain. I created this cesspool that I'm currently swimming in. Enduring that smoothie and this zit is penance.

Katherine is supposed to go on at 8:22. She's being interviewed by Lester Holt. When I arrive at seven thirty, I'm directed to the same dressing room we were in last time where I find Katherine getting her makeup done. She looks great in a charcoal-grey tailored suit with a white blouse open at the collar. If I didn't know any better and if my eyes were worse, I'd say it could have been her downing cosmos at Nobu with Nick.

I receive pleasant-enough greetings from both Brooke and Katherine. I was so afraid to see them this morning because if Brooke "Drew" had conducted the Great Article Source Inquisition she would have found out that I was the source. So I'm happy, and very surprised actually, to see them acting normally toward me. It's still possible that

Brooke knows but hasn't told Katherine, but the friendly vibes I'm getting from Brooke suggest otherwise.

Brooke is quietly going over talking points with Katherine so I grab some coffee from the machine and sit down on the couch.

"This will all be fine, Katherine. It's just you and Lester. I've worked with Lester in the past, and I spoke with him this morning before he went on the air. He's totally supportive of you; he told me his wife, Carol, loved your book. He's going to ask you about your reaction to the piece and then he'll let you defend yourself. Just be totally calm and maybe even a little self-deprecating. You'll be fine."

"Is there anything you need me to do?" I ask.

"No, we're fine. But thanks, Lucy. There's food down the hall if you're hungry," Brooke says, smiling at me. I actually like this new side of Brooke. Crisis Brooke.

"Great, thanks. Do either of you want anything?"

"No, thanks," says Katherine.

"I'm good. Thanks," says Brooke.

I head down the hall in search of what will hopefully be a table like you see in the movies, heaped with every kind of breakfast carb one could possibly desire on a stressful morning such as this. I am not let down, and I approach the carb cornucopia (a carbucopia?) with excited anticipation.

As I load my plate, I overhear two women in a corner speaking quietly—though not as quietly as they think, because I can hear them. One is holding a clipboard and has an earpiece. She looks like a producer or production assistant. The other is wearing a sensible dress. She looks like she's a guest on the show. I take my time filling my plate and listen in.

Clipboard: "She has no idea you're going to be here. We wanted to catch her off guard."

Sensible Dress: "Oh, really? I didn't know that. I'm not entirely comfortable with that, to be honest."

Clipboard: "No, no, I don't mean that we want to attack her. We just don't want her to be too rehearsed when Lester presents the other side."

I've heard enough at this point so I rush back into where Katherine and Brooke are.

"They're trying to ambush you!" I shout, bursting into the dressing room.

The first person I see is Theo.

"Hey, slugger," he says, trying to act normal. Katherine wouldn't understand if he didn't act normal.

"Hey, Theo," I say as I set my plate o'carbs on the table.

"What? Lucy, what are you talking about?" Brooke asks.

"I overheard a producer talking to a woman out in the hall. The producer was saying that they're going to try to catch Katherine off guard. There's another guest on your segment," I say, almost out of breath. I'm all fired up.

"Are you sure?" Brooke asks.

"Well, I'm sure about what I heard. But I'm not entirely sure they were referring to Katherine's interview."

"Huh. Fascinating," Brooke says. She stands up and purposefully walks out of the dressing room.

"Brooke—" Katherine calls after her but the makeup artist is applying mascara so Katherine stays where she is.

A few minutes later, Katherine's face is done and the makeup artist leaves the room. Katherine adjusts her suit and checks her hair in the mirror and then says she's headed out to find Brooke to see what's going on. Which leaves Theo and me.

"How's everything going?" he asks me carefully.

"Just dandy," I say snidely. I can tell he's looking at me, but I concentrate on my breakfast.

"I guess I should thank you for not telling Katherine."

"How do you know I haven't told her?"

"Because she would have gone utterly berserk on me and she has not gone utterly berserk on me. So, thank you."

"Are you going to man up and tell her?" I ask, looking at him in the eyes.

"No. I'm not. I don't think that information will serve Katherine well at all. Especially not now with how things are going. And that was the first and last time, so I think she's better off not knowing. *We're* better off with her not knowing."

"You mean *you're* better off with her not knowing."

Katherine and Brooke walk through the door.

"I can *not* believe this. That's so underhanded of them," Brooke says through gritted teeth. "But, okay, let's just take a second," Brooke paces the room a couple times. Katherine looks nervous.

"Okay, Katherine. Here's what you're going to do—"

"Katherine Whitney," a producer says, walking into the room we're all in. "Please come with me. You're on in two."

"Brooke?" Katherine asks, looking like a kindergartner being separated from her mother on the first day of school.

"It's okay, Katherine. You'll be fine. Just be yourself. You can do this!" Brooke says encouragingly, calling after her down the hallway. *Be nice to the other children, but if someone hits you, fight back!*

Brooke comes back into the room, looking like she might need a defibrillator. Or a shot of tequila. The three of us sit on the couch and stare at the TV. Theo turns the volume up on the remote.

When Katherine's segment comes on, she is indeed sitting on the set with Lester *and* Sensible Dress who turns out to be Dr. Elaine Ireland, a women's health physician with a specialty in working women. How convenient.

Lester begins, "Can working women have it all? Possible? Or impossible? There are as many answers as there are women asking the question. It's a hot-button issue that's not dying down anytime soon. To discuss it, I'd like to welcome my next two guests: two women with very different perspectives on *work-life balance and having it all,* Katherine Whitney and Dr. Elaine Ireland. Welcome, ladies."

"Thank you, Lester," Katherine and Elaine say at the same time. They're both seated on stools, both sitting up straight as arrows.

"Katherine, let's start with you," Lester says, looking at Katherine as the camera does a close-up on her face. She looks confident and ready. "A little over a week ago, you were a guest on *Today* to celebrate the six-month anniversary of the launch of your book *The Balance Project.* How are things going with the book?"

"Great, Lester," Katherine says earnestly. "Things are going really well with *The Balance Project.* It's been on *The New York Times* bestsellers list for the past six months, and we have been getting wonderful response and reviews from women all over the country, actually, from all over the world."

Lester continues, "That's fantastic. But we can't ignore an article that came out yesterday in the *New York Post.*" He looks directly into the camera. "For those of you who didn't see the piece, it called Katherine Whitney a fraud." Now he turns to Katherine and there's another close-up of her as Lester continues, "The writer quoted an anonymous source, several anonymous sources, but one in particular who said he or she works at your company and has witnessed firsthand that, though you publicly say you have it all and that your life is well-balanced, in reality, the opposite is true. How do you respond to that?"

"Well, to be honest, Lester," Katherine says, looking humble, "the article definitely rattled me. It's never fun to read something like that about yourself." She gives a sincere smile and recrosses her legs, and then her voice changes; it gets stronger and more serious. "But I have thick skin and have had to endure my share of criticism over the years. In fact, there's been criticism of me and of Green Goddess ever since Evan Hewitt and I started the company. This article contained so many outright lies, though. I do know who the anonymous Green Goddess source was, Lester, and while I'm not going to name names, it's fair to say that it's a woman at my company with whom I have a strained working relationship. I think it's sad that the *Post* would publish something like that. Something that's clearly wrong. I'm not saying, and have never said, that it's always easy dealing with everything on my plate. No working woman would say that. But to say that my life is a fraud and that I'm preaching ideals that I don't personally live up to is flat-out wrong." Point for Katherine!

"Let me turn to you, Dr. Ireland," Lester says. You're a leading expert in women's health and you specialize in working women. Did I get that right?"

"Yes, Lester, that's right," Elaine says. She comes off as very professional, no-nonsense. "I work with a lot of high-powered career women. I was an internist for many years but redirected my career when I noticed there was an epidemic among working women. Now, I work with these very same women to provide them with strategies and action plans to deal with the stressors in their lives and to help them achieve more balance and better overall health."

"So what do you think of the whole concept of having it all?" Lester asks, making air quotes around having it all.

"Well, first I want to say that I very much admire Ms. Whitney and all that she's done in her career at Green Goddess to promote health and wellness among Americans," Elaine says, looking right at Katherine and smiling at her.

"Thank you," Katherine says, a huge smile on her face. Clearly because she realizes this might not be as bad as the butcher job she and Brooke anticipated.

"But I have to say," Elaine continues, "with all due respect, that while Green Goddess & Company is truly revolutionizing healthy lifestyles in our country, I believe that Ms. Whitney's book is not serving women well at all."

Ruh roh.

"How so?" Lester asks, smelling blood. They cut to a brief close-up of Katherine who is doing her best to maintain a polite smile.

"Lester," Elaine says, "I'm finding in our society that the definition of *having it all* has changed. For the worse. What I find celebrated in the media is this notion of extremes. This idea of being a superwoman. That you can do everything—taking care of your career, your children, your marriage, and yourself—all really well and that everyone in that equation—your boss, your family, you—will be happy and sane and well all the time. But in reality, that's impossible. There are not enough hours in the day for a woman to come even close to accomplishing all of those things successfully each day." Katherine starts to speak, but Lester cuts her off. She looks like she has just had her palms slapped by Sister Mary Margaret.

"So you're saying that having it all is impossible?" Lester asks Elaine.

"I'm saying that you have to change your definition of *it all,*" Elaine says.

"What do you mean?" Lester asks.

"If having it all means *being a* superwoman," Elaine says, "then, yes, I believe having it all is impossible. Because having a full-time job is a full-time job. Being a full-time mother is a full-time job. Taking care of your marriage requires work and time. And taking care of yourself requires a good amount of hours devoted to sleeping every night, exercising most days, and taking time to eat well and do things that light you up. That list doesn't even include socializing, volunteering, and being spiritual. And all of those together amount to more hours than there are in each day. So if that's your definition of having it all, then you are kidding yourself. And it's pretty evident that that's the notion that Ms. Whitney is trying to perpetuate, and I think that's dangerous because it sets women up to fail."

"However, when women change that spurious definition of having it all, when they accept the fact that they have to make sacrifices, that they're not going to be able to do it all well, all successfully, all at the same time, then they are able to be well-balanced, healthier, and ultimately happier. And let me clarify one thing, I'm not saying women shouldn't be aiming for that corner office, shouldn't be leaning in, I'm saying that if they do that they have to be realistic about and comfortable making sacrifices in other domains of their life."

"Katherine, what do you have to say to that?" Lester asks.

A quick camera cut to Katherine shows her stunned, but she recovers quickly. At least she tries to. "Um, I, well, I believe that my book *The Balance Project*, um, provides strategies so women can be successful in all domains of their lives. And women come up to me at my talks, and, um, at the book signings I do and they tell me that these strategies are working for them, that they do feel balanced, and they do think they have it all."

Well, she tried.

"Dr. Ireland?" Lester asks.

Elaine continues, "I wouldn't contest what Ms. Whitney has heard from her fans. I'm sure that's all true. I'm just not sure how sustainable those strategies ultimately are long term, when things, let's say, start going wrong. For instance, when there's a big push going on at work and extra hours at the office are required. Or when a child's learning differences require more attention from the parents. Or when an elderly parent becomes ill. I have dealt with thousands of women in my private practice and through my seminars, and I can honestly say that when women are honest with themselves about what they can realistically accomplish in a given day, they lead more vibrant lives. Sure, I would agree that there is a subset of women who *are* making it, but that's not sustainable, and the slightest challenge will affect that perceived, yet ultimately impractical, balance. I think we, as a society, need to tone down this glorification of being busy, this myth of the superwoman."

There's a wide-angle shot of the set and you can see Katherine start to say something else, but again, she's cut off by Lester.

"And there you have it folks. Work-life balance, having it all, topics still up for discussion by American women. An issue that will be around for a long time. I'd like to thank my guests Katherine Whitney and Dr. Elaine Ireland. And we'll be back after these messages with more on *Today*."

Cut.

A couple seconds later, Katherine storms into the dressing room looking like an insane-asylum escapee. She slams the door behind her. "That was a fucking ambush. What the hell was that, Brooke?"

"I don't know, Katherine. But you held your own. You were fine," Brooke says, putting her arm around Katherine reassuringly.

"Theo, what did you think?" Katherine asks, wriggling out of Brooke's embrace.

"Well, I'm not going to lie to you. I don't think it was great. I think they had an agenda, and they clearly accomplished what they set out to do."

Katherine lets out a deep sigh and says, "Damn it! I felt so good, so confident, but then I totally lost my cool and I could barely string two sentences together. I tried a couple times to say something, but Lester kept cutting me off. That was a disaster!"

"Well, that didn't go entirely as we planned but we have to put that behind us and move on. We have to focus on tonight. Let's go back to your apartment, and we'll work on your speech." Brooke says.

"I think that sounds like a good plan, Kath," Theo says walking up to her and putting his hands squarely on her shoulders. "What's done is done. You have the opportunity tonight to say what's on your mind without any interruption or challenge. You will shine tonight, so let's focus on that."

Katherine shakes herself off and agrees to the plan. I ask Brooke if they need me this afternoon but she says no and that they'll be fine. She says they'll catch up with me tonight and to have a good day.

I tell her I'll try.

I decide to walk from Rockefeller Center, where *Today* is taped, back to my apartment through Central Park. But first I text Nick to see if he wants to meet me for a coffee. I'm pretty sure he won't text me back but it's worth a try. I'm not giving up on him and I want him to know that. The acute pain of his silence has lessened as each day has passed, but the dull pain lingers. I thought by now he would have at least asked to get together to talk.

Lucy: Good morning. I really miss you and want to talk. I'm in Midtown. Want to meet for a coffee?

Nothing. I told him I missed him and he didn't even respond. I stand there for a few minutes, checking my phone. Sad. Sad and waiting. I can't believe this is where I am right now in my life. I just can't believe it. I feel like a four-year-old who didn't manage to get any candy from the piñata. A six-year-old whose first dog has died. A twelve-year-old who didn't get invited to the slumber party. All at the same time.

I decide to go into Dean & DeLuca, which is across from the *Today* studio, to grab a coffee and something comforting from the café. As if the breakfast I ate less than an hour ago wasn't enough. I'll stop my wallowing and self-pity for a second to tell you that if you've never been to Dean & DeLuca, you are missing out. It is a culinary heaven, a gourmet-food lover's mecca. There's not a Dean & DeLuca on the Upper West Side or near my office so whenever I'm near one, I don't miss the opportunity to enjoy its gastronomic loveliness. They have a mail-order business, too. Go ahead, order a gift basket. I'll wait.

Before I get my coffee, I roam the aisles looking at the amazingly colorful produce, prepared foods, and land of cheese, hoping the sight of them will make me feel better, make me realize that though everything in my life sucks, there is still true goodness in the world. At least in the form of an unpasteurized fromage à raclette from the French Alps. Or so I'm told by the cute cheese guy who's wearing a striped apron and white cheese-guy hat. I indulge in an olive oil tasting and admire the bakery display cases that hold all sorts of sugary and buttery treats. I buy a large latte and a chocolate-chip scone and maneuver my way through the throngs of tourists milling around Rockefeller Center. It's a beautiful day and though the walk to my apartment will be long, it will give me time to think. And the exercise won't hurt either.

As I stroll up Fifth Avenue, staying close to the curb to avoid the packs of teen tourists who walk four across, arms interlocked, I start thinking about the state of my life and how I got to where I am now. My life was fantastic until a few months ago. I was cruising along with a great job and an even-greater boyfriend. Family dinners on Sunday night. A run now and then. Attempts to eat healthy. Dinners once a week with my best friend. Honestly, if my life had stayed that way forever I wouldn't have complained. So what's happened over the last few weeks is inconceivable to me.

Things are beyond crazy at work. Katherine sabotaged my chances at a job in digital media. I have no time for my best friend and my family. My exercise routine is fairly nonexistent unless walking up Fifth Avenue while eating a chocolate-chip scone qualifies as exercise. I completely sold my soul and, in a state of weakness, betrayed my boss

SUSIE ORMAN SCHNALL

and revealed her secrets to a newspaper. And the worst part of it all is that Nick wants nothing to do with me, and I may have screwed things up with us forever.

I've made it to Central Park, and I stop and try to enjoy the small street performances along the way: musicians, caricaturists, street dancers, rollerbladers. The air is still a bit crisp but the sun is shining so the park is filling up with strolling families, runners, and bikers. And all manner of Manhattanites on their brisk way to something very important.

Central Park has always been one of my favorite places in the world. When I was little, when things were still good between my parents, we used to come here as a family once a year. We'd rent a couple of rowboats—the four kids in one, my parents in another. My brothers and I would try to splash my parents with the oars, but my dad would row so fast we couldn't catch them. We'd explore the lake for an entire hour. "We need to get our money's worth," my dad would say. Then we'd head to the Sheep Meadow, lay down a blanket, and devour the massive picnic lunch my mom had packed. After lunch we'd play Frisbee and simply enjoy being a family. And when it was time to go, my parents would always buy us Good Humor ice-cream bars from one of the trucks parked on Central Park West. I think about all that now as I head through the meadow.

Nick, his proposal, and what will happen next have been on my mind constantly. And I've been thinking about marriage a lot, too: how I feel about it, why I'm so afraid of it, and all the things my brothers and sisters-in-law were telling me the other night at my mom's. I'm realizing that it's not *marriage* that I'm afraid of. It's a *bad* marriage that I'm afraid of. And I'm afraid of divorce and abuse and ending up like my mother. But why am I assuming that being married to Nick will be bad? There are zero indications that it would be.

I think of one of my favorite quotes: *Don't be afraid to fail. Be*

180

afraid not to try. Maybe Nick and Ava and my family have a point. And maybe I've been so consumed with what happened to my parents that I haven't been able to see my personal situation independently from that. I'm not sure what took me so long but I'm beginning to see marriage to Nick a little more clearly. A little more optimistically. Whenever I would think of marriage, I would picture this dark-grey, stormy sky, the kind in a movie that's always accompanied by eerie music and a plot twist. But now, as I sort out my feelings, analyze them instead of letting them consume me, I see the clouds lighten up and begin to clear.

I feel a tingle in my body as I let go of a little of the fear I've been holding on to. I'm not running to Crate & Barrel to register, but I am allowing myself to feel more comfortable with the idea that marrying Nick might actually be exquisite.

The third thing on the list was for me to decide whether I want to have kids. I'm not sure why he phrased it like that, because I've never been uncertain about having kids and he knows that. I definitely want to be a mother. It's what kind of mother I want to be, can be, that I'm conflicted about. I'd always pictured myself leaning in, having a full-time career with a paycheck that reflected my hard work and with responsibilities that challenged me and lit me up.

Observing Katherine, however, especially over the past couple of weeks, has taught me so much. Has opened my eyes to aspects of being a working mom that I'd never thought about because I'd never had to before. Being a full-time working mom with a nanny sounds good on paper but, depending on the job, depending on the kids, depending on the mom herself, it's clearly not that simple. I took what that Elaine Ireland said on *Today* this morning to heart. And after witnessing Katherine's messed-up life, and after listening to my mom's neighbor Grace and my sister-in-law Kelly, I'm realizing that you *can't* entirely have it all.

If I do lean in fully, I will have to make sacrifices in other places. And even though Nick says he's willing to be flexible with me about my career when we have children (assuming he still *wants* to have children with me), I'm not so sure I believe that. Because if I do concentrate so fully on my career, I will not be able to be the kind of wife and mother he wants me to be. And, to be fully honest with myself, the kind of wife and mother I realize *I* want to be. I'm not saying I want to give up my career and prepare a dry martini with two olives for Nick when he gets home from work every day, but I *think* I am saying, yes indeed, I *am* saying that I don't want a career like Katherine's. Not if it means the rest of my life will suffer so much. Will be so *out* of balance.

I make my way through the park and back to my apartment feeling a little lighter. I feel like I've made a decision that is going to change my life. I've seen a lot of sides of this balance equation and I know which side I want to be on. Hopefully, Nick will give me the opportunity to share that choice with him.

Chapter Sixteen

Later that afternoon, after I've done a few loads of laundry and spoken to Ava on the phone about what I thought about during my walk, I text Katherine.

Lucy: Hey. Hope the speech prep is going well. Thanks for offering to lend me a dress but I have something to wear. What time do you need me to meet you at the Waldorf?

Katherine: Thanks. It's going pretty well. Brooke has been making me rehearse all day. She finally left so I have a couple hours to rest and play with the girls. I'll have Pancho pick you up first at 6:30, then he'll swing by for Theo and me, and we'll head crosstown together.

Lucy: Okay, sounds good. Thanks for the ride. See you later.

I take my time getting ready. I blow my hair straight, add a few curls at the ends with a curling iron, and use the makeup Ava got me for Christmas. I have a lot of bridesmaid dresses, from all my brothers' weddings and a couple friends' weddings, but they all, even the short ones, seem too froufrou. I go with my old standby little black dress that I got at Bloomingdale's a couple Decembers ago. It's thick satin (although, it might be polyester) with a fitted sleeveless bodice and a flared skirt. It hits a bit above my knees, and there's a jeweled clasp at the back of the neck. I feel pretty in it, and even a little sexy. I put on my reliable black Steve Madden pumps and check myself in the mirror. Not bad. I stick my phone/money/keys into my black evening bag and grab my long black wool coat. I hang it over my arm because even though it's cold outside, I'm really hot from getting ready.

I head downstairs at six thirty and find Pancho waiting in the car, double-parked in front of my building. He takes one look at me and gives an approving head nod/smile combo. The cold hits me so I quickly head for the car.

"Looking good, Lucy."

"Why, thank you, Pancho," I say pleased, as I get into the backseat.

We arrive at Katherine's a few minutes later, and Pancho calls upstairs on his cell.

"I'm outside," he says into the phone, which is on Bluetooth so I can hear the conversation.

"Uh, okay. Uh, we're having a little delay here, Pancho. We'll be down in a few minutes," Katherine says.

"All right. No problem. I may have to circle so call me when you're on your way down."

At that moment, a car comes up behind Pancho and honks. There's only one idling spot in front of Katherine's apartment building. Pancho suggests I get out and wait in the lobby, that I'd be more comfortable that way. So I do.

I grab my bag and head out of the car, realizing as I shut the door and the cold hits me that I've forgotten my coat. I turn around but Pancho has already driven off. I run into the building. Cute Doorman takes one look at me and smiles.

"Looking good," he says.

"Why, thank you," I say for the second time in the span of ten minutes, delighted with the prevailing opinion.

I sit on one of the leather lobby couches for a few minutes, making happy small talk with Cute Doorman as I wait for Katherine and Theo to come down.

Eventually, I see Pancho pull up outside at the same time as Katherine emerges from the elevator. Sans Theo.

"Hi, don't you look pretty," she says quickly, giving me a tight smile.

"Hi. Thanks. Wow, you look beautiful," I say and she does.

"Thanks. Ready?"

"Where's Theo?"

"Oh, he's not feeling great. He's gonna stay home with the girls."

I realize at that moment that I need to tell Katherine about Theo, but I decide to wait until next week when things aren't so charged.

Katherine heads to the apartment building door and holds it open for me. Just then I hear my phone ring so I pull it out of my bag. It's Ty Collins, Nick's client, our friend. I slide the bar to answer.

"Hey, Ty," I say, walking outside.

"Lucy?" the voice on the other end says with an urgent tone.

"C'mon, Lucy, we've got to go," Katherine says, looking annoyed. I hurry up and walk toward the car.

"Ty. Hey. It's Lucy. What's up?"

"Lucy, Nick's had an accident."

"What? Oh my God. What happened?" I stop where I am on the sidewalk. I don't even feel the cold. Katherine is already in the car and calling for me to get in.

"I'm not entirely sure, but I just got a call on my phone from the ambulance guy. Something about Nick running—"

"Ambulance? He's not supposed to run! His heart!" I say in a panicked voice.

"Lucy, come on!" Katherine says.

I get into the car. Pancho steps on the gas.

"I know, Lucy. Just relax and listen to me," Ty says, all business now. He speaks clearly and slowly. "I guess Nick was unconscious so the ambulance guy dialed the last number that Nick had called on his phone and that was me. But I'm in Charlotte for a game. They're taking him to the NYU Hospital emergency room, which they said is on First Avenue at Thirty-Third Street. Lucy, can you go there now?"

"Oh my God, Ty. Yes, I will go there now," I say.

"What happened?" I hear Katherine ask. I ignore her.

"I told the ambulance guy to put you on the list so you can see Nick when you get to the hospital. Call me when you have any information," Ty says.

"I will, bye," I say, hanging up the phone. "Oh my God. I have to get out of the car," I say leaning toward the front seat. "Pancho, stop the car."

He swerves and pulls over to the side of the busy street.

"Lucy, what is it?" Katherine asks, looking concerned.

"Nick's in the emergency room. He's unconscious. He was running but he's not supposed to run because he has a heart condition," I say quickly. "I have to get to the hospital. Oh no, I forgot where Ty said the hospital is."

"Pancho, keep driving," Katherine says.

"No, Pancho! Stop the car! I need to get to the hospital," I say, the panic rising in my voice again.

"Yes, I know. Pancho will drive you there. It's okay. Everything's going to be okay," Katherine says as she puts my coat over my shoulders and grabs my hand. "Did they say which hospital Nick's at?"

"The NYU emergency room," I say, looking expectantly at Katherine.

"Thirty-Third and First, Pancho," Katherine says. "I had my girls there," she says to me calmly.

"But you'll be late to your dinner," I say to Katherine.

"It's okay, Lucy. We'll drop you at the hospital and then I'll go to the Waldorf. I won't be too late, if traffic cooperates, and even if it doesn't, this is more important," she says as she strokes my hand and tells me everything is going to be okay.

Pancho does his best to get me to the hospital as quickly as possible, and my mind starts racing as I stare out the window watching the lights of the city flash by. I think I mentioned earlier that Nick was diagnosed at his precollege physical with hypertrophic cardiomyopathy, a genetic heart condition. It means the walls of the heart are thicker than they should be. It's pretty common and usually something that people live with just fine. There are just restrictions. Nick is allowed to work out moderately; he can lift weights and do light cardio. But he's not allowed to do intense workouts like running or playing a full-out game of basketball. He's always been good about following those rules, so I'm totally confused about what happened.

Eventually, after what seems like forever but is only the reality of going crosstown in New York City traffic on a Saturday night, we pull up to the emergency room entrance. I say a quick good-bye and thanks to Katherine and Pancho and quickly walk inside. I have to wait at the desk for a few minutes because there are people ahead of me. I shift my weight from heel to heel impatiently. Nervously.

"I'm here to see Nicholas Heston," I say with urgency to the woman at the desk, when it's finally my turn.

She starts typing into the computer.

"Are you family?" she asks, eyeing me over the purple-rimmed reading glasses that sit at the end of her large nose.

"No. Is that going to be a problem?" I ask. Too bad I don't have an engagement ring to flash at her. "My name is Lucy Cooper. The ambulance guy was supposed to put me on a visitor list."

"Why didn't you tell me that to start with?" she asks, giving me a sharp look before she returns to her furious typing. Eventually she says,

"Okay, Nicholas Heston is in room twelve. Go through those doors, and it'll be on your right."

I exhale.

"Thank you. Thank you so much."

I rush through the main doors and find room twelve. Nick is lying on the bed asleep. Unconscious? White sheets cover him from his waist down, and there's a carefully folded white blanket on top of the sheets. His chest is bare and there are sensors attached everywhere. There's an IV tube running from the back of his hand to a half-full bag of clear solution hanging from a pole next to his bed.

I approach the bed, and I burst out crying out of relief and fear and sadness and love. I walk out of his room and scan the hall looking for someone to give me information on Nick's condition. There are doctors and nurses rushing around. One of the nurses catches my eye and walks toward the room.

"Is he still sleeping?" she asks in a kind voice.

"Yeah," I say. "So he's not unconscious?" I ask.

"Are you his wife?" the nurse asks.

"No." Hospitals are a shitty place to go when you haven't accepted your boyfriend's marriage proposal.

"Well, I'm not supposed to give out any patient information but you look so worried so I'll tell you that he's just sleeping and he's going to be fine. He was awake when we were running tests. He's been asleep for ten minutes or so." She smiles and pats my hand. I love her.

"Thank you so much," I say as I go back into Nick's room. I sit on the chair for loved ones, hoping that I still am, and wait. I watch Nick sleep, his chest rising and falling steadily, and the feelings of relief and fear and sadness and love come over me again. Too many emotions to process at once. I wonder what will happen when he wakes up. Will he be happy to see me or will he ask me to leave?

I don't have to wait very long for the answer because a few minutes later, Nick opens his eyes. He starts to sit up, confused about where he is, and looks around. His eyes land on me.

"Hey," he says.

"Hey," I say, smiling. I stand up and walk over to the side of his bed. "How are you feeling?" I try but am not able to stop the tears from filling my eyes.

"How did you know I was here?" he asks.

"The ambulance guy called the last number dialed on your phone and it was Ty. So Ty called me, and I came right over." I pause. "Is it okay that I'm here? Do you want me to leave?"

"Yeah, yeah, it's okay that you're here," he says as he tries to adjust his position.

"Do you need help?" I ask as I move the sheets over a little so he can get where he wants to go.

"I'm okay, thanks."

"What happened?" I ask, my tears making his face all blurry.

"I did something really stupid. But I got lucky, and apparently, according to the doctor, I'm going to be okay."

"So you went running?"

"Yeah," he says with regret in his voice. "I couldn't help myself. I was feeling so frustrated, almost depressed actually, and I wanted to get the endorphins going. I miss that feeling, and I needed it. I knew I was being stupid, but before my diagnosis I used to run hard and nothing ever happened, just shortness of breath sometimes. But I was always fine after. So I thought nothing would happen."

"What did happen?" I ask softly.

"All I remember is that I started feeling short of breath and the next thing I knew I was in the ambulance staring up at the EMT. He told me that I had collapsed and someone on the street called 911."

"Did you—" I pause, having trouble getting out the words. "Did you have a heart attack?"

"No, Coop. I didn't. I'm fine. The doctor thinks I fainted. I'm lucky nothing worse happened. And I'm lucky I didn't fall and hit my head on the cement. The EMT said that my head landed on some grass. I was in Union Square Park at that point, so I got lucky."

"I'm so happy you're okay," I say and we are both quiet for a minute. I'm not sure how to act around him. I want nothing more than to lower my head on his chest and kiss him and tell him how much I love him, but I'm trying to respect an invisible boundary. "You said you went running because you were feeling frustrated and depressed. What were you feeling frustrated and depressed about?" I ask.

"Seriously, Coop? You."

I attempt a small smile and boldly reach for his hand, the one not attached to the IV line. He doesn't pull it away. I'm so happy I could explode. Not happy, of course, that my boyfriend is lying in a hospital bed, but happy because what's going on here makes it seem like my worst fears about our relationship aren't substantiated.

"So how long do they want you to stay here?" I ask.

"Not entirely sure. They want to observe me for a while, they said, but they think I'll be able to go home tonight."

"That's great," I say. "Is it okay if I stay here with you?"

"Sure," he says quietly. "But from the looks of that pretty dress, I'm guessing you are supposed to be somewhere else. Hot date?" he asks, smirking at me.

"Definitely not," I say, smiling at him. "Katherine is being honored and is speaking tonight at the Waldorf for a working women's organization. I was going to keep her company at her table and lend my moral support."

"To tend to her?"

"To tend to her," I say.

"But instead you're tending to me," he says softly.

"Instead I am tending to you."

We stare at each other for a few seconds as we both absorb what's going on.

"Ty! Oh, shit, Ty!" I say suddenly.

"What?" Nick asks.

"I told him I'd let him know that you're okay," I say as I grab my bag from the chair in the corner and pull out my phone. I enter my password and then click on Ty's number from my recents list. The phone rings once.

"Lucy! Is he okay?" Ty asks in an expectant voice.

"He's fine, Ty. I'm sorry it took me so long to call you. He's fine. He's absolutely fine," I say and start crying again.

Nick looks at me and holds his hand out so I hand the phone to him.

"Ty, hey," Nick says. His voice sounds strong.

"Nick, man, are you okay?" I can hear Ty's voice through the phone.

"I'm fine. Really, I'm fine," Nick says.

"Man, you scared the shit out of me! Thank God you're okay," Ty says.

"Thanks, Ty. And thanks for calling Lucy. She came right over."

"All right, Nick. I gotta get back to practice. I snuck my phone in the waistband of my shorts so I could wait for Lucy's call. Good thing I wasn't practicing yet when the ambulance guy called or I wouldn't have gotten the message for hours. I'm so glad you're okay."

"Thanks, man. I'll be fine. Go back to practice, and I'll call you tomorrow."

"Okay, you take care, Nick. I'll talk to you tomorrow."

Nick hangs up and hands me back the phone. There are a million things I want to tell him: about Katherine, about the *Post*, about the epiphany I had this afternoon on my walk (that seems like days ago), about us.

"I know we have a lot to talk about," I say.

"Yeah. Sorry about that note at the Union Square Cafe. You didn't deserve that," Nick says.

"You had your reasons. And it didn't rattle me as much as it could have. I know you too well."

"Not the most mature way to handle things."

"I meant it when I said that I was willing to do the things on the list. For you and for me. I've even done some already."

"Really?" Nick asks, smiling and tilting his head.

"Yes. I told you last Saturday morning in that text that I wanted to do the plan."

"And then you stood me up."

"It wasn't like that, Nick. Katherine and Theo. . . . You never let me explain—"

"Actually, Coop," Nick stops me. "I am happy you're here. Trying to process it all, but, yes, I'm happy you're here. And I do want to talk all about this stuff but I'd rather do it when I'm feeling a little better so I can concentrate. My head's a little fuzzy right now."

"Of course. I totally understand."

We smile at each other, the beeping of the machines sound tracking the heaviness in the room.

"You want to watch some basketball?"

"Thought you'd never ask," he says and points to the remote on the table next to the bed.

Chapter Seventeen

Last night I arrived at the emergency room a little after seven. We didn't get out of there until one thirty Sunday morning. Nurses came in and out checking Nick's vitals, repeating EKGs, talking to us. Then there was the very bland and salt-free meal that we shared. And there was lots of basketball. We didn't talk again, after the first short interaction, about anything going on in our lives. When the doctor was happy with the state of Nick's heart, they sent us on our way and told Nick to make a follow-up appointment with his cardiologist for next week. And they told him to avoid engaging in any strenuous activity until then.

Nick felt fine so he was able to walk out of the hospital, instead of going in a wheelchair like the nurses offered, and we caught a cab back to his apartment. I enjoyed my job as caretaker and made sure Nick was comfortable when he finally, after a shower and a cup of tea, got into bed. He fell right asleep, and I, well, I just watched him sleep for a while. And I thanked God and the universe and NYU Hospital and the EMTs for delivering my sweet and good and beautiful man back to me so I could have another chance.

When I wake up Sunday morning, sun streaming through the blinds that I forgot to close the night before, I roll over and find Nick staring at me.

"Good morning, sunshine," he says, grinning at me.

"Good morning. How do you feel?" I ask.

"Fine. I feel completely normal."

"That's great."

"Except, there is one thing that's different," he says, looking troubled.

"What?" I ask, concerned, hoisting myself up on one elbow.

"You're back in my bed," he says, smiling.

"I'm back in your bed," I say.

"It's good to have you here."

"It is exceptionally good to *be* here. Too bad you can't—how did the doctor phrase it?—engage, that's right, engage in any strenuous activity," I say, laughing.

"It is too bad!" He says as he lightly whacks his pillow at me. "Too bad for you, that is," he says.

"Well, I probably should go."

"Why?" he asks, seemingly stunned that I'd even consider such a thing.

"I have to go home and make a really important phone call to someone," I say contritely.

"Who?"

"Well, you see, I've had this boyfriend for almost as long as I can remember. And we've been the best together. If you want to know the truth, I think we're perfect for each other."

"Wow. Lucky guy."

"But, you see, I did a couple things wrong and I need to talk to him about them."

"That sounds terrible. What did you do?"

"Well, I got extremely busy at my job. He wasn't upset with that, you see, because he's always been supportive of my career and he understands that my boss can be, how shall we put this? A little demanding and needy at times. But he was upset with the fact that I was neglecting our relationship, choosing her over him too many times, and getting sucked into this whole workaholic thing. He didn't think it was healthy for me. He didn't like that I felt so stressed all the time."

"Sounds like a thoughtful guy. Sounds pretty handsome, too."

"Oh yes, he's very thoughtful and terribly handsome. Not as handsome as you, but close," I say.

"So what's the second thing you did?" Nick asks.

"Are you sure you want to hear this?" I ask.

"Oh, yes. I'm sure."

"Well, you see, he proposed to me."

"Wow! Congratulations!" Nick says.

"Not so fast. I didn't say yes."

"But why not? I thought you said you were perfect for each other and that he was very thoughtful and terribly handsome."

"Oh, I did. And he is. He most definitely is. But I was really scared."

"What were you scared of?"

"I was scared of marriage. I was scared of committing myself to something that has no guarantees. I was scared of becoming like some other married couples I see. Some not-so-good ones. And I was scared that I couldn't be the type of wife and mother that I knew he wanted me to be. But all that's changed for me now. And now I'm ready to move forward with him."

"Hmmm. I can see why you two need to talk."

"Yes. So I better get up now. But if things don't work out with this thoughtful and terribly handsome man, can I call you?"

Nick grabs me and hugs me. Tightly. And doesn't let me go. We stay that way for a while, just holding each other and Nick says, "I love you so much, Lucy. I don't want to lose you."

"I don't want to lose you either, Nick," I say, pulling away and looking into his eyes. "So much has happened over the past week that I need to talk to you about. There's so much that has changed."

"Really?"

"Really."

"Okay, let's get up and make some breakfast, and we can talk."

Nick gets into the shower and I head to the kitchen to put the coffee on. While I'm in the shower and the coffee's brewing, Nick cooks eggs and toast, and we sit at the tiny kitchen table next to an open window and eat. We're both starving.

When we've finished eating, we head to the couch with our coffee mugs and I start talking. But before I get into everything Nick and Lucy, I decide to get all the other shit in my life out of the way. I tell him about how Ava asked me to be a source for the article on Katherine and how I was so disturbed by that and said no. I tell him about Katherine's breakdown in the office and how I was surprised to hear that Katherine isn't actually what she's telling everyone she is. I tell him about how I walked in on Theo. I tell him about the job opening in the digital-media department, about how Katherine said she would support me and put in a good word for me, and how I found out from Sera that Katherine had done just the opposite, sabotaged my chance at the job, and lied to me. I tell him about how furious I was at that and how despondent I was over him and in a state of absolute weakness, anger, and misery, I did something horrible.

"What did you do?" Nick asks. But not in an accusing voice. In a kind voice.

"I don't want to tell you. You're going to be so disappointed in me," I say shamefully, hiding my face in my hands so I don't have to look in his eyes.

And then, with my eyes still covered, I tell him how I gave the information to Daniel. But then I take my hands away from my eyes and tell him that I woke up the next morning completely disgusted with myself and that I tried to get in touch with Daniel and that I told Ava immediately to make sure Daniel didn't write the article. I explain the whole thing: how it was too late, how he completely butchered and embellished what I told him, and how the article was a hatchet job. I tell him that Katherine went ballistic and that she has no idea that it was me who was the anonymous source and how she was so kind last night when she had Pancho drive me to the hospital. But most importantly I tell him about the life decisions I made yesterday during my walk.

This whole time while we're talking, I'm mostly sitting cross-legged on the couch, with a pillow over my lap, staring straight out, and gesticulating wildly with my hands. Nick sits calmly, his back up to the end of the couch so he can face me, listening intently, with a serious expression on his face, sipping his coffee now and then, not interrupting even once.

I turn to face him. "I realize, now, Nick, that, yes, I do want to have a career as I get older. But I also want to be a great mom to lots of kids. And I want to have time to watch basketball, and have dinner at my mom's, and exercise, and not be stressed out all the time. I realize that I can't have all those things and have the kind of job Katherine has. And I'm starting to understand how marriage to the right person for the right reasons *can* be a beautiful and wonderful thing. And I want that. With the right person and for the right reasons." I say as I put his coffee cup down on the table and hold his hands. "I want that with you. Do you think you can give me another chance?"

Nick stares at me, a big grin developing on his face. He looks like he's trying to figure out what to say. "I don't even know where to start. I want to start with the last part but first, man, I can't even leave you alone for one week! Look at all this stuff that's happened to you!"

"I know!" I say and start to cry and laugh at the same time.

"And I was just sitting here in my apartment in these very same sweats all week, on this very same couch drinking out of this very same mug and trying to get all this Ty stuff worked out."

"I saw you, actually," I say, not able to hold it in any longer.

"What do you mean? Where?" he asks.

"At Nobu. With that blonde."

"You were there?" he asks, confused.

"I came to surprise you. Because I had that dinner with you and Grant on my calendar. But then I walked in and saw you with that girl and I left," I say sadly.

"That was Jenna. You've met Jenna. She's Grant's attorney," he says, calmly.

"Jenna?"

"Yeah, Jenna. Did you think I was on a date?"

"Yes," I say, a little indignation in my voice.

"It was far from a date. Grant was with us most of the night but he had to leave early. Did you get there after, like, nine fifteen?"

"Yes." The indignation is fading. "But the table was only set for two."

"When Grant left, they cleared his place."

"She was so pretty. And you know I can barely see. I didn't recognize her. I thought you were on a date and had lied to me."

"Oh, Coop," he says, laughing a little at me, but not in a mean way. "She's not nearly as pretty as you and I was not on a date. I spent all week despairing over you. Plus, she's so not my type. And she drinks cosmos," he says with derision.

I'm laughing now too, though a few tears might be mixed in. I'm so relieved and of course, I have no reason not to believe Nick. We talk for a while about what I'm planning to do about my job and the article, about whether I think Brooke will find me out, and about whether I should tell Katherine about Theo. I wait for him to bring the marriage thing up.

"So did I hear you say you're keen on this whole marriage concept?" he asks, taking a sip of his coffee.

"I did. I did indeed say I was keen on this whole marriage concept," I say and then I explain what happened the night I was late to Union Square Cafe. I'm so relieved that all this awful stuff is out of the way. That Nick knows everything that's been going on. That I've been able to explain everything to him. "And last night really drove it all home for me, Nick. As I was on my way to the hospital, I tried not to let my mind go to an awful place, but it did. And before I could reel the bad thoughts back in, I thought about what my life would be like without you. If things hadn't turned out okay for you last night. And that was inconceivable to me. You are everything to me. I love you so much. I don't ever want to be without you," I say.

I kind of expect at that moment that Nick might whip out the ring from under the futon cushion and get down on one knee to propose. That I might again be offered a ring and a lifetime in a state of Sunday-morning dishevelment. But he does no such thing. No such thing at all.

"About that," he says turning to me. "I think we should take some time," he says seriously.

"What kind of time? What do you mean? I thought you said that you don't want to waste any more time deciding?" I ask confused.

"Not time away from each other," he says. "But I want to make sure you absolutely mean it. I don't want the drama and scariness of last night to push you into a decision that you're not fully prepared to make. I want you to be sure," he says lovingly, pushing a stray hair off my forehead.

"I am sure," I say, smiling at him, still somewhat hoping he's kidding, making me sweat, and is going to sink to his knees *tout de suite.*

"I couldn't be happier to hear that. Honestly. But I mean it. I want you to be 100-percent sure. And things are so insane with both of our jobs right now. Let's let things settle down for a bit."

I get what he's saying. It does make sense. I mean it was only yesterday that I became certain of this whole thing. Maybe I *should* let it sink in for a bit.

"I guess you're right. And I still want to check everything off the list for both of our benefits. I know you created that list as a sort of prerequisite for marriage. But I saw the value in it for my life in general so I've claimed it as an Improve Lucy's Life List. And, I've made good progress."

"That's so great. I appreciate more than you can know that you took that list seriously. I love that you've claimed it for yourself, and I don't need you to do those things for me anymore. It's pretty clear that your perspective has changed in a monumental way. I think we're gonna be good, Lucy Cooper. You and I are gonna be good. I just want all this dust to settle and then, when you least expect it, and when your hair is combed, I will propose to you."

"And when you do, Nicholas Heston, I will say yes."

He kisses me softly on the lips. We talk for a long time more, and Nick fills me in on everything that's going on with his new company and Ty. He says that Grant, his old boss, backed down at the Nobu dinner when he realized that he had no legal grounds for accusing him, Nick, of any misconduct in landing Ty as a client because Nick did everything by the book. And he tells me exciting news about a couple other athletes who are considering signing with him. I'm so thrilled to hear that all is going well with him professionally.

We clean up breakfast and decide we'll hang out a bit and then see a movie. It's nice to be in our comfortable routine again. To be together. I've missed this so much.

Still, though, I have an unsettled pit in my stomach. I realize that a small part of it is a mix of anxiety and relief over Nick because I'm still so surprised that we *are* okay and that we're going to *be* okay. That indeed it was a blip and not an iceberg. But most of the pit is stress about Katherine, about my job, about what's going to happen at work. I realize that since I woke up Friday morning I've had this low-grade and constant sense of panic about what I did to Katherine. I'm so disappointed with myself that I had the capacity to do such an awful thing. And I'm terrified that she will find out it was me. A small part of me says the right thing to do is to own it and tell Katherine. That I'll never truly be able to look at myself in a mirror without regret unless I tell the truth. Another small, teeny, tiny part of me wants to tell Katherine that her suspicions were correct and I found out somehow that it *was* Maggie Stern who talked to the *Post*. But that would be wrong. And my conscience cannot withstand one more sin. I decide that the only thing I'm going to do about it today is let it stew. I'm going to actively immerse myself in this awful bile and make myself suffer a bit for the horrible thing I did.

I ask Nick if he wants to come with me to my mom's for dinner, but he tells me that he has some documents he has to revise tonight that are due to his lawyer first thing tomorrow morning. He had been planning on doing them last night so now he has to do the whole thing tonight, and it's going to take him several hours. Bummer. It would have been nice to bring my new boyfriend home with me tonight to meet the family.

I had turned off my phone last night after we talked to Ty at the hospital and hadn't bothered to turn it back on. I turn it on now so I can send my mom and my brother Matty a text about tonight.

The phone beeps and shows two texts waiting to be read: the first from Katherine at around eleven o'clock last night and the second from Ava early this morning.

Katherine: How is Nick? I hope everything is okay. Speech went great.

Ava: OMG, Lucy. I cannot believe Katherine did that. Twitter is blowing up. I saw the video. Call me. We must discuss.

What, Ava? What did Katherine do? What video? I grab Nick's iPad, google Katherine Whitney, and click on "Videos." There's a link to a YouTube video entitled "Katherine Whitney Goes Rogue at Ellevate" with an image of Katherine in what she was wearing last night. So I click on it and start watching what appears to be an amateur video taken by an audience member of Katherine's speech, and I can't believe my eyes.

Chapter Eighteen

Good evening. And thank you Sallie for that wonderful introduction. I am honored to be here tonight and honored that Ellevate, of which I'm proud to be a member, has decided to bestow this prestigious award upon me. I also want to congratulate Oprah Winfrey. I have admired Oprah for as long as I can remember and she is a true role model for so many women.

But I'm sorry to say that I am unable to accept this award. And I apologize to Sallie that I did not give her any notice. I was actually planning on coming up here and accepting the award graciously and giving a prepared speech to you all about how you should live your dream life, about how work-life balance is possible, about how you, like me, can have it all. And I was going to stand up here and make it all look so easy.

But as my name was announced and as I was walking up here to give that speech, I realized I could not say what I had originally planned. And that I could not in good faith accept this award. Because that would be a lie.

I do not have anything written down. I left the planned speech on the table in my handbag. Please bear with me as I try to articulate what I am suddenly feeling so clearly and deeply.

First I want to say I'm sorry. I'm sorry to all the people I have hurt and all the people I'm going to hurt by the end of this speech. All the people who have trusted me, who have supported me, who have invested in me. I was wrong and I am sorry.

There are a few things that happened today, that have actually been happening over the last several months but that came to a head today that led me to make this decision to, well, come clean.

This morning I received a diagnosis from my dermatologist. I, and I'm sure many of you can relate to this, have been too busy, or so I convinced myself, to go to the dermatologist for a skin check. I have had skin cancer scares in the past so it was, to say the least, unwise to put my checkup off as long as I did, but there was always something more important to do and the dermatologist appointment kept falling to the bottom of the list. Eventually I went. In fact, it was a week and a half ago. I was not surprised when my doctor found a spot on my forehead that he thought looked suspicious. I told him I had no time for a biopsy and ran out of the office. A week later, this past Wednesday, my husband practically forced me to go back to get the biopsy done. I went, and the procedure, a shave biopsy, was no big deal. What was unpleasant, though, was waiting for the results to come back. Oh, how my mind played with me. I had convinced myself that I had cancer.

Well, I got the call from the doctor this morning. And appreciation must go out to all the doctors out there who will call their patients on Saturdays so the waiting does not go on needlessly. I was lucky. I am lucky. The spot was diagnosed as a solar keratosis. It is not cancer. Millions of Americans are diagnosed with skin cancer every year.

Today, I was not one of them. I know how lucky I am.

What my doctor gave me this morning, in addition to that diagnosis, was a dose of perspective.

You see, I received the diagnosis while I was wallowing in self-pity. I had a dreadful experience on the Today show this morning. I was supposed to be on to defend myself against the article that was published in the New York Post yesterday that called me a fraud.

Let's just say the Today interview did not go so well. It was not the supportive fluff piece I had been led to believe it would be. Instead, and rightfully so, I was called out by the host Lester Holt and the other guest Dr. Elaine Ireland, who I spoke to for a while during cocktails here tonight and who, unknowingly, was one of the reasons I've decided to give this speech. They challenged me, my book, and what I stand for. And they were, I realized later that afternoon when I had time to reflect on it all, right. They were absolutely, unequivocally right.

So there I was, post-Today show interview, wallowing in my self-pity when I received a phone call telling me that I don't have cancer. And not to make this too dramatic, but I suddenly felt like one of those airplane crash survivors who says that she feels like she has a second chance at her life.

Suddenly everything came into laser focus, and I saw my life with the perspective that I so desperately needed.

It is true, well some of it, the gist of it at least, what the Post said about me. My life is unbalanced. I am doing a terrible job at doing it all. And I understand and agree with what Dr. Ireland was trying to tell me.

While I was trying to convince women that they can have it all, that it is so easy, that it simply takes commitment, and drive, and some well-proven strategies, I was having trouble in my own life.

I'll let you in on my secrets. I am completely overwhelmed at work. There is more on my plate than I think I can accomplish. I feel stressed out most of the time. My youngest daughter often calls our nanny "Mama." I have neglected my daughters and my dear and understanding and incredibly supportive husband, who I'm starting to suspect might actually be considering leaving me. I never have time to exercise, and as you now know, I put off going to the doctor. In other words, I don't exactly practice what I preach.

What I've learned is that you can't do all of it well all at the same time. Sacrifices, sometimes big ones, must be made and it's just a matter of deciding which sacrifices you are willing to make.

I apologize to all the women out there who I've met, who have sent me letters telling me about their struggles trying to balance it all. I apologize to all of you for saying it was possible. It is not. And I fear most of all that I've made women feel inadequate. That by acting like having it all and doing it all is doable, that they feel like failures for not living up to what I've told them is their potential.

So to all you women out there who feel badly about yourselves, who are trying to get by every day taking care of your job, your family, your marriage, yourself, you must know that you are doing a great job. That it isn't easy. And that if none of it seems like it's working out, which most days it won't, then you are officially a member of a sisterhood of women exactly like you. You are not alone.

So, thank you Ellevate for giving me this platform. Though this wasn't the speech I had intended to give and it certainly wasn't the speech you had intended me to give, I feel like it was the perfect audience to talk to about all this.

I would also like to say that I did not set out to be a fraud or to be malicious in any way. When I wrote my book, I truly believed everything in it, and I still think there are strategies in there that can help working women handle their responsibilities. But when things got harder in my life, I do admit that I didn't come out and speak the truth. I felt like I was too deep into this persona, that I could never find a way out of it. I thank you in advance for understanding that I did not mean to hurt anyone or, as I've been accused of doing, set the women's movement back. I hope by speaking to you tonight, I've made slight amends for my mistakes, and I look forward to making more.

Thank you for your time.

Chapter Nineteen

I check Facebook, Twitter, and Instagram and see that Katherine is trending everywhere. Social media is all aflutter about Katherine's "announcement," "admission," "fall from grace," "disgusting pity party." There's a long *Huffington Post* piece about the speech with hundreds of comments. Someone wrote, "I admire Katherine Whitney so much for what she did. That took a lot of guts. And it validates women to no end that someone at her level and of her prominence stood up there and told it like it is." Someone else wrote "Wah, wah. I feel so sorry for Katherine Whitney. Stop crying bitch." I spend time reading all the comments. I am in shock that Katherine did what she did.

At the same time, I feel so proud of her. I cannot imagine that was easy to do. In the video I watched, the sound was a little off and it was a little shaky, but I could hear in Katherine's voice how sincere she was. How emotional that was for her. She clearly spoke from her heart.

I try to put myself in the shoes of someone who doesn't know her. Would I think she was being authentic? Would I forgive her? It's hard to say whether strangers will believe she was being genuine, but from the majority of reactions on social media, it seems as if they will.

It takes me a moment to make the realization, and the pit in my stomach grows as I do, that I did indeed create Katherine's downfall.

But I think about all that she said in her speech and realize the *Post* article was just one piece of that puzzle. Sure it was the first piece, and sure it was the reason there was a *Today* interview in the first place, but it wasn't the only thing. And Katherine didn't sound like she had any regrets during that speech. It wasn't like she was someone who got caught doing something, that then the press exposed her, and she begrudgingly confessed. No, she would have been fine keeping her cover, convincing the media that the *Post* piece was a fluke, that she was still killing it in the balance department. No one forced Katherine to make that speech. She chose to get up there and come clean to all those people, to the world. And it actually sounded like she was glad she did.

Lucy: Hi Mom. Hi Matt. Coming tonight. Matt can you pick me up at station at 3:54?

Mom: So glad Lucy.

Matt: I can pick you up. See you later.

Lucy: Hi Katherine. Nick is fine. Thank God. Just a bad scare but he is going to be fine. Thank you for asking. I watched your speech. So proud of you. Talk tomorrow.

And then I call Ava. I tell her about Nick's accident and that we're officially back together. We discuss her amazing date last night. And then we discuss Katherine and The Speech. When we're about to hang up, she asks me if I've seen the quote she posted on Instagram this morning. I grab my phone and look at my feed: *Freedom is found when we let go of who we're supposed to be and embrace who we really are.*

Later, after Nick and I see a movie and engage in a lot of kissing (nothing strenuous, doctor), I start to leave his apartment to head to Grand Central to take the 3:07 to Rye.

"That was a really nice day," Nick says.

"It was a perfect end to this horrendous week that has been an unbelievable roller coaster of emotion," I say leaning against his door. He kisses me again.

"Have fun at your mom's. Tell everyone I say hey."

"Will do. Good luck with all your work tonight."

"Speaking of work, what do you think is going to happen at work tomorrow? Katherine and all?" He asks.

"Oh, man, I don't know," I say.

"If I had to guess, I would say that you'll go in and things will kind of be back to normal. Maybe a new normal, but normal. I mean, what's Katherine going to do? Quit her job?"

That's exactly what she did.

I head into work on Monday morning as nervous as a guilty baby daddy before a DNA test. I'm nervous because I've decided to tell Katherine the truth about being the source for the article in the *Post*. She may or may not already know at this point, depending upon Brooke's commitment to weekend sleuthing, but whether or not *she* knows, *I* know. She will never forgive me. I'm wondering if I'll ever be able to forgive myself.

I've also decided to tell her about Theo. She said something in her speech about suspecting Theo might leave her. I have no idea what that's based on, but as of Saturday morning, it was my understanding that Theo was not going to tell Katherine what happened. I try to put myself in her shoes and think about what it would feel like if Nick cheated on me and whether or not I would want to know. I know every situation is different so it's hard to decide for anyone else. But, personally, I would want to know. I would most definitely want to know.

And finally, I've decided to confront her about telling Ash not to consider me for the digital-media job. I have to get all of these secrets out of my body. Their poison is making me sick. The backlash is most definitely going to be a bitch. But the alternative, keeping it all in, isn't an option for me anymore. I'll deal with the aftermath when it comes.

I delay the inevitable with my usual soothing tactic: the bagel guy. I order my regular and head toward the elevator. It feels like there are crack-addicted trapeze artists in my stomach, and they are just beginning their routine. I see Evan waiting for the elevator, so I head toward him and we wait.

"Hey, Luciebelle. I've see you've got your normal fortifications," he says. "You'll need them. Gonna be a busy day." He says the last part in a taunting, sing-song voice.

The elevator door opens and we both walk in. Evan presses our floor and the doors close. It's only the two of us in the car.

"What did you think about the speech?" I ask, taking a sip of my coffee.

"What speech?" Evan asks, looking at me with a confused expression.

"Umm," I stammer, not entirely sure what to say. Certainly Evan must have heard about The Speech.

"Kidding, Luciebelle. Kidding," Evan says.

"Not funny, Evan," I say with a smile and a cock of my head.

"What did I think of the speech? If I had a dime for every time I've been asked that in the last twenty-four hours, I'd be a richer man than I am currently am. You know, to be honest, I'm still trying to digest it all. I will say that I'm proud of Katherine for being so honest. I know that was really hard."

"Did you talk to her yesterday?" I ask.

"Of course," Evan says. "Several times. I spent a few hours at her apartment and we discussed all the implications . . . for Green Goddess, for the book, for her."

"And, what do—" I start to ask as the elevator doors open.

"Gotta run. Talk to you later," he says, rushing off and flicking his fingers in a good-bye to me.

I proceed to my desk slowly. A dead man walking.

"Lucy, is that you?" I hear Katherine call from her office as I get to my desk and start setting my things down. I keep my coffee and head into her office. I'm stunned by what I see.

"Katherine? What are you doing?"

"I'm packing," she says sounding as normal as if she had said, I'm going to have a salad for dinner.

"Packing for what?" I ask, though I already know. I look around her office and it's a sea of brown boxes, some wide open revealing their contents: books, frames, vases. Some already taped closed.

"Packing up my office." She stops, puts her hands on her hips, takes a deep breath and says, "I'm leaving, Lucy. I've quit my job. Today's my last official day." She sounds so content, so determined.

"What? Why?" I ask and collapse into a Kelly chair.

"Well, for a lot of reasons," she says and takes a break from packing to sit at the edge of her desk. "Wait, first of all, is Nick okay?"

"Yes, thank you. He's fine. He's going to be just fine. Thank you."

"Thank God. I'm so happy to hear that."

I smile.

"I stunned myself with that speech. Up until the minute Sallie called my name, I did not plan on giving that speech. And then something came over me. I thought, *to hell with it all.* I was sick of the charade, Lucy. I've been holding it together, clearly not very well, and I couldn't convince myself that it was worth it anymore. I know it all sounds very unlike me to give up like that, but maybe it's more like me than I even know." She gets up and starts walking around her office. "I really took Elaine Ireland's words to heart. Sure, I'd heard that same argument hundreds of times, but I'd never truly allowed myself to let the words register. I'd always felt like that was a cop-out. And I realize now how arrogant I was and how stupid I was. And that's what all came into my brain in that immediate moment before I went on stage. I left my speech on the table, and as I walked up to the dais, I was scared. In my head, there were voices shouting at me saying, *Don't do this* and *Turn around and get your speech.* But, as I said, something came over me and I kept going."

"It was a really good speech, Katherine."

"Thanks," she laughs. "I felt like I was possessed, in a way. I didn't feel like I even had control over what I was saying. Don't get me wrong, I knew what I was saying and I wanted to make that speech, but the words somehow seemed to formulate themselves. Anyway, when I was done and I started walking back to my seat, it was like a cacophony in my ears, though I found out later that the audience was dead silent. But to me the noise was deafening. And I didn't really know what had just happened. I had to read the transcript of the speech when it was printed online the next morning to remember what I had said." She smiles, calmly tucks her hair behind her ears, and takes a sip of her Glow juice.

I smile back as best I can and she continues.

"I have to say that I'm happy I did it. Well, most of me. Part of me wishes I had thought that whole plan out a little more," she laughs. "I might have gone about it differently. I might not have spilled so many personal secrets. Ugh, like about Theo. And I could have used some time to think about how this would affect everyone else. In that moment I was only thinking about how I couldn't keep the facade up any longer. Anyway, at the end of it all, I'm happy it happened the way it did." She seems so light. Liberated.

"But why do you have to leave Green Goddess?" I ask.

"Oh, I can't stay here, Lucy. It's too much of a distraction for the company. I had a long talk with Evan yesterday. He tried to convince me that we could make it work. That we could smooth things over with shareholders and the board and all that, and that we could spin it all in a positive way. I get what he's saying, and I can see some validity in it. But the main reason I'm leaving is because I can't do this job . . . ," she gestures around her office with her hands, "anymore. It's too much. The commitment that this particular job requires is no longer what I'm willing to give. I'm officially a corporate cliché," she says and then changes her voice to one of a news broadcaster, "Katherine Whitney is leaving her job to spend more time with her family."

"Couldn't they make your job a little less demanding?" I ask.

"This job requires someone who is going to make a 100-percent commitment to his or her career. And I'm not willing to do that anymore. Ah, that sounds so liberating. And, to be honest, scary as hell." She comes over and sits on the chair next to me.

"What about London. And the book?" I ask.

"There are plenty of people to take control of the reins for London. And almost everything's ready for the launch anyway. And the book, well, I'm not sure what's going to happen with the book and the website yet, but I'm not worried. Things have a way of working themselves out when they need to."

"Couldn't you do a different job here?"

"I could. But I don't want to. You know how important my career is to me. But something inside is telling me I should make a clean break from all of this and start over. And I want to listen to that voice. I think it knows something."

"So what are you going to do now?" I ask, my voice breaking a little. I'm starting to feel really, really sad.

"Oh, Luce," she says and grabs my hand. "I'm not entirely sure, but everything's going to be fine."

"Katherine," I say, gathering my courage. I need to do it now. I need to have it be done. "There are some things I really need to talk to you about," I say. The *Post*. Theo. Ash.

"What's on your mind?" she asks, slapping her hands down on her thighs (clad in jeans, I should add).

"You ready, Katherine?" Evan asks as he walks into Katherine's office.

"Lucy, sorry, Evan and I have a call with London right now to go over what's happening here. Can we talk later about what you wanted to talk about?"

"Sure," I say, mostly relieved. I close the door behind me as I leave Katherine's office and sit down at my desk.

And then it hits me. I don't know what took me so long. If Katherine is no longer the COO of Green Goddess then I no longer have a boss, which means I am no longer anyone's employee, which means I do not have a job. I let that sink in a bit and then I call Nick.

"She quit," I say quietly when Nick picks up on the first ring.

"No way."

"Yep," I say.

"Wow. Totally not what I thought she'd do."

"She's here, but she's packing up her office."

"So what happens to you?"

"You'd think I would have asked that, right?"

"Well, yeah."

"We were in the middle of talking about everything, but then she had to get on a conference call. So now I'm at my desk, whispering on the phone to you, while people walk by my desk staring at me and at Katherine's closed door. I was so startled and flustered by her telling me about *her* job that I didn't even think about *my own* job."

"How long is she going to be on the call?" Nick asks.

"I have no idea," I say.

"Well, as soon as she gets off you should ask her what this means for you."

"Yep, that's the plan," I say.

"And if it means you no longer have a job at Green Goddess, then we can sit down tonight and come up with a strategy together."

"Okay, thanks, Nick."

"Speaking of tonight," his tone changes.

"Yes?"

"Can you come over after work? Or can I come to you? I had my cardiologist appointment early this morning, and I'm cleared for strenuous activities. I'd like to be strenuous with you."

"It's a date. I would like to be strenuous with you, too," I say, laughing.

As the day goes on, Katherine remains behind closed doors on a series of calls. Evan is in there most of the day, too, slipping out only to ask me to grab them lunch. I still answer her phone and conduct business as usual because there has been no official press release announcing Katherine's resignation. As far as the public knows, Katherine Whitney is still the COO of Green Goddess. I guess I'm happy to have my job for at least one more day. One of the fears I had originally about telling Katherine the truth about the *Post* is that I knew I would lose my job. But I guess I don't have to worry about that part. My job is already lost. Karma is a bitch.

Late in the afternoon, around four o'clock, Katherine's door finally opens and she strides out, her bag on her shoulder.

"I'm going home, Lucy," Katherine says.

"But—"

"We can talk about everything tomorrow," she says and quickly walks away toward the elevator.

What was that? I find out about a half hour later.

"Katherine Whitney's office."

"Lucy, it's Katherine."

"Oh, hi, Katherine."

"Can you come by my apartment in about a half hour? At five? There's something I'd like to talk to you about."

"Um, sure. Yeah, that's no problem. I'll see you in a half hour."

I hang up the phone and I just stare. I could not read her tone. It wasn't exactly unfriendly but it was nowhere near the tone of our little banter this morning. Which doesn't necessarily mean anything. But it could mean everything. Maybe she just wants to talk to me about what's going to happen with my job. Maybe she decided not to come in tomorrow so she wants to let me finish the conversation I started with her earlier when Evan walked in. Maybe she's going to tell me that she pulled some strings and I have the job in digital media. Or maybe it's something else entirely. I slowly gather my things and send a quick text to Nick.

Lucy: Katherine wants to see me at her apartment. Heading there now.

Nick: Why?

Lucy: Not sure. Will let you know after. In fact would love for you to head to my apartment so I can tell you in person when I'm done.

Nick: I can do that.

Lucy: If it's bad news, I might need some strenuous drinking in addition to the other strenuous activities you had in mind. Be prepared.

Nick: Done. Good luck. I love you.

Luck might be exactly what I need, I think as I head toward the elevator. Toward Katherine's.

Chapter Twenty

Cute Doorman and I smile at each other as I walk into Katherine's building.

"Go ahead," he says. "I'll tell them you're on your way up."

"Thanks," I say and head toward the elevator.

Apparently, five o'clock is a sort of rush hour in New York City doorman buildings. I'm never home at five on a weekday nor do I live in a doorman building, so I've never gotten to observe this phenomenon.

There are no fewer than six kids and what appear to be two nannies and a mom waiting for the elevator. There's a stroller, two soccer balls, one baseball bat, and a scooter. There are two sippy cups, one half-eaten bag of popcorn that's now spilling over onto the pristine marble lobby floor, and three bottles of water. There's pushing, crying, whining, and kicking. And there's me, observing it all. Empathizing with these caretakers. Happy, for the time being, that I'm not them.

I let them all cram into the elevator when it comes and am relieved that another elevator comes soon thereafter. I don't want to be late to meet with Katherine. I've mentally exhausted every iteration of this conversation, and now I just want to get it over with.

I knock on Katherine's door, and Theo opens it.

"Hey, slugger," he says glumly.

"Hey," I say.

"Come, she's in the library."

I follow Theo into the library. In large Manhattan apartments inhabited by the very wealthy, the library is more often than not an intimate room painted either in an oxblood red or midnight-blue lacquer. There are solid-wood bookshelves displaying hundreds, if not thousands, of books. There is almost always a leather couch laden with decorative pillows as well as various other upholstered chairs or benches assembled to form a central seating area. And there is a coffee table that always holds a scented Diptyque or DayNa Decker candle, a beautiful low arrangement of single-hued flowers, a crystal dish filled with nuts or wrapped candies, and a neat stack of urbane coffee-table books published by Rizzoli. If you don't believe me, look through any issue of *Architectural Digest,* and you'll see what I mean.

As I enter the library, I see Katherine curled into one side of the espresso-colored leather couch, a decorative pillow atop her lap. The DayNa Decker Tuberose is lit and it gives the room a warm glow. Katherine's wearing sweats and a cashmere sweater, her hair in a ponytail. She has obviously been crying and she continues to do so, tossing spent tissues into a small leather wastebasket on the floor by her side.

"Katherine," I say, shocked by what I see.

"Lucy, how could you?" Katherine asks with venom in her voice. And I realize she knows.

"How—" I start, unsure of what I'm going to say.

Katherine interrupts. "I know you were the source for the *Post.*" She looks at me with daggers in her eyes.

"Is that true, Lucy?" Theo asks.

"Yes, but—"

"But what? But what, Lucy?" Katherine asks angrily as she tosses another tissue into the garbage and plucks a fresh one from the box next to her on the couch.

"Katherine, I'm so sorry," I say in a wretched voice. "Please, can I explain?"

Katherine makes a disgusted sound.

"Let her explain, Katherine," Theo says. He and I have been standing up till now. He sits down next to Katherine on the couch and gestures toward a small bench on the other side of the coffee table facing them.

I sit in my assigned seat and take a deep breath.

"I'm so sorry. I've never been more sorry about anything in my entire life. I tried to tell you earlier today when I was in your office because I couldn't keep it from you any longer. And it's not all exactly how it seems."

"It never is," Theo says.

"I found out from the assistant grapevine that you told Ash not to hire me for the job in the digital-media department. His assistant Sera's desk is where a bunch of the assistants assemble to gossip, and I guess someone overheard you having a conversation with Ash in his office." One last lie, but I will not snitch on Sera.

I see something come over Katherine's face, but I'm not sure what it is.

I continue. "I was so mad, Katherine. I've never been madder in my life. I felt like I had done so much for you, that I had worked so hard all the time for you, and that seemed like such a betrayal. And you flat-out lied to me and said you had spoken to Joan and that you'd support me."

"I—" Katherine starts.

"Let her finish," Theo says softly, touching Katherine's shoulder.

"I didn't even start this whole thing, Katherine. It wasn't my idea. This story is kind of confusing, but I'll try to make sense. That assistant journalist guy, Daniel, who was here with *People* magazine overheard all kinds of things you were saying that day to me. And they didn't come off so well. He even recorded stuff you were saying on his phone. Well, his day job is at the *Post*. My best friend Ava works at *Cosmo*. Daniel used to work at *Cosmo*, and he and Ava are friends. Ava and Daniel had lunch a few days after the *People* interview, and Daniel told Ava all about how you were acting toward your assistant during the interview. Ava told him that I, her best friend, was your assistant. Daniel said he was going to write an exposé about you for the *Post* and asked Ava if she would ask me if I would give him information about you. I immediately said no, of course. I would never do something like that to you. You'd always been so good to me. But then I found out about what you told Ash. And that you had lied to me. And that was a couple days after you were crying in your office and admitted to me that things were so bad with you. Plus, my mom's neighbor told me that what you were doing was making women feel so badly. And I was just so mad. Madder than I ever remember feeling. And in the absolute heat of that anger, I fed Daniel some information. I immediately regretted it the next day and as soon as I woke up I called Daniel to tell him to not use anything I had said. I didn't even know at that point that this was going to be a big story. I didn't realize he had other sources. I thought it was just me. But it was too late. Not only was it already in the *Post*, but he distorted the things I did say, and added all sorts of things that I didn't say." I am speaking so fast, not making entire sense, trying to get it all in. I take a deep breath and wait for Katherine or Theo to speak. They don't. I can barely meet their eyes.

"But, Lucy, giving information to the *Post*?" Theo asks, accusingly.

"Haven't you ever done anything wrong in your life, Theo?" I ask.

"Yes, yes I have," Theo says.

"I feel so badly about the whole thing, Katherine. I know what I did is wrong and awful and I've never done anything like that before in my life and I am disgusted with myself that I even had the capacity to do it. I take full responsibility for what I did and I'm so, so sorry. I don't expect you to ever forgive me."

There's silence for a moment. I'm still looking down. Waiting.

"Well, that's good then, because I don't think I ever will," Katherine says.

"Kath," Theo says to her softly, his tone implying that she shouldn't have said that.

"What, Theo?" Katherine asks. "What?"

Theo doesn't say anything and the two of them look at me. I look down at the flame dancing in the wooden wick. I want to run out of that fancy library. But I feel like a child who needs to wait for permission to be dismissed from the table.

"You do realize that you ruined my life, right?" Katherine asks, staring at me. "Because of you my career, my reputation, my livelihood . . . they're all in complete jeopardy."

I look up and catch her eye. This is all too much. But I deserve every ounce of it.

"I know, Katherine. And I'm so sorry. I really don't know what else to say. Maybe I can write an article and get it posted somewhere admitting that I was the Green Goddess source, and what I said was untrue."

"But it doesn't even matter anymore. Don't you realize that?" she asks, her voice filled with rancor. "That article and its veracity are completely irrelevant at this point. I already gave that speech. I already admitted everything. That I am a fraud," she says, spitting out that last word. "So your apologizing or your coming out with some heroic public apology won't change anything, Lucy. The fact is that you did it in the first place. The fact is that you started this whole thing in motion and none of it would have happened if you had kept your mouth shut. God! I can't believe this!"

Theo stands up. "Lucy, why don't you come with me?"

I stand up and follow him out of the library. I'm practically shaking. I've never felt so horribly in my entire life. Theo walks toward the front door, and I trail behind him.

"Listen, let me talk to her," he says softly, opening the front door.

"You might as well not even bother," I say. "It's not going to change anything. She's absolutely right. I'm an awful, horrible person and I ruined her life. I wouldn't forgive me either."

"Well, let me talk to her. I don't know what will come out of it, but she's really angry right now and you don't need to sit there and get all that dumped on you. We can talk about it again when she's had some time to let it all sink in." Theo moves aside so I can leave.

"Thanks, Theo," I say walking out the door.

"You got it, slugger. I owe you one."

"That's for sure," I say snidely. "You know I almost told her about you this morning. I think she deserves to know."

"You're right," he says, looking behind him to make sure Katherine's not there. "I have been thinking about it and I agree with you. She does deserve to know. But Lucy, goddamn it," he says angrily, gritting his teeth, "she deserves to know from me. I think you've done enough for now, so please, let me handle this. I will tell her."

"Okay, Theo. Okay," I say and I see him visibly calm down. "You're right. She does deserve to hear it from you. And I realize it's not the best time right now."

"I will tell her, Lucy. Just give me a little time," he says agitated.

I leave, the apartment door closing heavily behind me. When I'm back out on the street, I text Nick.

Lucy: On my way home. Worse than expected. She knows.

Nick: So sorry. I'm at your place. Want me to meet you somewhere?

Lucy: No. Going to walk home. Give me time to think. I'll be there in 20 min. Don't go anywhere.

I decide to walk up Central Park West toward Eighty-Third Street. There are throngs of people walking by me quickly, on their way home after a long New York City day at work. I've always liked sitting on benches in the park or at a bus stop and watching these New Yorkers and their dogged purposefulness. And I've always liked imagining everyone's story: oh, that guy got a new job and he's smiling like that because he's about to go home and tell his pregnant wife that he'll have a steady paycheck when the baby comes. That woman is heading to her apartment to make her famous lasagna because her husband, the war correspondent, is on his way home and they haven't been together in months. And so on. I walk by a woman sitting on a bench at a bus stop on Sixty-Eighth Street waiting for the M10. Our eyes meet. I wonder if she's imagining my story.

My story is so confusing at this point. And so out of control. But what I'm starting to realize, as I replay Katherine's hateful words, is that she didn't take any responsibility for the role she played in all this. And I was so flustered in her apartment and so focused on explaining myself that I didn't even make her answer for what she did. Sure, I did something mean and spiteful. But she did, too! I saw something in her eyes, on her face, when I said that she had lied to me and that one of the assistants had overheard her talking to Ash. So I know she heard me say that. But she didn't own up to what she did and admit that it was wrong. She just dumped all over me. I realize I deserve her acrimony, but something about that exchange felt off to me.

I'm walking quickly now and mumbling under my breath. People stare at me and I don't give a flying fuck. I'm so angry. Mike-Tyson-biting-an-ear angry. I turn left on Eighty-Third Street and head toward

Columbus. The circus performers on crack are starting up again in my stomach, and I realize that by ruining Katherine's life, I've also done a number on my own, because not only do I not have a job, but I have no hope of ever getting one at Green Goddess. For that matter, any employer who sees the Green Goddess job on my résumé is going to ask for a recommendation from them, maybe even expect some glowing written recommendation from Katherine herself, and what will it say about me when I can't produce one? So basically I can't ever get another job anywhere, ever. I guess I could just have a baby and stay home with him or her. Or them.

As I'm tossing that last thought over and over in my head, I unlock the main door on my building and head up the stairs, happy that Nick will be there to make me feel better.

I open the door to my apartment and I immediately see Nick, all dressed up in a suit, sitting at my kitchen table. On the table, all laid out nicely, is a bouquet of red roses in a vase, a box of mini cupcakes, two empty water glasses, an open bottle of champagne sitting in an ice bucket, and one brand-new bottle each of tequila, vodka, scotch, and gin.

"I didn't know what you were going to want to drink," he says, shrugging his shoulders. "Oh, and we're going to have to register for glasses. Wine glasses. Booze glasses. Shot glasses. Lots of glasses. These will have to do for now," he says pointing at the water glasses. He turns more serious. "How did it go?"

"It was a disaster," I say, sinking into the yellow love seat.

"What happened?" he asks, turning his chair to face me.

"She knows it was me. That's basically all there is to it. She knows it was me, she hates me, and she will never forgive me. That's what she said. She said I ruined her life. But she didn't take any responsibility for what she did, which led to all of this!" I say angrily.

"How did she find out?"

SUSIE ORMAN SCHNALL

"Brooke found out. I mean, she didn't exactly say that, but I know that's how. I'm sure it wasn't that hard to get the information out of that Daniel."

I recount our entire conversation. What she said. What I said. What Theo said. What I wish I had said. Nick helps me process what happened, and I start to feel a little better.

"So what happens now?"

"Well, if you weren't here, I'd take this opportunity to inhale the two pints of ice cream I bought last night. This is nothing a little Chunky Monkey can't fix," I say with a sad face.

Nick stands up and opens my freezer. He grabs the two pints of ice cream, puts them on a cookie sheet that I keep in my oven, pulls a spoon out of the drawer, and places it all on my lap.

"Don't let my being here stop you," he says, cocking his head toward the side in sympathy.

"You're the best. You know that?" I say, opening the lid on pint number one.

"Been told," he says.

"I just feel sick about this whole thing. About what I did to her."

"I know. And unfortunately that's something you're going to have to live with for a while. It sucks, but the guilt will fade with time."

"I hope so," I say, filling my spoon with a huge portion of ice cream and stuffing it in my mouth. I take a moment to savor the ice cream's exceptional therapeutic prowess. "I really don't know what I'm going to do, Nick. I know this sounds very dramatic, but I don't know who would give me a job. There's no way I'm going to get a recommendation from my past employer."

"Somehow everything will work out, Coop. You could always do some work for me, on my website and all, and then when you apply for a new job, *I'll* be your past employer and I'll write you an unbelievable recommendation."

"Oh, yeah?" I ask, holding my next spoonful in midair before stuffing its contents into my mouth. "What would you say?"

"I'd start with how you're so passionate about everything you do. And then I'd say that you take your tasks very seriously. That you are always concerned with how everyone else on the team is doing and feeling and that you're very responsive to other people's needs. That you never leave a task until it's entirely finished. Hmmm, what else?" Nick asks, rubbing his chin and squinting his eyes.

"How about the fact that I'm very flexible?" I suggest.

"Oh, yeah. I forgot about that. You're very flexible in the most demanding of situations."

"Thank you, Nick," I say, smiling at him.

"For that glowing recommendation?" he asks.

"No, for making me feel better. I mean, don't give yourself too much credit, I still feel like shit. But talking to you helps a lot. Not nearly as much as this ice cream, though," I say, smiling.

He comes over to the couch and gives me a kiss. I decide that I'd like to get out of my brain by getting out of my clothes. That maybe the distraction will have a way of making me feel better.

"So about those strenuous activities?" I ask.

"Yeah?"

"I'm ready."

I tell Nick to grab the bottle of champagne and lead him by his finger into my bedroom. I take the bottle out of his hand.

"To us," I say holding the bottle up.

"To us," he says.

I take a sip of the champagne and pass the bottle to him. He takes a sip and then puts the bottle on my dresser and sits me down gently on the bed. He starts to kiss me and I feel the little champagne bubbles with my tongue in his mouth. He tastes so good and we kiss more forcefully.

Nick pulls back and stares at me while he unbuttons his shirt. And as he takes it off, I hear myself gasp a little. I have always been so turned on by Nick's body. He reaches over and pulls my sweater off and puts his hands on my shoulders. I lean forward to kiss him but he keeps me at shoulder distance. He gently leans forward and gives me the most delicate kiss, parting my lips at the last minute with his tongue. He stops, picks the bottle of champagne up off the table, and offers me a sip. I accept and hand the bottle back to him.

He takes a sip and kisses me again. I taste the sweet champagne on his tongue. But again he pulls away. He slowly eases my bra straps off my shoulders, then reaches behind my back and unclasps it entirely. It falls to the floor.

Nick looks in my eyes and then looks down as he cups my breasts in his hands. "You're so beautiful," he says and kisses me again. As we're kissing, he slowly lowers me down on the bed. We stay there for a while, just kissing.

Nick turns his body so he's resting on his left hip. He watches me as he traces a line with his finger from my left ear to my lips. He leaves his finger on my lips. I kiss the tip of his finger. Then Nick stands up on the side of the bed and takes off his pants. As he's doing that I shimmy out of mine and drop them on the floor beside me. I get under the covers and pull the sheets down for him on the other side.

I stare at Nick's naked body before he climbs back into the bed and I'm breathless from how beautiful he is. He gets into the bed and we lie on our sides pressing the fronts of our bodies into each other as we kiss. We stay there for a very long time, feeling each other, touching each other, kissing. At one point our faces are so close, our bodies flat against each other and our hands are grasped together. I feel so safe with Nick. So happy. So loved.

Eventually, we need to be even closer than we already are, and when we finish, we stay there for a long time, the side of Nick's face resting on my chest, neither one wanting to part with the other. When we separate ourselves, we both lie face up on our pillows looking at the ceiling.

"I hope that wasn't too strenuous," I say smiling, turning my head to look at him.

"Nope. Not too strenuous. Perfect, but not too strenuous," Nick says, smiling at me.

"Well, I guess we're going to have to keep at it then. To see how strenuous we can get."

And so we do.

Chapter Twenty-One

I wake up on Tuesday morning confused about what I'm supposed to do. Nick's in the bathroom brushing his teeth.

"Good morning, sunshine," he says, walking back into the bedroom to get dressed. His hair is wet and he's wrapped in a towel from the waist down.

"Good morning. Where are you off to?"

"The office. I mean, my apartment," he laughs. "I think I should start looking at office space and make this baby official."

"That's a great idea, Nick. Speaking of going to the office, do you think I'm supposed to go to work?"

"I don't know," he says, letting the towel drop to the floor as he gets dressed.

"I don't know, either," I say, watching him. "I haven't technically been fired. But I don't technically have a job either."

"Is Katherine supposed to be in the office?"

"No. Yesterday she told me it was her last day."

"So then why don't you go in and see what happens. At least it'll give you an opportunity to clear your desk and get your stuff in order." He gathers his things.

"That makes sense," I say as I get out of bed and head toward the bathroom.

"I'm gonna run," Nick says, giving me a kiss on my forehead. "Keep me posted."

"I will. Thanks, babe. I love you."

"I love you, too, Coop. Everything's going to be okay. I promise."

Twenty minutes later, I head down the stairs of my apartment building. I put my headphones in and click on my Sad Lucy playlist. I walk out of the building and turn left, Christina Perri's "Jar of Hearts" playing in my ears. I jump when I feel someone tapping my shoulder, and I pull my earplugs out of my ears.

"Jeez, Lucy. How loud is your music?"

"Pancho," I say, startled. "Jesus! You scared me. Why did you do that?" I feel my heart pounding. A million racehorses.

"I was calling your name, but you didn't hear me. I'm parked in front of your building," he says turning and gesturing toward the Escalade, which is parked in front of a hydrant.

"My music is loud," I say, pointing at my headphones.

"Yeah," he says. "Anyway, I'm here to pick you up."

"For what?" I ask.

"To go to Katherine's," he says, confused.

"To go to Katherine's what?" I ask, just as confused.

"Her apartment," he says, in a tone that means I should know what the hell he's talking about.

"For what?"

"I don't know, Lucy," he says, starting to sound a little frustrated with me. "Can you just get in the car before I get a ticket that I can't afford to pay?"

We get in the car and Pancho starts driving toward Katherine's.

"How long have you been outside?" I ask.

"About a half hour. Katherine said she didn't know what time you left your apartment but she wanted to make sure I caught you so she had me start waiting earlier than she figured you'd leave," he says. "Saw your boyfriend though," he says, smirking at me in the rearview mirror.

"Soon-to-be fiancé," I say, not wanting him to think I'm a hussy.

"Fiancé!" Pancho says. "Way to go, Lucy."

"Thanks, Pancho."

"Marriage can be pretty cool," he says, looking at me again in the mirror.

"Are you married?" I ask him, realizing that I know absolutely nothing about Pancho. Shame on me.

"Seriously? I've been married for sixteen years. Three kids, too. My oldest one just got into Bronx Science for the fall," he says beaming. "It's one of the best high schools in the city, you know."

"That's amazing, Pancho. Congratulations!"

We talk a little more about his kids and his wife but soon we're pulling up to Katherine's. I walk inside and Cute Doorman (does he ever sleep?) tells me they called down already. That they're expecting me.

When I get off the elevator at Katherine's floor, Theo's waiting for me, holding the door open to their apartment. I haven't even had a second to think about what this could be about, my being summonsed to Katherine the Great's apartment, because I was talking to Pancho the whole time in the car. But now, as I stand on the threshold of the apartment, I feel a bit panicked.

"Morning, slugger. Come on in. Coffee?"

"Will I need it?" I ask Theo, giving him a scared look.

He laughs. "Coffee can never hurt." I wait in the foyer while he pops his head into the kitchen, and I hear him ask the housekeeper to bring the coffee into the library. He nods toward me, and I follow him into the library where Katherine is sitting on the couch. She definitely looks more presentable than yesterday. She's still wearing sweatpants and a cashmere sweater, which I realize now is her lounging-around-the-apartment outfit, but it's a different set than yesterday's. I smile when I consider my own lounging-around-the-apartment outfit, which is considerably more casual: flannel pajama pants and a ratty old Pearl Jam T-shirt that I stole from one of my brothers.

"Hey, Lucy," Katherine says, and I'm not sure if she sounds contrite or irritated.

"Hey," I say softly, taking my assigned seat from yesterday on the bench across the coffee table from where Katherine is sitting. The pistachios in the crystal dish have been replaced by individually wrapped Godiva chocolates. Theo sits down on the couch next to Katherine.

The housekeeper walks into the library balancing a silver tray. She sets it down on the coffee table. On it are two giant mugs (for Theo and me, I gather when I see Katherine sipping tea), a silver coffee pot, a small glass pitcher filled with steamed milk, and another crystal dish filled with sugar. We're all silent as Theo pours the coffee. I thank him and then add milk and sugar. I take a sip and look up. The prisoner is ready for the execution.

"Thanks for coming," Katherine says.

"Sure," I say. *As if I had a choice. As if I wasn't just abducted by your driver.*

"You know Lucy, when I found out yesterday that it was you," Katherine says starting off slowly, calmly, "I felt like someone had shot me in the stomach. I really couldn't believe it. I never would have guessed in a million years that you were, as you said yesterday, capable of something like that. And I was going to cut all ties with you. I didn't want to ever see or talk to you again. But Theo had more faith in you. He convinced me to let you tell your side of the story. That's why we asked you over yesterday."

She stops and takes a sip of her tea. I take another sip of my coffee, unsure of what I'm supposed to do or say in this scenario.

Katherine continues, "And I'm glad he convinced me to do that. I couldn't think of any reasonable explanation for what you did. How you could have been so malicious. What could have possibly been your motivation to expose me like that. But now I understand. And you're right. I did something awful to you. I was selfish. I lied to you, and I did tell Ash not to hire you. Because I couldn't fathom how I could possibly do my job, do my life for that matter, without you. And I can understand how you could have seen that from your perspective. I owe you an apology, Lucy."

I finally get the courage to look into her eyes. I'm so pleasantly surprised that she's owning up to what she did.

"I'm really sorry, Lucy. I'm sorry that I sabotaged your chance at getting the job you wanted. It was selfish, and I'm sorry."

"Thank you for saying that," I say.

"Can you forgive me?" she asks.

"I can. And I do." And I absolutely mean it. If I want Katherine to forgive me, if I want her to believe that what I did was out of character and wrong, then I feel I owe it to her to forgive her. And I think we both learned something valuable from our terrible actions. So, yes, I do forgive Katherine. I will move on.

"I'm glad to hear that. Theo and I have been talking about all of this, a lot. For hours and hours, we have been talking about this," she laughs softly. "I have analyzed it from every angle and at some point late last night, I had a complete attitude shift about the whole thing. I realized, and this is insane considering how mad at you I was yesterday, I realized, Lucy, that you did me a favor."

Suddenly Katherine *is* sounding insane, but I'm willing to hear her out as it appears that my star might be on the rise.

"Despite the very public beating that I received, at the end of it all, I'm better off for it. I guess in a way, and this *is* absolutely insane and I realize that, I guess I should be thanking you."

"You can do that," I smile weakly.

"I should thank you because if it weren't for you, I would still be in my job and my life would still be falling apart. But because of you and your crappy little tête-à-tête with the *Post*, I had to give that *Today* interview, which led me to listen to that Elaine Winters, which led me to give that speech at the Ellevate dinner. And that speech totally liberated me. I'm free of the lies. And I'm free to live my life more authentically and in a way that's better for me. And for my family." She looks at Theo and puts her hand in his. "And for our marriage."

Katherine has gone from yesterday's curled-up crumple of a distraught woman to, well, Katherine. She takes a sip of her tea and smiles at me. I'm trying to take this all in.

"Do you remember when I asked you that day in your office why you don't come clean?" I ask Katherine.

"Yes," she says.

"And you said something like you could never reveal yourself like that?"

"Yes."

"I sensed in your voice that day that you wished someone would do it for you."

"Really?"

"Really. I may have just imagined it. And I may have hoped it was true so I could justify what I later did, but despite all the bad stuff that has happened in the last few days, I hope I'm not crossing any lines to say that it all seems to have turned out for the best."

"In some ways, I guess, yes," Katherine says and raises her eyebrows. "There's a lot of fallout from this though, Lucy. A lot of details left to be figured out."

"I imagine there are, Katherine. And again I'm so sorry. What I did was awful and I had no right to play with your life like that."

"Thank you, Lucy. I appreciate the apology. I will never know what would have happened, how long I could have lasted in the state I was in had you not given that information to the *Post*, but something tells me that I would have eventually ended up where I am right now."

"So what are you going to do?" I ask, taking a sip of coffee, suddenly feeling very relieved.

"I'm not sure. I imagine there are going to be a lot of media interviews once the press release comes out later this morning. So that will keep me busy for a while. And then I don't know. Maybe I'll do some consulting for Green Goddess. Or maybe I'll find a board or two to sit on. I might not be welcomed everywhere with open arms, but America loves a good redemption story. Look at Bill Clinton. I will work in some capacity. Sure, I want to spend more time with the girls, but I know I would be a terrible stay-at-home mom. Plus, the new nanny is starting later this week so we're in a better place with help. But for now, I'm just going to see what develops."

"And what's going to happen with my job?" I ask.

"Well, I'm fully prepared to call Ash when we're done with this conversation. I will give you a glowing recommendation and ask him to seriously consider you for the job."

"Really?" I'm completely shocked. "Thank you, Katherine. Thank you so much. Are you going to tell him that I found out that you told him not to hire me?"

"No. I don't see how that will serve anyone well. I'll tell him that now that I'm otherwise disposed, you are available for your true calling and that he should snatch you up while he still has a chance. He doesn't have to know that you ever knew about my first conversation with him. And then I'll be sure to tell him that he better treat you well and never betray you," Katherine adds.

I give her a look.

"Kidding, kidding," she says and bangs her hand down on the couch, laughing and shaking her head. "What is happening to my life?"

She asks no one in particular.

Theo and I give each other a look.

Theo rubs her shoulder and tells her everything is going to be okay. The girls run into the library and jump all over me, excited to tell me what they're going to do today. I am laughing and talking and trying to keep up when I look over at Katherine and Theo on the couch. He's rubbing her face gently with his finger and again I hear him say, "Everything's going to be okay."

A little while later, after the girls have told me their latest news, Katherine walks me to the door.

"Oh, Brooke might be in touch with you later this morning to go over how to handle phone calls that come in. Thanks for agreeing to stay in your job for a couple weeks while this whole transition gets sorted out."

"Of course. But I'm not sure how happy Brooke's going to be to talk to me," I say reaching for the door handle.

"What do you mean?" Katherine asks, looking at me with a perplexed expression.

"Isn't she the one who found out from the *Post* that it was me?" I ask.

"No."

"Then who told you?" I ask.

"Maggie Stern."

"Maggie? Seriously? How did she find out?"

"Her husband is some high-up executive at News Corp. News Corp. owns the *Post*. She had heard through the Green Goddess office grapevine that I thought it was her who talked to the *Post* so she wanted to find out who it really was so I wouldn't put her job in jeopardy in any way. Maggie Stern did not like being falsely accused. Just before I left the office yesterday afternoon, Maggie called me on my cell and told me that her husband found out through his own contacts that it was you. I don't know how he did it since journalists aren't supposed to reveal their sources but I guess he had his ways. I didn't believe her right away but she had a very convincing story. I half expected you to deny it when you came over yesterday and then my hunch about Maggie lying would have been true. But you admitted it, so I knew she was telling the truth."

"Maggie didn't deserve to be blamed. I probably owe her an apology for letting that go on as long as it did."

"Don't worry. I'll talk to Maggie. She'll be fine," Katherine says as I open the door.

"Oh, Katherine, do you know when you'll have a chance to call Ash? I want to talk to him today but I want to wait until you've spoken to him."

"I'll call him right now."

"Thanks. And sorry, again," I say.

"Me, too, Lucy," she says.

"Keep me posted about what you're going to do."

"I will. You can't get rid of me that easily."

I had no idea at that moment how true that was.

Chapter Twenty-Two

It doesn't take me long to get to the office from Katherine's and when I arrive, I settle myself in and start dealing with all her voice mails and e-mails. I also call Sera to see if Ash has filled Kyle's position yet. I am pleasantly surprised when she tells me he hasn't, that Ash has interviewed a couple people but things have been moving slowly because he's been really busy with other projects. While I'm on the phone with Sera, I watch the office manager Sal move boxes out of Katherine's office. He stacks them on a wheeled cart, heads down the hall to the mail room, returns with an empty cart, and begins again.

Brooke calls and spends fifteen minutes carefully giving me the lowdown on how I should handle everything. As we're about to get off the phone, she surprises me.

"I knew it was you the whole time, Lucy," Brooke says. I had suspected Katherine told her what Maggie's husband had found out, but I wasn't sure.

"How?"

"It's always the person you least suspect. I watch a lot of *CSI*."

"Why didn't you say anything?"

"I did. I told Katherine right away it was you, but she wouldn't listen to me."

"Have you talked to Katherine today?"

"Yes, I was on the phone with her right before I called you. She told me about your explanation. I guess you two are even now, huh?"

"I guess so."

"Well, I don't hold grudges, darlin'. That would be impossible in this business," she says with a snorting laugh. "Anyway, do what I told you with Katherine's e-mails and voice mails, and we'll all move on from this little clusterfuck."

"To be honest, Brooke, I'm surprised it took as long as it did for someone to find me out. I thought for sure you were going to go all commando on the *Post* and find out on day one."

"Commando is an understatement. I went batshit on the *Post*. But that little cocksucker Daniel whatshisname who wrote the article didn't crack. I gotta give it to the guy. He held on pretty impressively. I have no idea what tactics Maggie Stern's husband used, but I'm going to have to find out because I am impressed with his moves."

I laugh. "Sorry about all this, Brooke. I know that I made your life a living hell, too."

"That's okay, Lucy. I will find a way for you to make it up to me. In the meantime, I've got to go find myself a new high-profile client. My current one has officially left the building."

We say our good-byes and then I pay a visit to Ash.

"Hey Lucy, c'mon in," he says when he sees me at the door to his office. As I walk in, I hear Sera push her chair back to listen in.

There's no reason to discuss with Ash any of the preceding drama that went on behind the scenes with me and this job. As Katherine and I discussed earlier, Ash doesn't need to know that I know about the nature of his first conversation with her.

"I'm just checking in on Kyle's position. I know Katherine called you this morning to put in another good word for me. Are you still interviewing candidates?"

"Yes, I am still interviewing, and I'd like to make an appointment for you to come talk to me about the job. Sorry that's only happening now. The process was delayed a bit," he says holding his hands up in front of him. "But we're full steam ahead again, and I look forward to talking to you about the job. I can't guarantee what's going to happen, but Katherine has put in an awfully good recommendation for you," he says, smiling.

"Great. That's great, Ash," I say.

"I do have to be honest with you, Lucy," he says, becoming a little more serious, a little less friendly. "There are a lot of applicants for this position, and we are going to run a fair process to make sure the most-qualified person gets the job."

"I totally understand. I would expect no less."

As I walk out of his office, Sera stops me.

"Lucy, I don't know what's going on, but right after you called me this morning to ask whether the position had been filled, Katherine called Ash. I put the call through and after he hung up, he called me into his office and told me to set up a time for you to talk to him about Kyle's job."

"That's great. Thanks, Sera."

"I guess that means you're pretty happy that Katherine's leaving the company."

"No, not happy. But if the reality is that she is leaving, then I'm happy it means I can move on with my future as well."

When I get back to my desk, I walk into Katherine's office and see Sal stack the last box onto his cart. A couple of maintenance guys come in and Sal tells them to start moving the furniture out.

"Why are you moving all the furniture out?" I ask Sal.

"Because the new lady wants her own stuff."

"What new lady?" I ask, taken aback. Completely surprised that there's already a new lady.

"Don't know," Sal says. "I'm on a need-to-know basis."

And I guess I am, too.

Later in the day, Maggie Stern comes by. She takes a quick peak into Katherine's office and then stands in front of my desk. This is one interaction I have not been looking forward to.

"Hi, Lucy."

"Hey, Maggie."

"I have no idea why you did it but you must have had a really good reason."

"It's a long story, but let's just say I had my justification, and Katherine and I are okay."

"I was shocked when I found out it was you," she says with a look I interpret to mean that she didn't think I had it in me.

"Seems to be the prevailing opinion," I say, smiling.

"Sorry I had to throw you under the bus like that," Maggie says, with a pained expression.

"Water under the bridge. I understand why you had to do it."

"Yeah, I kept hearing around here that everyone thought I was the source. Like I've had any time to call up the *New York Post* and feed them information. Plus, everyone should have known it wasn't me right away because if I *had* decided to speak badly about Katherine, I certainly wouldn't have wasted my time with the *New York Post*. *Forbes* or *The Atlantic*, perhaps, but not the *New York Post*." She shakes her head and chuckles to herself.

"And I apologize. I can't say I worked too hard to squelch that rumor."

"That's all right, Lucy. I can see why everyone thought it was me. I know I'm not the best at being, how shall we say this, nice. Unfortunately, it's not enough that I'm overqualified for my job, an effective negotiator, and a competent manager," she says with frustration. "I have to be nice in the workplace, too. You never see anyone complaining that the men around here aren't nice. Just another double standard for women in the workplace. Anyway, I don't know why it's hard for me, but I'm working on it."

I smile.

"So what are you going to do now?" Maggie asks.

"I'm interviewing for a job in digital media. That's what I've wanted to do with my career this whole time."

"That's great. Good luck."

"Thanks, Maggie. I appreciate it."

"I'll see you around, Lucy."

"See you around."

She starts to walk away and then she stops. She walks back to my desk, looks around to see if anyone can hear her, and says to me quietly, "You know, if the new job doesn't work out, I'd love for you to consider working for me."

"For you?" I say confused.

"Yeah," she smiles widely and gestures toward Katherine's office. "It's still not public. The press release goes out Monday."

"Wow, Maggie. Congratulations. That's great." Huh, the new lady.

"Thanks."

"Well, if things don't work out with the digital-media job, I'll let you know."

"Sounds good. See you later." She smiles and taps her hand on my desk.

Strange times. Strange times.

Thursday, a couple of days later, I have my interview with Ash, and it goes really well. I'm able to answer all of his questions articulately, I pose a few well-thought-out questions to him, and I am confident with my proficiency in all of the skills he puts forth as necessary for the job.

"You did great," Sera whispers to me when I walk out of Ash's office after the interview.

"Thanks," I say. "How's the competition?"

"Pretty steep, actually. Not gonna lie. Lots of people from outside Green Goddess. I think you're the only internal applicant. But you're the only one with a recommendation from the COO of the company."

"Former COO," I say.

"Whatever. Anyway, I heard him talking to Joan from HR, and they're going to make a decision by the end of the day tomorrow."

"Well, hopefully it will be good news for me," I say.

"Hopefully is right. It would be nice for us to be in the same department," Sera says.

"Agreed. Wish me luck!"

"Good luck, Lucy!"

Later that day, I'm helping Evan with a project, trying to keep busy when my phone line rings.

"Hey, it's me."

"Hey, Katherine. How are you doing?"

"Really well. Beyond really well. There's something I actually want to talk to you about. Can you come over after work? Maybe around six?"

"Sure. Can you tell me what it's about?" I ask curiously.

"Nope. Can't. You'll have to wait and see," she says, barely containing the glee in her voice.

"Do you want some tea?" Katherine asks when I arrive at her apartment later that day. She's wearing ripped skinny jeans and a tailored white button-down shirt, her feet are bare, and her blonde hair is in a high ponytail.

"Have any coffee?"

Katherine laughs. "Sure!"

As we walk to the kitchen, we pass her dining room. I stop short in the doorway as something catches my eye. The long dining table is covered with two open laptops, empty plastic Glow juice cups scattered around, stacks of papers, and what look like piles of letters. This is most definitely headquarters for some sort of operation.

"Oh, that," Katherine says when she sees me staring. "That's what I want to talk to you about."

We walk into the kitchen, and I sit at her counter on a tall stool. Katherine stands on the other side of the counter and starts preparing our drinks.

"First, and I'm so sorry to have to tell you this, but I don't think it's going to work out with the digital-media job with Ash."

"Really?" I say, and my shoulders immediately slump down. I'm stunned. "You spoke to Ash?"

"No."

"Then how do you know that?"

"I have a hunch."

"Katherine, what are you talking about?" I ask completely confused.

"The reason I don't think it's going to work out with the Green Goddess job is because you're about to get another job offer that I hope you're going to find more compelling," she says, a wide grin spreading across her face.

"What?" I ask, not following.

Katherine stops what she's doing, puts both of her hands flat on the counter, and looks at me. "How would you like to be the director of digital media for a new organization I'm starting?"

"What? Seriously? What do you mean?" I ask shocked.

"Well, I've been doing a lot of reading and soul-searching over the past several days, and I've decided that I want to start a new organization whose mission, among other things, is to affect substantial change in this country for working women. It's going to be called Project: Balance. And I want you to start it with me."

Katherine and I spend the next half hour discussing her vision for Project: Balance and her vision for my role. I am so impressed by how much thought and work she's already put in, and I'm excited by the prospect of what I would be able to add as a woman from a younger generation. I also love what Katherine outlines as the plan for the website and her offer that I take ownership of all things related to it.

"You should also know that I hired an assistant this morning so you would have no administrative duties, besides what we would all pitch in and do together, considering it's a start-up. I've loved having you work for me for all these years, Lucy, but you are most definitely ready to have more responsibility and ownership over your projects."

"I really appreciate that. I've learned so much from you and you've given me so many opportunities, but I do not want to be someone's assistant anymore."

"I completely understand. And you've more than paid your dues."

"I hope I'm not speaking out of turn, Katherine, but what's to stop you from getting completely overwhelmed in this job? Especially since it will be your own company. Won't you be swamped and isn't that exactly what you said you don't want your life to be like anymore?"

"Fair question. And I've thought about it a lot. I am profoundly committed to making considerable changes in my own life, to make it more balanced. And since part of the mission of this organization *is* balance, I will ensure that our lives are sane. Predictable hours, time for our family and friends and ourselves. No more crazy lives, Lucy. I promise that. I know that sounds unrealistic since it's a start-up and there will be so much work to do, but I won't sacrifice us for the sake of the work. Slow and steady. It can be done that way."

"There's so much to digest. Can I have some time to think about it?"

"Of course. Go home and think about it, and tell me when you're ready. No pressure. But I know you'd be great at the job, and I would love for you to start this with me."

I leave Katherine's and decide to walk home to think over everything she proposed. The new organization sounds incredible and the job opportunity is exciting. But there are downsides to working for a start-up and for, rather with, Katherine. It's a lot to think about. Nick and I are having dinner tonight at Carlo's so I'm looking forward to discussing it all with him. I have a feeling I know what he's going to recommend.

I stop for a coffee and as I wait in the long line, I check my Instagram feed to see Ava's post of the day. The hairs raise up on my arms and a wave of excitement rushes through my body when I read what Ava and Deepak Chopra want me to understand: *All great changes are preceded by chaos.*

Epilogue: Six Months Later

"Welcome back to *Today*. Our next guest is Katherine Whitney. Welcome, Katherine," Matt Lauer says.

"Thanks, Matt," Katherine says with a glowing smile.

Katherine looks flawless. But different. She's wearing a pair of dark skinny jeans, a gorgeous but simple white blouse, a chunky gold necklace, and a pair of charcoal-grey leather ankle booties. She looks casual but hip. Perfect.

"So, a lot has transpired since the last time we talked," he says.

"It certainly has," Katherine says, laughing.

"For those of you who haven't been keeping up with Katherine Whitney, all five of you, I'll give you a rundown of what's happened in the last six months."

The camera zooms in on Katherine. She's sitting back in her chair, legs crossed, looking cool and confident.

Matt continues, "Katherine Whitney was the darling of corporate America the last time she and I spoke six months ago. She was the COO of Green Goddess & Company, the multibillion-dollar health and wellness company based here in New York City but with restaurants across the country and in London, a website, juice bars, a magazine, and so much more. And she was celebrating the six-month anniversary of the launch of her bestselling book *The Balance Project*.

She was also a fixture on New York City's social and philanthropic scene, and a shining role model for working women everywhere. But everything changed for Whitney in what seemed like the blink of an eye. After a scathing exposé in the *New York Post* this past April that called her out for being a fraud, Whitney decided to come clean. She did so at an awards dinner. Katherine, why don't you talk a little about that night."

"Well, Matt, in the course of a few days last April everything changed in my life. When I wrote *The Balance Project*, my life *was* very balanced. I was doing everything I wanted to do. My kids and my marriage were doing great. My job was fantastic. All the pieces of the puzzle were in place. But soon after that interview I did with you to celebrate the anniversary of the book, my life started to get difficult. I was in denial for a while. And it took that *Post* article, a cancer scare, and the wise words of Dr. Elaine Ireland to jolt me out of my haze and open my eyes to what was really going on. I honestly hadn't realized until then that what I was doing with *The Balance Project* and what I was doing through my speeches were actually having a *negative* effect on women. My intention had always been to *help* women. I figured that *my* life was so full and I was able to do it all, and I wanted to share that with other women. Well, it turned out I was wrong."

"How so?"

"It's unsustainable. Sure, there are times in your life when everything is going smoothly and it all seems very well-balanced. But those times aren't the norm. The norm is when things are crazy at work, or when your carefully coordinated child-care plan hits a snag, or when your husband feels neglected. That's the reality for women out there. And I learned that by telling women, as I did, that it was absolutely possible to have it all and do it all and have your life in perfect balance, I was doing them a disservice. Because trying to live up to that ideal only makes most women feel badly about themselves, incompetent even. And that's not good for anyone."

"So tell us about the night at the Ellevate dinner. The night you, essentially, blew your cover."

"I was so honored to be given the Working Woman of the Year Award. But as my name was called and I was heading up to the dais to give my speech, I realized I could no longer pretend that my life was perfect. And balanced. So I started telling the truth."

"You finished your speech that night by saying that you hoped you had made some amends and that you looked forward to making more. What did you mean by that?"

"Honestly, Matt, at the time I said it, I had no idea. But a lot has changed since then."

"In what way?" Matt asks.

Katherine uncrosses her legs and sits up straighter. "Well, right after that speech, I quit my job at Green Goddess. It was a heart-wrenching decision. I was one of the founders of that company, and I love it with all my heart. But I knew that what had been going on with me would become a distraction for the company. I also knew that I could no longer do the job I was doing at the level that it needed to be done. So after a lot of soul-searching, I decided to quit. I didn't know exactly what I was going to do next. In fact, I was in a complete haze of self-doubt and confusion about how I wanted to live my life."

"Then what happened?" Matt asks.

"I started reading the letters I had begun receiving after the Ellevate speech. I had been letting them pile up in my dining room. I hadn't read them because I thought they would all be so hateful. But I'm thankful for whatever compelled me to not throw them away."

"What did the letters say?"

"There were all kinds of letters, actually. Mostly positive," she laughs. "I did receive a lot of hate mail, to be fair. But for the most part, women from all over the world wrote me and thanked me for talking so publicly about what it's truly like to be a working woman. They told me they felt validated. And they told me that rather than it being the case that women can't have it all because there aren't enough hours or because the systems in place don't allow it, they wished that instead of that being our fate, that we could change the systems. That's when I had my lightbulb moment, and I decided what I wanted to dedicate my life to."

"So tell us what you're doing now."

"Well, a short while after I left Green Goddess, I founded an organization called Project: Balance," Katherine says proudly.

"And what is that?"

"The mission of the organization is to affect policy changes in the American corporate structure to support the unique position working women find themselves in, whether they are mothers or not. There have been a lot of cosmetic changes and lip service in American corporations over the past years in terms of making the workplace better for women. But what's needed, and what Project: Balance is aiming to do, is create radical changes, truly out-of-the-box changes that will, for once and for all, stop hindering women from realizing their full potentials."

"Isn't that a little ambitious? How are you going to do that?"

"Hell, yeah, it's ambitious. But that's what's needed in order to create serious change in our corporate infrastructure. A lot of other countries are doing this way better than we are. Our first initiative for Project: Balance, and I'm beyond excited about this, is a competition. A huge competition, actually. We've put out a call for radical, groundbreaking ideas to affect change. And we've provided incentive in the form of a cash prize of two million dollars. Twelve American companies have put their money where their mouths are and are sponsoring this competition: Green Goddess, American Express, Amazon, Facebook, Procter & Gamble, General Electric, Nike, Estée

Lauder, Google, Whole Foods, Johnson and Johnson, and Apple. And we've assembled a judging panel made up of politicians, business leaders, and women's advocates, people like Maria Shriver, Sheryl Sandberg, Dr. Elaine Ireland, Michelle Obama, Oprah Winfrey, Sara Blakeley, Kirsten Gillibrand, Melinda Gates, Indra Nooyi, Arianna Huffington, Ellen DeGeneres, Meg Whitman, Gwyneth Paltrow, and Tory Burch. The competition went live on our website last night, and we're so excited to see what the brightest minds come up with."

"Wow, that sounds like an amazing plan."

"Thank you, Matt. We're very excited."

"So everything has turned out well for Katherine Whitney after all," Matt says.

"It has, Matt," Katherine laughs. "Six months ago, I couldn't have imagined that this is where I'd be, but life has a funny way of working itself out."

"It does, indeed. Thank you, Katherine Whitney, for joining us. Will you come back soon and give us an update on Project: Balance and the competition?"

"I would love to."

"And this is *Today* on NBC."

Cut.

I click off of Hulu where I'd been watching *Today* live on my computer and get back to work. I hear my phone ping.

Nick: That went well.

Lucy: Yeah. She really sounded great.

Nick: How are you?

Lucy: Fantastic. You?

Nick: Also quite fantastic. See you after your dinner?

Lucy: Counting the minutes.

Nick: Have a good day at work, you digital media goddess.

Lucy: Thank you, you sports agent to the stars.

I take a sip of coffee and enter my password into the content management system. A jolt of happiness runs through me every time I log into the system because it reminds me that careerwise I'm finally doing what I've wanted to do for years. I can say with absolute certainty that I love my job. It's everything that I could have hoped for.

My life has been so much better since I stopped working as Katherine's assistant. It's been, well, balanced. I still work hard, but normal New York City hard. My hours are predictable, and I have time to exercise now and then, see Nick and Ava and other friends, and do my laundry. And I have much less Sunday-night anxiety, so Sunday dinners at my mom's are a regular thing.

I put my headphones on, click on my Happy Lucy Work playlist, and dive in. I'm typing away, deep in my thoughts and work, when I realize there's someone talking to me.

"Hey, Lucy, can you hear me?

I take off my headphones.

"Sorry. Lost in thought. And Pharrell," I say.

"That's okay! What did you think?"

"You were great, Katherine. I thought you sounded amazing! And Project: Balance and the competition came off sounding so incredible."

"Oh good! I'm so glad you thought so!" Katherine says, clapping her hands together.

"You want to scream?" I ask.

"I guess it depends what kind of scream. What's up?"

"Since the competition went live last night, the registration packet has been downloaded over a hundred times!"

"That's amazing!" Katherine says.

"I know! I really think we're onto something here."

"I think you're right," she says in a sing-song voice.

"Katherine," Aimee, her assistant calls from across the loft.

"Yes?"

"Brooke's on the phone for you. She wants to tell you, and I quote, how *fabuloso* you were on *Today.*"

"Tell her I'll be with her in a second," Katherine says, laughing. "So, dinner tonight at seven. Are we still on?"

"Hell, yeah. It's about time we had a proper celebration dinner for this organization. And now we have some things to celebrate: a terrific coming-out party on *Today* and over a hundred downloads!"

"Okay, we'll plan on leaving here at 6:50 to walk to Carlo's. I'm so excited to finally try that place."

Six months ago when Katherine offered me this job, I spent that night going over the pros and cons with Nick. I realized that this was an amazing opportunity and I decided it would be crazy to pass it up. Part of me wanted to wait to see if I got a job offer from Ash, but I was certain I wanted to work with Katherine, and if Ash *did* make me an offer it wouldn't have reflected well on me to then turn it down. Plus, I didn't want to burn any bridges at Green Goddess in case Project: Balance didn't work out. That next morning, Friday, when I got to the office, I immediately told Ash that I was withdrawing my name from consideration. I still don't know if he was planning to make me an offer. According to Sera, she doesn't either.

I met Katherine for lunch that day, assertively negotiated a generous salary for myself, *with full benefits*, and officially accepted her offer. I had one more week at Green Goddess, then I took a week off to, well, do all the things I never get to do (organize my apartment, sleep in, binge watch *Orange Is the New Black*), and started working with Katherine after that.

It's been better than I could have expected. The work we're doing is stimulating and important, Katherine and I work incredibly well together, I feel so proud of what we're trying to accomplish, and I'm excited about all that's in store for us. Katherine has stuck to her word about working slowly and steadily, and her life has been so much better, too.

Soon after Katherine and I started Project: Balance, she asked me to meet her for breakfast before work one morning. Once we had ordered, she told me, quite matter-of-factly, that Theo had admitted to cheating on her. That he had cried for hours to her the night before and begged her to forgive him, that it had been a one-time thing, that he regretted it entirely, and that he was devastated that he might have put his marriage in jeopardy. And because, as he said, he wanted to put everything out there, he told her that I had witnessed it. Katherine completely understood why I hadn't said anything to her; in fact, she thanked me for letting Theo tell her when he was ready. She said that he had made an appointment for them to go to therapy later that afternoon. And she said that she was unsure whether she should leave him or not (*Once a cheater, always a cheater*), but that she was willing to go to therapy and see if they could save their marriage. And they did. It was rocky at times, and, at one point, Katherine was going to leave him, but somehow they made it through. Katherine says that even though she can't forget what Theo did, in many ways their marriage is even better because of it. I still have a hard time forgiving Theo for what he did, but I've decided that if Katherine is willing to move forward, I should, too.

At 6:50, Katherine, Aimee, and I head out of the loft, which is located equidistant from my and Katherine's apartments, to walk to Carlo's. We have been looking forward to this night all week. We've accomplished so much in the past six months and the announcement on *Today* was a culmination of those efforts. We are ready to celebrate.

We walk into the restaurant and Katherine gives her name to the hostess, who leads us through the main area toward the backroom.

"You booked the backroom?" I ask Katherine.

"I wanted us to have some privacy."

"Big room for just the three of us."

"I invited some others to help us celebrate," Katherine says as we enter the room.

The room is filled with people, and I'm completely stunned because it's my entire family: my mom; Matty, Shannon, and the boys; Tommy, Kelly, and Ella; Sam, Allie, and their new baby Finn; Theo; Ava. And Nick.

"Hey, you!" I say giving him a kiss, so happy to see him. "I'm so confused, what are you all doing here?"

Nick doesn't say a word. He looks at me for a second and then before I even know what's happening, he's down on his knee.

I see Nick take a deep breath.

"Lucy," he says.

I start to laugh and cry at the same time. JJ and Parker get up from where they'd been sitting and come over to where Nick and I are. They stand right next to me to see what's going on. Everyone laughs.

"Lucy," Nick continues, smiling. "I'm gonna try this again."

More laughter in the room. My mother starts to cry, and Matt goes over to where she is and puts his arm around her. I stare down at Nick, at his beautiful face; I'm smiling so wide and the tears are flowing. A sun shower.

"Why are you crying, Aunt Lucy?" Parker asks in a concerned

voice.

"Because I'm so happy," I say.

"And why is Uncle Nick on the floor?"

We all laugh again. "Because I have a very important question to ask Aunt Lucy, buddy," Nick says to Parker.

"Okay. What are you waiting for?" Parker asks, and Nick takes that as his cue to go on. I guess this is what happens when you get engaged in front of your entire family. Nick grabs my hands in his.

"Lucy, the past eight years have been the happiest in my life because I've spent them by the side of the most beautiful, intelligent, funny, and intriguing woman I've ever met. You are everything to me. And everything we've been through together has shown me that you are the woman I want to spend the rest of my life with. Lucy Olivia Cooper, will you marry me?"

"Say yes, Aunt Lucy," JJ says jumping up and down.

"YES!" I say, laughing and crying and now kissing Nick as he stands up and grabs me in his arms.

Everyone in the room cheers and applauds. I see my mom crying into Matt's shoulder. As everyone quiets down, Nick pulls a small velvet box out of his pocket and opens it. I gasp. The ring is so beautiful. As he extracts it from its silver velvet nest, I consider saying something, but I wait and let him place the stunning diamond on my waiting and very happy finger.

"Congratulations, you two!" Matty yells out.

A chorus of "Congratulations!" follows.

At that moment, waiters come into the room and start handing out glasses of champagne. John Legend's "All of Me" starts playing. It's perfect.

Shannon is standing closest to us, so she comes over and gives me a big kiss and hug, "Congratulations, Lucy," she whispers in my ear. "This is going to be better than you could have ever imagined. You've made the right decision. Nick is a wonderful man, and I'm so happy for you."

I hug her tightly, and then she pulls away and holds up my left hand so she can see my ring. All the women circle around me, giving me kisses, wishing me congratulations, and looking at my ring. Ava gives me a high five.

My brothers are all around Nick, slapping his back, giving him hugs, making various and sundry remarks that he better not ever break their little sister's heart.

Then the circles switch and the ladies go over to Nick, while the men surround me.

"Congratulations, little Lucy," Tommy says. "We love Nick and we're all very happy for you."

"Thanks, Tommy," I say.

"Lucy!" Sam says. "Nice work, little sister. Congratulations!"

"Thanks, Sam," I say.

"Way to go, slugger. You deserve all the happiness in the world."

"Thanks, Theo."

Then it's Matt's turn. He pulls me to a corner of the room.

"Lucy," he says and he can't control his tears. "I love you so much, and I'm so happy for you."

"Thanks, Matty," I say, and he's got me crying even harder than I was before.

"You really are making the right decision, you know."

"I know," I say softly.

We hear a big cheer in the dining room so we turn around and see that the waiters have brought out large platters of food. There's a long rectangular table set for sixteen with place cards. Nick and I sit next to each other at the head on one end of the table with Matt to Nick's left and Ava to my right. My mom is at the other head, Theo to her left and Katherine to her right.

As everyone gets settled, I turn to Nick. He takes my left hand in his right and looks into my eyes.

"That was fun," Nick says. "Way more fun than the last time I proposed to a girl."

"Oh, yeah?" I ask. "What happened then?"

"She didn't say yes."

"Bitch!"

"Well, no not exactly. She had some pretty valid reasons. Well, in her eyes they were pretty valid, but she's come around."

I look up at Nick and we kiss.

"Nick, there's something I want to say to you, too. I almost said it when you were about to put the ring on my finger, but I decided I wanted to say it to you privately."

"By the way," he says. "Sorry to interrupt. But are you bummed I did it in front of everyone? I wasn't sure if I should."

"I loved it! It actually makes the whole thing fun and festive, like a little engagement party. You did good," I say. "And this time, my hair is combed."

"Did you like my little lie this afternoon when I said I'd see you *after* your dinner? I totally threw you off, huh?" he says, proud of his sneakiness.

"You did. I was not expecting this at all."

"Sorry I interrupted you. What did you want to say?"

I hold both of Nick's hands and look into his eyes. "These past six months have felt like a lifetime for me in terms of things that have happened and realizations I've made about how I want to live my life. Things that will affect me, affect us, for years to come. I'm so ready for all that we're about to embark on together. I couldn't be happier or more excited or more certain of anything I've ever done in my entire life."

"Then I'm so glad we waited a bit to get engaged."

"Yeah. I wasn't sure that was such a good idea when you had suggested that we put off getting engaged until we were both more settled in our careers. But you were right."

"Yeah. Things were so hectic and I felt like both of our lives were going through such a transition."

"And now that we've both gotten through those transitions, incredibly successfully I should add, I'm so happy to know that we are in this together."

"For the long run, Lucy Cooper."

"For the long run, Nicholas Heston."

Dinner is wonderful. The food is delicious. Carlo himself comes out of the kitchen to congratulate Nick and me. And there are lots of small toasts throughout dinner, including this one from Katherine: "I want to make a toast to congratulate Nick and Lucy. I couldn't be happier for them and I'm so honored to be a part of this special occasion. Thank you all for entrusting Lucy in my care these past years. We went though a bit of a rough patch, but we've come out on the other end better than either of us could have ever imagined. Together we are building something magnificent, and I want you all to know how spectacular Lucy is at her job. She comes into our office every morning with an enthusiastic smile on her face and has the most incredible work ethic I have ever seen in my career. Nick and Lucy, I wish you both true love and pure happiness. Congratulations!"

And this one from Ava: "I also want to take this opportunity to congratulate Nick and Lucy. And I am so happy that you two are finally engaged. Not that I minded dealing with the drama it took to get the two of you here, but I'm happy you both finally realized that you are exceptionally perfect for one another. Lucy and I love quotes, and I wanted to find a perfect quote to share with you all tonight. That proved to be an impossible task. There are so many wonderful quotes on love, on destiny, on being true to who you are. How to choose just one? Nothing seemed perfect enough. Finally, though, I found this quote. It's not exactly a summation of all the emotions that surround an engagement and new beginnings, but it is the perfect summation of Lucy. It's by Mandy Hale: *Just be yourself. Let people see the real, imperfect, flawed, quirky, weird, beautiful, magical person that you are.* Congratulations, Nick and Lucy. I love you both."

And finally, this one from me: "I don't have the words to express how happy I am right now. Tonight was a complete surprise, but it was the best surprise I've ever gotten in my life. There is so much I could say about how I've gotten to this place in my life, this amazing place. But that would go on forever, and you're all probably tired of hearing me talk about how great it is that I've found balance and how I've learned so much over the last six months, and blah, blah, blah. So I'll spare you the reflection and just say that I am so excited to embark on this next stage of my life. Building this organization with Katherine. And building this life, this new family, with Nick. Because right now my future is bright, and I'm looking forward to enjoying this next adventure in my life. With authenticity. With love. With balance."

Acknowledgments

As a working mother, I am extremely interested in and curious about how women I admire manage the tragically glorified "doing it all" craze. So in January 2014, I started a series of interviews on my website called The Balance Project. Each week I post candid interviews that feature inspiring and accomplished women talking about balance. I've interviewed authors and entrepreneurs, bloggers and nonprofit executives, fashion designers and creative geniuses: brilliant women, all of them. I've even featured the male perspective.

Through The Balance Project interviews I learned that there is not a woman out there who is "doing it all" when "all" is defined by consistently giving full attention to her career, her family, and most importantly, herself. That is truly unrealistic and unsustainable. Everyone makes sacrifices somewhere. That realization made me feel a lot better. It took some of the pressure off as I struggled to find my own balance.

My takeaway has been that when we define "it all" realistically, then yes, we most certainly can have it. Setting manageable expectations ensures success. Shonda Rhimes said it perfectly, "Anyone who tells you they are doing it all perfectly is a liar."

When I was thinking about what I wanted my second novel to be about, I decided I wanted to focus on an issue that was important to me. My award-winning, debut novel *On Grace* focused on being authentic when presented with a new life chapter, feelings I had faced when I turned forty. I wanted my second novel to have personal meaning as well. So The Balance Project became the inspiration for *The Balance Project: A Novel.*

There are so many people who have been supportive of my work and who have helped me with *The Balance Project.* . . .

Thank you Crystal Patriarche and the whole team at BookSparksPR and SparkPress. Crystal, you believed in me and I am so grateful for that. I am impressed by what you have accomplished as a pioneer in the changing world of publishing, and I'm so happy to be along for the ride. Thank you for helping me achieve my dream of being a published author. And thank you, Sara Chambers, for the expert work promoting this book; I've really enjoyed working with you.

Beth Kendrick, you may have given me stomachaches, but you also ensured that I created a better book. Thank you for being such a thoughtful, insightful, constructive, and encouraging editor.

David Orman, Dad, sorry I made you work during your visit! Thank you for your comments and edits which were wonderful and very much appreciated.

Thank you Wayne Parrish for your excellent and thorough copyediting skills and for your heart-warming enthusiasm for the project and its theme (sorry about Nick!).

Thank you Julie Metz for, once again, coming up with a perfect and stunning cover. I fell in love when I saw it.

Thank you Jennifer Unter for your guidance and honesty over the years.

Thank you to all of the interviewees of The Balance Project: Jessica Mindich, Veronica Beard, Emily Liebert, Lyss Stern, Lauren Slayton, Elizabeth Moyer, Annabel Monaghan, Holly Gordon, Jill Salzman, Jennifer Levinson, Jenny Hutt, Angela Santomero, Carola Donato,

Tiffany Washington, Emily Giffin, Alana Sanko, Cara Lemieux, Liz Fenton, Lisa Steinke, Nikki Mark, Colleen Oakes, Jill Bryan, Cindy Callaghan, Stephanie Hirsch, Whitney Dineen, Jo-Laine Duke-Collins, Whitney English, Jennifer Gooch Hummer, Melissa Amster, Nigel Marsh, DayNa Decker, Amy Selling, Heather Sonnenberg, Allison Winn Scotch, Bibi Kasrai, Karen Sutton, Samantha Ettus, and Pam Yudko (as of press time). This endeavor is so close to my heart, and your participation and enthusiasm mean the world. I look forward to continuing the interview series and hope that some of my readers will participate as well.

Thank you to the wonderfully benevolent book bloggers who are so supportive of my work and the authors who are incredible advisors and sounding boards for me as I navigate life as a novelist. I am blown away by the kindness of the women's fiction community and am grateful that they have welcomed me in. Special thanks to bloggers Jenny O'Regan, Melissa Amster, Erin Baker, Rhiannon Johnson, and Tara Caudle, and authors Kristin Harmel, Jennifer Gooch Hummer, Emily Liebert, Annabel Monaghan, Colleen Oakes, and Eileen Palma.

Thank you from the bottom of my heart to the readers who take the time to read my novels and write reviews, who contact me to share their thoughts on what my writing means to them, and who humble me with their generous praise.

My friends have always been my biggest cheerleaders, my first readers, and my most vocal and enthusiastic advocates. Special thanks to the ones who put up with me the most: Sharon Cooper, Karen Cousin, Sally Paridis, and Allison Wohl. And thank you to my first readers, Rene and Mike Benedetto, for your early enthusiasm and encouragement, which were so motivating.

My family has always been wonderfully supportive of my efforts and generous with their love. Thank you to Nancy Norris, David and Marsha Orman, Terry Orman Gevisser, Mike and Leslie Norris, Greg and Joanne Norris, Joy and Robert Schnall, Jodi and Geoff Quintiere, and Lisa and Andy Smukler. Ira Norris, I miss you so much. I love spending time with my nieces and nephews, and I had fun naming a character after each of them in this book.

To my three amazing boys, Jason, Will, and Judd: thank you for understanding when I needed to write and when I needed to celebrate and for indulging me in both. Your pride in and love for your mama brings me the purest form of joy. You are all such incredible champions of my work, and I am so proud of the young men you are becoming.

And to Rick, you could have an illustrious career in editing if you choose. Your astute thoughts were instrumental as I shaped and wrote the first draft of this story. Thank you for your enthusiasm for this book, your support of my career, and your true and steadfast love. I am eternally grateful to have you as my partner and my love.

Book Club Discussion Guide

We hope this guide enhances your book club's discussion of *The Balance Project: A Novel*. Please note that the questions below will give away elements of the plot, so we recommend you read the book before reviewing the guide.

1. For readers with children: before you had your kids, what did you think you were going to do professionally when they were born: Go back to work full time? Be a full-time stay-at-home mother? Work part time? Something else entirely? Did you change your mind once they were born? Six months later?

2. For readers with children: how have your feelings about combining work and motherhood changed as your children have grown up?

3. For readers who are planning on having children: what are your thoughts on combining work and motherhood? How have those feelings been influenced?

4. Do you think women judge each other's choices on this issue too harshly?

5. What are your thoughts on work-life balance? How do you balance your own life?

6. What are your thoughts on having it all? Do you think you can, like Katherine wrote in her book *The Balance Project*, or do you ascribe more to Dr. Elaine Ireland's opinions on the matter?

7. Why do you think some women feel this need to do "it all"? What is it in our society that feeds that?

8. Lucy puts her career advancement (applying for a new job in digital media) on hold out of loyalty toward Katherine. Have you ever done that? Tell about a time when you boldly went for your professional goals.

9. Did you think Lucy was justified in giving Daniel, the *New York Post* journalist, information for his article about Katherine?

10. Did you feel badly for Katherine when the *Post* article came out or do you think she got what was coming to her?

11. Lucy said she thought Katherine wanted someone to blow her cover. Do you think Katherine meant that? Have you ever wanted to blow the cover off something about yourself? About someone else? Have you done it? If not, do you plan to?

12. Lucy feared marriage because of her parents' experience. Do/did you have fears about marriage? What in your own life prompted those fears? If you were able to overcome them, how did you do it?

13. What did you think of the two-word note Nick left Lucy at Union Square Cafe the night she was very late for their date?

14. In chapter nine, Katherine talks about having imposter syndrome. Have you ever felt like that?

15. Should Lucy have told Katherine about Theo's affair as soon as it happened? Have you ever been in that position?

16. Kyle Jackson calls Lucy a "meant-to-be girl" in the cafeteria in chapter eleven. Do you think Kyle was right about Lucy? Has

anyone ever called you anything that made you so mad but that you realized was true and that spurred you to do something?

17. Should Lucy have forgiven Katherine and vice versa? Do you think either of their transgressions was worse than the other?

18. Were you surprised Katherine quit her job at Green Goddess? Why or why not?

19. What do you think of the new organization Project: Balance? Do you have any out-of-the-box ideas for changing the climate for working women?

20. Were you surprised about what awaited Lucy when she went into Carlo's in the last scene? How and where did you get engaged? Was it a surprise? What would your dream engagement look like?

21. Quotes are a big part of Lucy's life, and Ava and Nick both recognize this. What is your favorite quote in the book and why? Do you have a favorite quote? If so, please share it with the group.

22. In chapter twenty-two, Maggie Stern says: "I know I'm not the best at being, how shall we say this, nice. Unfortunately, it's not enough that I'm overqualified for my job, an effective negotiator, and a competent manager. I have to be nice in the workplace, too. You never see anyone complaining that the men around here aren't nice. Just another double standard for women in the workplace." What are your thoughts on this?

23. Whom do you think Lucy learned the most from: Katherine? Theo? Her family? Which lesson was most valuable? What's the most valuable lesson you ever learned from someone you respect?

24. What's your biggest takeaway from this book?

25. Do you wish it had ended differently? If so, how?

26. Could you identify in any way with Lucy or Katherine? Or both at different stages in your life? In what ways?

27. If you read Susie's debut novel *On Grace,* how did her two books compare? Which did you like more? Did you enjoy Grace's cameo in *The Balance Project: A Novel?*

Be sure to take a photo of your book club with each member holding up a copy of *The Balance Project: A Novel.* Post it to Susie's Facebook page (SusieOrmanSchnall) or tweet it to her (@susieschnall), and she may share it with her followers!

The Balance Project Questionnaire

The Balance Project: A Novel was inspired by the interview series, also called The Balance Project, Susie does on her website. Now you can participate in The Balance Project! Fill out the interview questions below or online at www.susieschnall.com. We promise you will find the exercise enlightening!

Name:

Age:

Where you live:

Job:

If you're a parent, ages/genders of kid(s):

Do you think "having it all" is realistic or overrated, and why?

What part of "balance" can you just not seem to figure out?

What part of "balance" are you getting better at?

Have you changed jobs or adjusted anything in your career to have more balance?

If you're a parent, is the job you have now the same one you had before kids? If not, how and why did you change directions?

What was the best advice you ever heard on balance . . .
    From a mentor/coworker?
    From your mother?
    From your spouse/partner?
    From your kids?

If you had one extra hour in each day and you couldn't work or be with your family, how would you spend that hour?

What do you wish you'd known when you were twenty?

What do you hope to know by the time you're sixty?

What one part of your home life do you wish you could outsource?

What/whose job do you wish you had?

What/whose job are you glad you don't have?

Favorite book(s)?

What are you reading right now?

Biggest activity vice?

Biggest food vice?

Biggest website vice?

How many hours do you generally sleep at night during the week?

What do you read every morning?

Complete the following sentences however you'd like:
I think I:_____
I wish I: _____
My kids:_____

Do you have a personal motto or favorite saying?

Anything else you'd like to add?

About the Author

Susie Orman Schnall grew up in Los Angeles and graduated from the University of Pennsylvania. She lives in New York with her husband and their three boys. Learn more about and connect with Susie at her website and via social media:

www.susieschnall.com
Facebook: SusieOrmanSchnall
Twitter: @SusieSchnall
Pinterest: Susie Schnall

About SparkPress

SparkPress is an independent boutique publisher delivering high-quality, entertaining, and engaging content that enhances readers' lives, with a special focus on female-driven work. We are proud of our catalog of both fiction and nonfiction titles, featuring authors who represent a wide array of genres, as well as our established, industry-wide reputation for innovative, creative, results-driven success in working with authors. SparkPress, a BookSparks imprint, is a division of SparkPoint Studio, LLC.

To learn more, visit us at gosparkpress.com.